BITTER STEEL

BITTER STEEL

TALES AND POEMS OF EPIC FANTASY

by

Charles Allen Gramlich

THE BORGO PRESS

An Imprint of Wildside Press LLC

MMX

CONTENTS

DEDICATION

To Robert E. Howard,

And to the current, future, and ex-members of
REHupa, The Robert E. Howard
United Press Association

PREFACE

Most of the stories and poems in this collection would not exist if it weren't for Robert E. Howard, a Texas pulp writer from the 1920s and 1930s whose characters are probably better known than Howard himself. Who, for example, hasn't heard of Conan the Barbarian?

Howard created Conan, although most people who know *of* the character have a very distorted view of him. Howard didn't actually *use* "the Barbarian" descriptor for Conan, and he didn't show him as a muscle-bound oaf. He didn't have Conan running around in a fur loin-cloth; Howard's Conan had the sense to wear armor into battle. People's mistaken impressions of the character come primarily from the movies, cover art, and from the post-Howard glut of comics and pastiche novels that have featured Conan. Most of these have not struck true to *Howard's* original vision.

Conan wasn't the only iconic character Howard created. Kull, Solomon Kane, and Bran Mak Morn also arose from Howard's fertile imagination, and the comic book character Red Sonja and her fantasy world are based on Howard's work. Red Sonja and Kull films already exist, although both are generally panned by Howard's most devoted followers, and there are plans for movies about Solomon Kane and Bran Mak Morn. Far more words have been written about Howard's characters by later authors than Howard ever wrote himself in his short, thirty year life.

The true importance of Howard, though, lies in his legacy. Howard took the most ancient form of storytelling, the weaving of epic adventure tales around the first human campfires, and brought it into modern print. He combined history, horror, fantasy, and mythology to create a new literary genre, which came to be called Sword & Sorcery. Fritz Leiber, with his Fafhrd and Gray Mouser tales, and C. L. Moore, with her Jirel of Joiry stories, were other early practitioners in the new field. They created original Sword & Sorcery characters and told original stories about them.

Later writers, such as Karl Edward Wagner with his Kane stories, David C. Smith with Oron, Charles Saunders with Imaro, and David Gemmel with Druss the Legend, mined similar ground and turned up gems. These are all writers I admire and respect, and in following their footsteps into the Sword & Sorcery landscape I hope I've done them some honor.

Among the pieces in this collection are several direct homages to Howard. The opening poem is a personal response to one of Howard's best poems, simply called "Recompense." The poem that ends this collection was written *about* Robert E. Howard and was nominated for the Rhysling Award in 2002. "Slugger's Holiday" is an outright pastiche that tells a new story about one of Howard's lesser known characters, Sailor Steve Costigan.

The rest of these stories introduce original characters in Sword & Sorcery settings. Six of them are about Thal Kyrin, the first Sword & Sorcery hero I created. That was at age fifteen or so, back when I often used daydreams to escape my chores on the Arkansas farm where I grew up. The remaining stories are standalones.

Except for "Coin and Steel" and "Sundered Man," all these stories have been previously published. However, I'm not a writer who can leave his stuff alone once it's finished, and everything here has been revised for this printing, sometimes dramatically.

So, let's gather around the campfire now, where the smoke stings our eyes. We'll drink from the common bowl and hear the thud of the drums driving blood in our hearts. We'll think of the whispering darkness outside our camp, and we'll shiver even though it is not cold. And soon, one of our number will lean forward to begin a tale. It happened to him only a moon ago and we know it must be true. He has the scars to prove it.

—Charles Allen Gramlich
April 2010

RECOMPENSE REPRISE

I have not heard the harps of heaven, nor yet the chants of
    Hell.
But I have tasted a night's despair that rang me like a bell.
I have not heard the guns of war, nor killed a man in hate.
But I have felt the brooding black that names them both
    my fate.

I have not seen the rocket's flare across the blood-soaked
    sand.
But I have dreamt a soldier's road where I made my own
    last stand.
I have not known the peace of man nor yet the love of god.
But I have left a woman's heart bleeding where I trod.

I have not stood in white as king beneath the spotlight's
    glare.
And I have not led ten thousand men into death's cold
    stare.
And though I've fought one on one where nothing was at
    stake.
I wonder if I have the courage a hero's life would take.

I have not crossed Viking seas on ships enlaced with rime.
But I have walked wild woods at night and bided there a
    time.
And I have swum in waters cold that tasted copper green.

And I have felt strange movements deep beneath me in the
    sheen.

I have not loved the evil fire that roils the minds of men.
But I have felt the beast inside and reveled in my sin.
And I have dressed myself in honor and known it was just
    pride.
And I have told a friend a "truth," knowing that I lied.

I have felt the pallid breath of the dying on my face.
I have seen the dead forgot without a memory trace.
And I have known since childhood that life is never long.
That thought wets a sweeter edge to every sadder song.

A GATHERING OF RAVENS

I.

The ravens gathered, their voices as harsh in the twilight silence as the turning of ungreased axles. It was to a dead place they flocked, a place of white bone and spilled blood, a place where warriors had come in the morning and stayed until late at their work. But it was to just such places that ravens were drawn, and these scarcely stirred when the woman rode from the forest and joined them among the slain.

It was not easy at first to tell the rider was a woman. Armor covered her breast, and back, and thighs. A helm cloaked her features. But when she stripped off that white-plumed defense and the hair fell silver to her shoulders, then it was clear she was female. No man ever had such a delicate face, nor lips that seemed so made for smiling, despite the fact they'd been drawn rictus-tight for many days past. No, she was not a man, though she had taken the lives of many who claimed that title of late.

At a shout of hooves, the war-daughter turned in her saddle and drew her sword, its steel no longer bright as it had been at dawn. She was glad when she found no need to stain it further, for it was only her guards riding to join her on battle-weary horses.

II.

Trajan Vittus, Commander of the Royal Guard, had considered chiding Jedess for riding off ahead of her troop, but he thought better of it when he saw the Queen's green eyes and the dark circles like cicatrices around them. He could not meet that gaze, nor mutter condemnation to it. He said only: "My Liege."

Beside Trajan rode a male version of the Queen—or nearly so. The man was tall, as was Jedess, and they both wore the same hair and eyes. But the resemblance ended with the cruelness in the man's handsome features. Angrily, Lord Janik hurled a broken lance at the ravens that squabbled over a nearby corpse.

"Swiving birds!" he cursed.

"Leave them be, Janik," the Queen said. "It is in their nature. Just as killing is in yours."

"In yours as well then," Janik retorted. "Sweet sister."

"Yes. But I try not to enjoy it."

Janik was about to respond further when Vittus pushed forward with a question for the Queen, though his main goal was to stay the exchange he feared was about to occur. Janik hated his older sister, who had always bested him before their father, but Vittus cared nothing for the Prince's feelings. He did care about the Queen of Seth-Loeril, and her mood of late ached in him like an arthritic limb. Jedess had been born a daughter of war and it was not like her to brood so much over the dead. But then, this war was different. The enemy were her own people.

"Is there anything you need, my Queen?" Vittus asked.

She glanced at the soldier, her attention drawn from her brother, as Vittus had hoped. But that did not alter the haunted place built these last few weeks behind her eyes.

"Yes, Commander," she said after a moment. "There is something I need." She gestured to a body that lay at her courser's hooves. "Tell me how old this enemy is. Commander."

Vittus looked where the Queen pointed, and winced as he saw in the grass the unlined face and slender shoulders of a youth. He spoke, hesitantly: "Nineteen years. Eighteen perhaps."

Jedess snorted. "Don't try to protect my feelings, Trajan. I've killed as many men as you. That boy can be no more than fifteen at most."

"So," Janik interrupted. "He was a rebel and a traitor. And did we not win this battle?"

Jedess replied without looking up from the corpse. "Ask that of the dead, my brother. Perhaps *they* can tell you."

She then turned and rode away through the ravens. The birds didn't notice; the dead didn't care.

III.

The Queen made no further attempt to outpace them and her exhausted guard kept up all the way to the broad valley where the royalist army of Seth-Loeril lay encamped. Vittus rode at Jedess's left as a shield, but his thoughts were on the war. He admitted, as would the Queen if pressed, that the rebels had once had cause for their rebellion. But he also knew those reasons had died with the King, with Jedess's father, who had taxed his people unmercifully in some stillborn plan to make Seth-Loeril a power among the raw young cities of the Virulian Coast. To that end he'd hired mercenaries, blond killers from Reyasvik with their spume-crusted beards, ebon horsemen from Kuthana and the stone prairies, a thousand others whose lives were given to coin and steel. To the people of Seth-Loeril, it seemed their money paid only for such men to swagger in their streets and abuse their hospitality.

To Jedess, empire dreams were for storytellers, and mercenaries were only another kind of raven. She had planned to disband the hired troops as soon as she returned from the northern frontier where news of her father's death reached her. The rebels had given her no time. War had erupted before Jedess could even reach Seth-Loeril, and it was only her strength of will that had driven the rebels from the city.

Most of the mercenaries quit when they realized neither side could afford them. But one troop, under a captain named Doremos Kuchuan, had joined the rebellion. Doremos was born out of Tudisa in the south, and his natural talent for self-aggrandizement had brought him far in the employ of Jedess's father. Without the strength of that one trained legion, the rebels would soon have broken. Instead, the throne was at risk.

Doremos worried Trajan Vittus. Unprincipled and vicious though the man was, the mercenary was also an excellent strategist. His one legion and the various rebels under his command had fought Jedess's royalists to a standstill, even though they were outnumbered and Jedess was herself no mean general.

His respect for Doremos made Trajan suspicious of how easily today's battle had gone. But Kuchuan's best troops had not been among the thousand rebels that walked headlong into Jedess's army, so perhaps it was the mistake of some underling. It had been a needed victory for the Queen's men, however, frustrated as they were by repeated stalemates.

Trajan only wished the Queen could share her men's joy.

IV.

Her tent was waiting when Jedess rode into camp and dismounted. A squire came for her horse, and another followed into her quarters where a hot bath had been drawn and slices of meat and fruit had been spread on wooden platters. She waved the retainer away and undressed herself, foregoing more than a bite or two of food in order to join the bath and soak away the sweat and blood that painted her.

Tomorrow, her army would move toward the Naaritik River where scouts had reported Doremos's main force. Plans must be made, but the river was a week away and strategy would wait until morning. Tonight she needed this bath, this food, and some sleep, though she feared what dreams might bring.

v.

In a narrow valley scarcely five miles from where Jedess bathed lay the campfires of a second army, the army of mercenaries, thieves, and outlaws that fought for Doremos Kuchuan. They were inclined to call themselves rebels, and there were those among them who fought for such ideals as liberty and justice, but those were in the minority and Doremos was not one of them.

The mercenary captain sat now beneath the silk of his tent, flanked by tall warriors with blue irises and blond war-braids who held axes tight in calloused fists. He seemed almost small beside his blond savages, his body lean and boyish, but no one who ever looked into his grey eyes would joke about his sparseness of chin hair. Right now, his eyes were warmed a bit with laughter, despite the thousand men he had lost today. He was pleased because of news he had just heard.

Doremos looked toward the green-eyed messenger standing before him. His voice boomed with hearty laughter, and he drained a silver chalice of its taste of wine and tossed it aside.

"So tell me, Lord Janik," he said. "Do you think the crown will sit well on your head?"

"Better than on hers," Janik replied. He too was in a jovial mood, and he too drained a cup that was twin to the one Doremos had just discarded. Janik should have taken more note of that gesture.

"No doubt," Doremos said. "You are sure, of course, that she does not know where our camp lies?"

"I'm sure. You know I direct the royalist scouts. Everything Jedess sees, hears, and smells comes through me. And I fear I have distorted things a bit for my beloved sister. Good idea on your part, though, not to tell your advance force you'd be following so closely. Vittus and his slaughterers took prisoners, and the prisoners talked, but the fools told only what they believed true."

"That my legion still camps beyond the Naaritik," Doremos interjected.

"Yes. The Queen and her harlequins sleep peacefully tonight, secure in victory, secure in their absolute knowledge of your whereabouts."

Abruptly, Doremos stood, pushing back his chair. "Then we need to remind them there are no absolutes in war," he said.

A single order set already laid plans in motion, and Doremos strode across to grasp Lord Janik's shoulder in a comradely way. "Soon, my friend," he said, as the sounds of an army breaking camp welled up outside. "Soon, you will be King in Seth-Loeril. We will even bring your sister to you in chains if you wish."

"I would enjoy seeing her one last time," Janik agreed. "Afterward, you can do what you will with her."

"It will be a delight, my Liege."

They turned together and left the tent to take up swords for battle. Janik was first through the flaps and did not see the rebel captain stroke a dagger and smile at his back. Doremos had no intention of seeing Janik rule in

Seth-Loeril. No, he expected the new King to meet with unfortunate death at the hands of some fanatic or another—a civil war always brings out plenty to choose from. That would leave only one person with enough strength to hold the state together.

Doremos liked the idea of being King. He had always felt he was born for it. For now, though, he mounted his charger and rode out a few steps behind Lord Janik, as befitted a loyal soldier.

VI.

The harsh baying of alarm tocsins tore Jedess from her dreams. For a moment it was hard to separate the screams of nightmare from the screams of reality. Then an arrow ripped the silk of her tent, spilling the gray light of morning across her bed. It struck the pillow near her, and she could see it was already once-fleshed and painted red.

She exploded onto her feet and through the tent flaps before the arrow shaft stopped quivering, and she had a sword in hand though she could not have said how it got there. It mattered nothing to her that she was naked. But it mattered to Trajan Vittus, who had been racing to fetch her with half his armor slung about him.

"Doremos!" he shouted, pushing Jedess back into the tent and passing her the garments and armor laid out for her.

"Impossible! His army is miles away."

"No, my Queen. Somehow our scouts missed them. They've surrounded the camp. Their archers are wreaking havoc among the troops as they try to arm."

Jedess slung on a breastplate and grabbed her white-plumed helm from Vittus's hand. "Get our own archers to set up screens for the men," she ordered. "I'll gather what warriors I can and try a counter-thrust to ease the pressure."

Vittus turned to obey, she right behind him, and the tent was ripped open by swords and the armored forms of warhorses and men materialized out of the dawn. In a spray of horse spittle and nostril steam, amid dark shapes cloaked in chain mail and boiled leather, there grew a storm of steel.

Some unit deserted their posts, Jedess thought, as she saw Trajan go to his knees beneath a slashing blade and use his own sword to eviscerate his attacker's horse. The stallion screamed as it birthed its own intestines; Jedess tossed her helm aside and started forward; Trajan began to rise from his knees; a crossbow quarrel took him in the face. Jedess came in among the raiders with sword bared and lips twisted in a killing rage.

VII.

It was not yet noon when Jedess awoke. A fungal taste filled her mouth; a copper stench clung on her body. One eye was swollen nearly shut, but she got the other open fully and used it. She sat in a clearing with her back to a tree, not by choice, and before her was a black and white tent that drooped limply in the dead air. She had no idea how she came to be bound here. All she remembered was Trajan Vittus falling, and nothing after but fractured mother of pearl images carved out of violence.

How had she been such a fool, she berated herself? She'd known that Doremos was an apprentice of the unexpected. But why hadn't the scouts detected sign? How could the mercenary have hidden his entire army? What had she missed? Then she heard the stomp of cavalry boots on hard ground and looked up to see how it was she'd been so misled.

"Janik," she said. "You bastard! How did you manage this?"

"You may address me as King," Janik said, Doremos standing at ease beside him. "I soon shall be anyway. As to how. It seems Captain Doremos never really left our employ. He only pretended to join the rebellion so he could destroy it from within. This morning he finally maneuvered the enemy into the position we wanted. They attacked, thinking to surprise us, and were themselves surprised when Doremos's legion turned on them from the rear. Together we crushed them. Unfortunately, as sometimes happens in war, an accident occurred."

"And I was killed," Jedess snarled.

Janik shook his head sadly and tsk tsked deep in his throat. "Most horrible," he said. "I will, naturally, commission a statue in your honor. Maybe we could even have the sculptor make you a bit more attractive. A bit higher in the bosom, perhaps?"

Jedess ignored the insults. "Somebody will recognize the lie soon enough," she snapped.

"Oh will they? What I've described is exactly what our soldiers saw. It makes no difference that it was staged."

"There have to be people who know the truth."

"A few. But the glory of mercenaries is that they kill whomever you tell them to. They don't care if it's somebody different today than yesterday. As long as the coin is paid."

"And what of the rebels who fought for weeks beside the honorable Captain and saw his blade running red with royalist blood?"

"Well... I imagine the executioners will be busy for a while. And if they don't get every rebel with a tongue, what matter. Who will believe them? Or be able to do anything about it if they do? You'll be dead. I'll be on the throne, with Doremos as my loyal janissary. I'm sure he'll be quite zealous in pursuit of my enemies."

"You bastard," Jedess said again.

"Why, sister. You're not being at all original. Surely you can think of a more appropriate insult. I always thought you a wit. Certainly so whenever you humiliated me before father."

Jedess's lips curled at the unintended challenge but she couldn't resist taking it. She might not have another chance.

She glanced at Doremos. "By the way, Captain," she said. "Have you enjoyed the Prince yet?"

Doremos looked blank.

"In bed, I mean. I'm told my brother is quite good when he's found the right man to play the catamite fo—"

"You bitch!" Janik screeched. He had been leaning over Jedess to gloat, and now he whipped a dagger from his belt and slashed downward across her cheek and mouth, slicing deeply through the pad of the lower lip. Blood spurted and Jedess cried out, then cried out again as Janik drew his blade back across her face from the other side. The fire-hardened steel split her right nostril and opened her upper lip to the teeth. The sound of metal and bone grating together locked her throat on a scream, and her mind dimmed but did not go out. Distantly, she heard her brother and his pet butcher talking.

"Kill her," Janik said. "And make sure she's unrecognizable when it's done. I've made a start for you."

"And what of yourself, my Liege?"

"I must get back to the army. Then to the city."

"Best, perhaps, to leave a good part of your men to hunting rebels, my Liege. Your sister has a point about wagging tongues."

"Uhm... I suppose you're right. I won't need the army in the city anyway. And they'll only slow my ride to the throne."

"Exactly my thoughts, my Lord."

"All right. I'll take the scouts with me to Seth-Loeril. Make sure your men do their part of the rebel spearing, though. There should be enough to go around."

Jedess did not hear Doremos's reply, for the two had turned away. A moment later, horses galloped from the camp. She assumed it was her brother riding to Seth-Loeril. The people would be just sick enough of war to buy whatever he told them. They had always been fonder of Janik than had his own family anyway. They liked his theatrical flair and his penchant for scattering sweet gold amid the crowds during feast days. Of course, Janik never told them it was his father's gold.

Well, none of it mattered now. She heard Doremos returning and looked up to watch her death. She was ready for it, and was startled when she heard the mercenary's words.

"Take her to my tent and dress her wounds," he commanded his guards. "And clean the filth off her body."

VIII.

It was evening when Doremos came to visit her. Jedess was alert and wary, though still bound. Her facial wounds burned but no longer screamed liked banshees. The pain had become a dull throb, but as the pain receded her rage deepened. It thrashed now to free itself, and she held it back by force as Doremos strode over to her and stood looking down. He was half drunk, though it was said he seldom touched more than a bit of watered wine.

"I have to kill you, you know," he said, and Jedess was surprised to hear regret in his voice. "Yes. Otherwise you would upset my plans too much."

He gestured meaninglessly with the cup in his hand, spilling purple wine over his fist. Then he smiled. "I see no reason we can't become better acquainted first, though. We have much in common, you and I."

Jedess's surprise evaporated. "Do it," she said, despite the pain of speaking. "I've expected it from the moment I woke up alive. But don't insult me by claiming kinship with my plight."

Doremos lifted one eyebrow, then laughed out loud as understanding struck him. "I'm afraid you mistake me," he said. "Rape is not something I'm likely to prove adept at. In fact... Well."

With that, the mercenary dropped his emptied cup and drew off his surcoat and the mail beneath. The undergarment was cotton, and when it was gone Jedess gasped in astonishment. Doremos's chest was hairless, and where the nipples should have been were two massive circular scars. They marked where the mercenary's breasts had been removed.

"You're a woman!" Jedess said

Doremos snorted. "Perceptive. What gave me away?"

"But your voice? Your...build? How?"

"I was always big for a female child," Doremos explained. "And with a good deal of muscle from filling a boy's shoes for my father, who was a farmer. As for my speech. Well, there is a plant that grows wild in my homeland. Called kahurra. Eating it swells the vocal chords, deepening the voice. Mothers use it for their sweet-tongued sons, lest the prelates cut them for keeping in their choirs. Frequent use makes the muscles bulkier, and some wrestlers and gladiators take it before their matches, as it is said also to enhance aggressiveness.

"And the breasts?" Jedess asked.

"I took them off myself. They were small anyway, and not of much use in the life I decided to lead."

"I don't understand why you would do this."

"Oh, I think you do. You've surely seen the peasant women. Like my mother. Toiling in the fields. Beaten to their chores like slaves. Dropping their get in the corn rows. You've seen the men. Like my father. Rutting with anything in skirts, even their daughters. Yet, it's always their perfumed town-slut who gets the fine clothes and sweet meals. But even the sluts have it none too easy, if you think about how they have to pay for it. Warring may be hard, but it is far cleaner than other ways I could have lived."

"But it's not that way for all women."

"No. You're right. Some find men to love them. But those are lucky, and I was sick at the thought of depending on luck to live my life. Perhaps if I'd been born a princess I might have been happy to spread my banquet for the lords to feast upon. But maybe not. I see you, too, have picked up the sword. Why is that, Jedess?"

The Queen gave no answer.

"It's because you're like me," Doremos continued. "Just like me."

"No," Jedess stated flatly. "I'm nothing like you. I didn't have to pretend to be a man to rule."

"Your father's throne, not yours. Through an accident of birth, you called yourself Queen for a few weeks. Until a man took it away from you. But that, too, will be temporary. Soon now, if not already, your brother will be dead. Then I'll be King, having taken the throne on my own terms."

"And how will that fill the void where your soul should lie?"

The mercenary's gaze darkened. "Thank you," she said after a moment. "Those words will make it easier to kill you."

Doremos drew a dagger and leaned toward Jedess, and the Queen saw movement at the tent's flap. Even half drunk, the mercenary caught the flick of Jedess's eyes and reacted by falling forward onto her belly. A crossbow quarrel slapped the cloth above them, and Doremos rolled and came to her feet, dropping the dagger and dragging her sword from its sheath.

Janik stood in the tent's doorway. He smiled and tossed the emptied crossbow aside, drawing his rapier instead. Behind him in the camp, sounds of battle broke out as men who had fought together hours before now pulled steel against one another.

"Ah... My dearest friend, Doremos," Janik said. "How fortunate to find you at home. About to entertain yourself with my delicious sister?"

Jedess heard the smug lilt in her brother's voice and realized he'd not yet seen the mercenary well enough to recognize the import of the chest scars.

"My King," Doremos said, as if to see whether a bluff was still possible. "I find myself confused. I thought you would be seated on your throne by now, not standing in the quarters of a loyal servant trying to shoot him in the back."

"Yes.... Unfortunately, I was accosted a while ago as I rode along the way into the city. It seems, though, that the raiders mistook another for me, perhaps because of the royal garments he was wearing, and I was able to take them from behind with my guard and cut them up rather badly."

"Good news indeed, my Lord. And most wise to dress another in your clothing. You do realize, of course, that I would never be so foolish."

"So I had surmised," Janik replied, his voice gone cold. "Until I stumbled upon this." He drew from his tunic a blond braid hacked from the head of one of Doremos's northern guards. He tossed it at the mercenary's feet.

Doremos glanced at the braid, then back at the man who wanted to be King. All bluff was gone from her expression, and from her speech. "I guess I'll have to kill you myself then," the mercenary said. "Before I rule in Seth-Loeril."

"I think not, Doremos. The army already has word of your treachery. The city will know soon enough. I've made sure."

"Very...well," Doremos said, her voice gone quiet, yet strained with the unendurable tension of ruined dreams. "Since...you've ended my game, I'll just...kill you...for the...joy in it."

She stepped toward Janik, moving into the light, and when the Prince saw her ruined chest he gasped. He did not know about the drug kahurra. He did not know how it drove its devotees insane. But now, he saw its effects. The mercenary's eyes rolled and her whole body twitched as she ran her sword down across the ridged whorls of her absent breasts and let it bite.

Janik gagged, and Doremos closed the gap and was upon him. The Prince whipped up a small, hand-held crossbow and fired its poisoned dart straight at the woman's face, but his instant of weakness let her slip past the bolt unharmed. A side-armed blow sent the man reeling, though he managed to get his rapier high enough to keep steel from his flesh. The mercenary kept coming, straight ahead.

IX.

As soon as Jedess saw the hand-bow, she understood Janik's willingness to face his former ally alone. She was relieved, though, when the dart missed, just as she was relieved when Doremos's first sword stroke was turned without drawing blood. It let her reach the mercenary's fallen dagger with her feet and drag it close.

Jedess's hands were tied in front of her and she wedged the blade into her belly so she could saw at the bindings of her wrists. The strands began to part, the process maddeningly slow. And during that time Doremos drove Janik around the tent at will, the Prince just able to keep the mercenary's steel from biting on his bones.

Jedess knew that her brother styled himself a swordsman. But she also knew he had seldom fought in single combat where his life hung on his skill. Oh, he had learned to dance around the fencing arena so he looked good for the noble ladies, but there was a very different kind of lady involved now, one that streamed sweat and had eyes full of crushed metal blades. Janik fought well, but was really no match for Doremos's talent and speed. He went down with a killing wound just as Jedess managed to pull her hands apart. One dagger stroke against the ropes binding her ankles and she gained her feet.

Doremos heard Jedess behind her and turned, delaying a stroke meant to take off Janik's head. The mercenary's face was flushed, her chest heaving. Jedess had never seen such intensity, a mixture of rage, and fear, and the insanity of the kahurra.

"Afraid we haven't time for more lovely talk now, my Queen," Doremos cackled. "I've got to finish you!"

"Jedess! Here!" Janik yelled, as with his parting strength he flung his sword to thud at his sister's feet. He was dead by the time Jedess scooped up the blade and felt it socket itself into her palm. She didn't know why Janik had thrown it to her, but she spared one thought of thanks as her brother's due. Then she opened her mind to a rage that mirrored her enemy's.

With a higher pitched shriek than anything yet spilled from the mercenary's mouth, Doremos hurled herself forward, her own blade glimmering evilly. The two warriors met and their swords caromed and sang, scattering bits of ablated metal.

Doremos was good, as she had to be in her profession, and in her lies. But Jedess was just a little better, perhaps because she didn't carry around the same garrote of self-loathing that had nearly strangled Doremos's will to live.

The two swords met and rebounded, gonged and licked and entwined, and when they came apart again it was because Doremos's weapon had slipped from her hand, and because Jedess's steel had slipped into the mercenary's heart.

The two faced each other for a moment, in a gyre of silence as their berserker emotions cooled. Doremos did not look at the blade that had killed her. She tried to talk instead. But when she opened her mouth it bubbled blood that ran down her chin like melting wax. The mercenary's eyes could still speak, however, and Jedess read their message and swallowed her pity. In another moment even the eyes went quiet, and the body of a warrior crumpled to the floor, the Queen's blade standing up between the terrible scars.

Jedess listened to the battle raging outside the tent, and to the silence that dwelt within. Then she plucked up Doremos's sword and slit the cloth wall at her back so she could slip into the night. There were riderless horses aplenty and she quickly chose one. She did not turn its head toward Seth-Loeril.

Let them have the Republic the rebels agitated for, she thought.

Doremos had been right in one way; the throne had never really been hers. But there would be something, somewhere, that *would* be hers. She promised herself that.

X.

Just after dawn, Jedess rode onto the narrow plain where the day before she had lost a throne. She found where Trajan Vittus had fallen. The carrion birds seemed especially thick there. She reached up and touched lightly on the wounds of her face before turning and riding into the morning. As if sensing the future, the ravens lifted from the battlefield and followed her for a ways, sunlight spilling dark from their wings.

THE HORNS OF THE AIR

I.

His hair hung pale to the shoulders; his eyes were the brown of good earth; his name was Jys Martel. He came up through Horse Hair Pass astride an ocher stallion, riding up into the high blue of the Tourmals where the shadows of the peaks slice down like memories across the hanging valleys. A dark sword arched up over his back, an ivory death's head for the pommel, and the afternoon sun on the ancient rock stirred winds in his face.

Behind him, ten days fast ride away, lay a dead man, a minor Duke in a minor corner of the Drang Empire, and though the creature had needed killing there would still be the Priest-Lord's justice to be paid. The Empire was a theocracy, the Duke a theocrat who had purchased much favor with his gold. Jys could have killed a peasant or petty merchant and spent a week in the foothills of the Tourmals while it was forgotten. But then, it had not been a peasant or merchant whose horse had ridden down an old woman too slow to get out of the way. It was not the horse's fault and Jys did not touch it. The Duke he butchered, along with four escorts who tried to intervene.

Afterward, Jys had ridden swiftly for the mountains, but not fast enough to avoid pursuit. That very night he had seen the fires behind him, and he knew who was following, the Priest-Lord's enforcers, the warrior monks known as Katai—night sword. Had it been a normal posse he might have turned to rend them. After all, he had been raised a Slayer, a brother of the Katana assassins, though he had since put aside the braid of that order. But the Katai were nearly as well trained as he, and they outnumbered him. So, though galled by the need, Jys pushed his horse hard up into the quiet hills, up into Horse Hair Pass and toward the stone valleys beyond.

Where he topped out at the height of the pass, Jys was at about 8,000 feet, still below tree line. A cairn of flat stones marked the place and he added another to the crown. At one time—before the coming of the Drang fanatics—the cairn might have had a spiritual significance, built, perhaps, as a ward against mountain demons, or to honor Siri, mother of Yhesak the stormer. Now it made only a small sign of a strength left unconquered.

Beyond the piled stones lay the entrance to a hanging valley. Rising smoke and a barking dog told Jys the valley was occupied, and his stomach told him *it* was empty. He scratched the horse behind the ears and turned its head up along the edge of a steep drop toward the promise of food.

The barking dog had only three good legs and sat at the edge of the village beside an old man cutting santhe wood sticks to peg the skulls of the dead, this too a small resistance to the Priest-Lord's rule. Jys wondered who had died, or who was about to die. Perhaps it was the old man himself. His eyes certainly seemed crowded enough with ghosts, and his face was nearly a skull already beneath a leather patina of skin.

Beyond the dog and the man, at the stoop of the first hut, there sat an old woman weaving yellow thread on a grime coated loom. She wore a woolen skirt and a vest that had once been red. The woman did not understand Jys when he spoke, and he thought her deaf. He showed her a copper coin so worn that the Priest-Lord's face was nothing but a smudge and pointed at his mouth. She understood that tongue and smiled black teeth at him as she went into the hut and returned with a few half-dried vegetables. Jys purchased potatoes and a handful of lentils. She gave him an onion that was nearly fresh and he bit it there before her.

She gave him, also, a cup of fresh snow-water, and he sat his horse in the cool evening and drank in the cool liquid. The village seemed empty, though he heard faintly the sound of distant voices and of goat-bells ringing. The rest of the village must be up on the mountain, and coming down by the sound of it. Well, he would ride on soon, perhaps before they came into the huts. It would not do to shelter here, not even for a night. The Katai were unforgiving of those who comforted fugitives, and Jys did not want a burned out community to rub his conscience raw.

Yet, he hesitated. It was pleasant here in the shelter of the huts, in the perse blue of falling evening. *Perhaps—* But his thoughts broke on a sudden shout and a scream. Jys wheeled his horse from the old woman, who cried out something he did not understand, and spurred hard toward the other end of the village and the sound of agony.

As it swung past the last hut, the thin dirt road that ran the length of the hamlet turned abruptly to the right. Some hundred yards up a hill beyond was a flat space ringed by a foot high wall of rocks. In the center of that circle was a single rough-hewn stone, a menhir nearly ten feet tall. A youth sitting on the stone began the iron ringing of bells, and beneath him a nude woman was leather-strapped to the harsh basalt.

Whip marks striped the woman's breasts, and legs, and stomach. Her face bled in streams where her nose had been hacked off. Around her jeered half a hundred men, women, and children, and in their midst was the taupe robe of a Kraal monk, the second rank of the Priest-Lord's servants. Even Jys knew the word the people shouted over and over.

"Kehries, kehries—witch, witch."

A few of the crowd turned heads at the sound of running hooves, and calloused hands gripped tightly their weapons of stones, and wood axes, and scythes. The few raised their voices and the monk turned as well, still holding a knife that writhed with blood. The priest's dark eyes met Jys's brown ones as the youth hauled his stallion up short of the stone circle. They knew each other at once for enemies.

Jys watched the monk move as the man came from the crowd to face him. Still a Kraal priest and not a Katai, he thought. Not yet so well trained. But dangerous still. And a bit overdramatic, as well, Jys added to his thoughts, as the monk struck a pose and thrust a finger at the mounted warrior's chest.

"What do you here?" the monk shouted. "In the Priest-Lord's name, I command you answer."

Jys chose instead to raise his arms, palms forward. The sleeves of his fur-lined jerkin slid back and he heard a gasp as the people saw the tattooed skull-snakes that twined his arms from elbow to wrist. It was from such people as these that the Katana—night whisper—and their skulls had been born. It was out of mountain people who smelled of goats and cheese and carried fangs in their eyes that the Slayers had risen. That had been on another side of the peaks and in another century, but yet these people remembered, and the memories held them back

Even the priest hesitated. He had not expected a Slayer. Not here. Not now. But he could show no weakness before his flock.

"Katana!" he said at last, nearly spitting the name. "You have no place here. The power of your sect is broken in these mountains."

"Perhaps not broken entirely, robe. But no matter. I am no longer Katana. But I would still have from you the woman."

"This is the Priest-Lord's affair," the monk said. "And

none of yours. The woman is a witch and a whore."

"The woman has been beaten with razor straps and is bleeding her beauty from out of her face! Is that not sufficient?"

"Not nearly so. She must burn."

"On whose authority?"

"On Kraal's, the Priest-Lord's, God's" the monk thundered.

"Then let Kraal burn her up," Jys said hotly. "If he wants her soul for witchcraft then let him take it. Cut her free and see. Or are you afraid your god will ignore you?"

"You blaspheme, Katana dog. And I will kill you for it."

"Then come," Jys said. "The horns of the air wait to embrace you and your god alike."

The reference to the pagan gods of the mountains, the horns of the air, turned the Kraal priest's face red. He brought up the clawed stave that marked his office, and from its heart slid a twenty-four inch rapier. Jys held his own draw. The monk yelled and charged, the villagers surging up behind.

No, Jys thought, the man was not yet Katai. Nor would he ever get there by attacking a man on a war-trained horse from the front. A faint pressure of Jys's right knee turned the stallion to the left, and the ex-Katana drew his Slayer's blade in one motion and struck. The blood channeled sword was half a foot longer than the monk's rapier, and it opened the man's skull to the shoulders before he was even in range to use his own weapon.

While the crowd held up for an instant at sight of their priest's gory death, Jys spurred his mount forward. Hooves lashed out and Jys laid the flat of his blade across faces and shoulders. In an instant the crowd had broken and fled, leaving behind one corpse and one girl tied in agony to a stone. Jys cut the girl free with a few sharp blows of his sword and she collapsed onto the earth. Dismounting, he held a water skin to her lips. She swallowed convulsively a few times, though she spilled as much as she got down.

Jys wore an undershirt of linen and stripped it for bandages to cover the lower half of the girl's face. Fortunately, such wounds as hers did not bleed much. The nose carried no major veins and the fluid coming out had already slowed to a thin ooze of pink froth. She could not rise, however, and Jys carried her to his horse. He sat her on the saddle and quickly mounted behind her, then booted the stallion up the mountain away from the village. The stones, and huts, and cries of outrage soon faded away into the gathering purple mists of night.

II.

In a sheltered grotto off the trail, near where a stream rilled down from snow caps above, Jys found a skull place, the white heads pegged through the eyes to the rock by santhe wood. It would have taken many days to drill those holes with nothing more than iron bits on hand turned tools, but time had always meant little in the stone and thatch eyries of the Tourmals. Now, time passed long between visits to these holy places and the ground was seldom used. The newest of the skulls here was at least ten years old, almost the time since the ritual had been outlawed by the Priest-Lord.

The Katana have no gods save death, but Jys had always felt the quiet of the mountains as something more than the weight of stone, and he knew what the skull ritual was for, to feed the spirits of the dead into the high cold with their gods. Sometimes, Jys almost prayed to the sky and sun himself. But he preferred his steel and did not feel as if he were violating spirits to stop here. It was a relatively safe haven for them both, and the girl was in no condition to argue his choice of campsites.

Jys helped her from the horse and half carried her to one side of the grotto where she could rest against a tree. She shivered within the jacket he had wrapped her in and he quickly pulled what blankets he had from his saddle roll to bundle her up. Then he bent to her face. She did not protest as he unwrapped the clotted bandages to check the wound. The nose was almost completely gone, leaving a gaping hole that leaked fluid.

One thing few people knew about the Katana was that they were trained as healers as well as assassins, and Jys had a small wealth of unguents and salves in his bags. He rummaged about until he found one used for sword wounds and then smeared the sticky paste liberally over the girl's injury. More of his undershirt went for bandages. He anointed her whip stripes with salve as well, but did not bandage those. They were not deep and would benefit from being left to the open. No bad air existed in the mountains.

Wood aplenty lay near the stream and Jys lit a fire to heat water, adding some potatoes and lentils to make a stew. It wasn't much—she needed meat—but it was all he had. Even so, she took only a bite or two and he did not force her to eat more. Nor was he particularly hungry, though he made *himself* eat. The girl had his jacket and blankets and he would need the warmth of food this night. After he had finished cooking, he built up the fire further, not worrying much about it being seen within the low depression where they camped. Besides, they had no choice. They would freeze without it.

As much as the girl needed warmth, Jys felt she also needed to talk. She'd not said a word since their escape and Jys thought he knew a bit of her pain. Her old life and what she would have thought of as her beauty were gone. She was without family or friends and must feel horribly alone.

He went over to her and stood looking down, and

when she refused to look up, he spoke: "Is the salve helping? It has saka root for the pain."

She did not answer.

"I saved your life," he said. "I think you owe me an answer to a simple question. It is an important one."

"You should have let me die," she said.

"I could not."

"Then it was your choice! I do not owe for what you say you had to do."

Jys smiled. At least there was still room for anger in her. That meant room for hope, as well. But Jys also needed to know some things, like where to find better shelter and food.

"We'll camp here for the night," he told her. "But tomorrow we will have to find a better place. I need more bandages and you need to be out of the cold. Is there another village near here?"

"The closest place is six days ride," she said. "But they would not accept me there either." Then she turned her face from him and would speak no more.

Jys went to his bed but did not sleep well.

At dawn, Jys changed the girl's bandages a third time, exhausting most of his salve and the remainder of the shirt he'd been using for wrappings. They would have to find shelter soon, he thought. And the cursed Katai were probably still on his trail.

At least the girl seemed hungrier this morning, and Jys let her have most of the leftover stew. Glancing at her while she ate, he realized she must have been very pretty before the mutilation, in the mountain way where women develop early and often age as fast. She was probably, he guessed, around seventeen, only a few years younger than he. Most of her age mates would already be wearing the braid of marriage and he wondered why she did not.

She caught him looking, and her voice and anger startled him. "I don't need or want your pity!" she shouted.

Jys's own frustration erupted. "Then stop acting as if you do!" he yelled back.

"And what is that supposed to mean?" she demanded.

"It means you should stop moping and help me figure out how we're going to live. I know you've been hurt but you're not the only one with problems. A dozen Katai are on my trail and they'll do a lot worse to me if they catch me than that damn monk had planned for you. Burning is at least a clean death."

It was the girl's turn to be startled. "Katai are after you!" she said. "Why?"

"It doesn't matter. All that matters is they are coming."

And then Jys found out how much strength the girl had in her. It awed him.

"I'm sorry," she said. "There may be one place we can go."

III.

The horse pushed on into the teeth of a chill breeze, Jys riding in front and the girl behind, both wrapped in blankets against the wet weather. They were above the tree line now, in a pass called Mouth of the Wind. It was appropriately named, the stone having been scoured clean of snow by a mistral that carried ice-blades in its grasp.

The girl, Marilan, had told Jys of a place and of a man who might offer them shelter. She called him Teskaharie, which translated into something like "pale man." She had not said why, only indicating that he lived in a valley beyond this pass and that it was because of a chance association with him she had been labeled witch.

The man was rumored a sorcerer and a black artist, and it was forbidden for village peoples to enter his valley. Marilan and two friends disobeyed and a late spring snowstorm had trapped them while they picked berries. Her friends died and Marilan survived only because Teskaharie had found her and returned her to her village.

The whispers started soon after. One had lived while two had died. And was not the girl fey as well? Did she not have an affinity with animals? Did she not walk at night unharmed? It took only the coming of a Kraal priest to turn whispers to wrath, a wrath that mindlessly sought her out. The pale man had helped her once. Would he again? He was the only hope they had.

It was nearing dusk when Jys at last brought his stallion down off the Mouth of the Wind and into the nameless valley beyond. It was much warmer there than he'd expected and shrubs and grass grew thickly. Too, squirrels chattered in the stunted trees and a few smaller rodents rooted in the leafy carpet beneath the branches. There were birds, as well, all swirling in the sky above a single point in the valley. Toward that place, Jys rode. On the way they passed a fane of toads and Jys smiled grimly.

"That was not here when last I came," Marilan said. "What is it?"

"A warning," Jys told her. "One used by sorcerers. Obviously, your pale man did not like it that you and your friends came here to pick berries. He's probably telling you not to return."

"Then he *is* a sorcerer!" Marilan said.

"Or he wants everyone to think he is," Jys added. "Anyway, we'll soon know how serious the warning is."

They found out sooner than Jys had expected. As they were riding down a slope carpeted with angel-nugget blooms, a jagdyke wearing a collar of entwined silver snakes trotted out of a clump of jittergrass and stopped to look at them. Jys halted the stallion carefully and pinched the animal's nostrils as it puffed up to bugle.

Jagdykes were not friendly animals and did not take well to noise. They had been bred long ago from dogs, though now they generally killed their former species mates on sight. This specimen stood about four feet at the shoulder, about average, and carried its weight in the forward quarters. It was also an albino, very unusual in the animals. Jys grasped the sword at his side and waited for the beast to make its move. It did nothing but sit down on its haunches and lick its front paws.

A moment later, a short man with a bow strode from the tall grass and stopped beside the animal. Some communication passed between the two and the jagdyke promptly got up and disappeared into the greenery. It seemed as if only seconds passed before the grass stirred again and a second man came out to join the first. Jys started. The second man, like the jagdyke, was an albino, and he wore the same silver snake torc around his neck. He raised a white and weaponless hand in greeting, and Jys removed his own fist from his sword and held it up.

"We come in peace and seek help," the youth said.

"I know the girl," the man said, his voice thick and heavy, incongruous with his appearance. "What has happened to her?"

Jys told him and saw the man shake his head in disgust. "Bring her," he said, as he turned to go.

"There is something else I must say before you offer help," Jys said.

The man turned back. "What?"

"I am pursued by Katai. I could leave the girl and go on, but in rescuing her a Kraal monk was killed. They probably want her too."

The man turned away again. "Bring her," he said.

Jys followed behind on the horse until they came to a stone keep. He dismounted then and helped Marilan up the steps behind the albino.

IV.

"She is exhausted but resting well," the pale man said, as he came from Marilan's room and started down the stairs. Jys walked down with him.

"Would you care for wine?" the man asked, as they reached the long front hall and turned into a small library.

"I seldom drink," Jys said. "But I would have water if it is available."

"Water is always available here," the man said. "We live beneath the snow caps."

"Of course."

A bell was rung, and the short man who had carried the bow in the forest came and then left again to fetch them drink. Jys saw now that he had a slight limp.

"By the way," the albino said, when the other had gone. "My name is Seriph Tosturo."

"And your servant?" Jys asked.

"Tleeh."

"I am called Jys and the girl is Marilan."

"I did not know her name."

"Is there anything you can do for her?"

"What do you mean?"

"I mean, are you a sorcerer and can you use such to heal her?"

"What makes you think I'm a sorcerer?" Seriph asked.

"I saw the fane of toads at the valley entrance."

Seriph chuckled, then shrugged. "I have some skills but they do not lie along that line."

"I saw the Jagdyke as well," Jys said.

"Yes. Uhm— Well— I am no sorcerer. I have not the power to heal her."

"Then you can do nothing?"

"Perhaps there is something I might do. Though I do not know if she will care for it."

"Tell me."

"Come. I will show you instead."

They went out, meeting Tleeh on the way, and Jys drank his cold water as they went down a long passageway into the heart of the keep. They came at last to a door that opened easily under the albino's hand. Inside was a work-shop with forge, bellows, and anvil, with hammers, chisels, and a dozen small edging and scraping tools. Stone—marble and granite and quartz—lay on the floor or leaned against tables. On shelves and in niches in the walls stood statuettes of various stones and hung masks of several metals. On the floor were bigger pieces, some finished, others only outlines. Here an arm lifted a flower with granite petals. There a face screamed out from stone. Jys was shocked at the pain there.

Seriph did not glance at the sculptures but turned instead to the masks. He picked up a silver half-face with high cheekbones and a patrician's nose. The openings for the eyes were ample and the metal above them of slightly darker alloy.

"This one perhaps," he said. "Though the inside will need thinning. The girl has lovely eyes and this will cover the nose and raise the cheekbones some. She will have her beauty back, or the illusion of it.

"Some illusions can be as good as reality," Jys said.

"Yes. I think you are right," Seriph agreed.

Jys took the mask and looked it over, then handed it back with a yawn.

"The girl will sleep for some time and Tleeh will watch over her," Seriph said. "Why don't you sleep yourself? I think I will start down here on the mask, but see Tleeh in the kitchen and he will get you something to eat."

"Perhaps I will," Jys said, but Seriph had already turned away to his work.

Jys found Tleeh in the keep's kitchen preparing a rabbit stew. There was, as well, a cobbler made from berries. Jys ate hungrily, and, afterward, Tleeh prepared him a pallet in the corner of the room where he could sleep near the stove, and near the door. During the night, Jys dreamed of the old Katana keep and of times when he had slipped from his bed and down the stairs to sleep by the stove in the cold. He dreamt also of the cook, who scolded him, though only when it was time for him to awake. And when he felt a hand on his shoulder Jys thought it was that cook. But it was Seriph, who held up a mask in the morning light.

"What do you think," he asked.

Jys took it from him and studied it. The workmanship was exquisite. "It is beautiful," he said. "If you can get her to wear it."

"I will show it to her this morning. Perhaps you should not be there."

"Why?" Jys asked.

"It will be hard for her. Besides, do you not know she is attracted to you? She would not choose to be embarrassed before you."

"I scarcely know her."

"Your words mean nothing. She sees a youth near her own age who rescued her, in you. She sees a Slayer, in you. And her people have long held such in awe."

"I am no longer Katana," Jys said.

"That is not something you shed as if it were a cloak."

"I am beginning to find that out."

"Do you think the Katai will be able to follow you here?" Seriph asked, changing the subject.

"I do not know. I left no clear trail on the stone of the Mouth of the Winds, and there are many valleys to check. But the Katai are trackers, and some in the village will remember *this* valley. Our hunters may expect us to come here, certainly if they can find us nowhere else."

"Then we may have some time," Seriph said.

"Perhaps a week or two. Perhaps much less."

"There are others who live here with me. They are gone now, except for Tleeh, into other valleys with our goats. They are expected back in some ten days."

"It is not your fight," Jys said. "Nor your people's."

"It is the girl's now, and I will help her."

"Do not be offended," Jys said, "but it would be better for me to work alone. The Katai are very very good."

"I have some skills," Seriph said. "My teacher in the old days was Setai—day sword—though I was never initiated."

"I know of the Setai," Jys said. "What was your teacher's name?"

"Karit Ollmas."

Jys started. "Karit! He who was known as the dance of knives?"

"Yes. He."

"Then perhaps I should stay out of *your* way," Jys said, smiling.

Seriph laughed, Jys with him. It seemed then they were friends.

v.

In the sapphire mists of evening, Jys stood at a corral by the stables and brushed the winter coat of his horse. Shadows crept down the hills with the declining sun, and darkness began to gather close to the keep, bringing down night.

A harp-owl cried a threat to its prey, and long dark bats stroked broad wings in search of insects. Silk whispered behind him and Jys turned to find Marilan. She wore gray that stretched taut over her breasts and fell in ruffles about her slim waist and legs. She wore her hair down in the back and in black waves at the side. And she wore her mask. She was beautiful and Jys told her so.

She breathed out air in a laugh that held no humor. "All an illusion."

"I think not," Jys said. "Dresses such as that only flatter what lies beneath."

He blushed as soon as he had spoken and saw her glance quickly away as a faint pink crept up her throat as well. For a while there was no sound beyond a small wind.

"I am sorry," he said at last. "I did not mean to disturb you."

"It is no matter," she said, looking back at him. "Perhaps it is good I can still be disturbed. Anyway, I came to thank you for saving my life. I must have seemed terribly ungrateful before. It was only that so much had changed for me so fast."

"You don't have to explain to me," he said.

"I know. And for that—" She stopped talking then and came up to him. She lifted on her toes to kiss him lightly at the corner of his mouth before turning to go back inside the keep. Jys stood there still for a while, until the horse butted his shoulder with its head to inform him the brushing was not yet done.

VI.

They spent a week in Seriph's valley and there came no rumor or sign of the Katai. Marilan began to openly express the thought that the enforcers had missed their trail, and Jys began to hope she was right. But no snow came to fill the pass and hide the small scuffs of their passage on the stone, and Jys could not shake thoughts of black cloaks and swords.

Only when Jys tarried with Marilan did he, for a time, forget. On the sixth day, she smiled without pain. On the seventh, she laughed richly. And on the eighth they knew they would not escape a fight. Tleeh came to them that day and told of six riders dressed like crows.

"My people have not yet returned," Seriph said, "but we can go higher into the mountains if you wish, and meet them there. That would give us the numbers."

"I do not believe we could outrun them now," Jys said. "I will fight here. Though perhaps you should take the girl."

"Do not speak as if I am not present," Marilan said. "I will not go."

Jys looked at the black of her eyes and knew it would be hard to force her. But perhaps he would not have to. After all, there were only six Katai. The number had been a dozen before, but the others must have turned back. Jys smiled as he thought of possible reasons. Perhaps someone besides himself had lifted a sword to the theocracy.

"Stay then if you will," he told the girl. "But you will stay inside out of my way."

Marilan bristled a bit but did not argue. "I will stay out of your way," she agreed.

"And I'll fetch my sword," Seriph added. "While Tleeh goes to track our foes."

VII.

Seriph and Jys waited like statues at top of the broad steps leading into the keep until Tleeh came back to them from the woods and said he was followed. Even as the limping scout went in and up the stairs with his bow, the Katai rode from the forest and out into the open space before the hold. All carried weapons and wore them well. All were young save one, and that one was leader. It was he who rode out and told the two at the door what he wished.

"That man," he said, speaking to Seriph but pointing at Jys, "is mine. The girl, too, we will have. She is a witch and has nearly missed her burning."

"They are under my protection," Seriph said.

"The girl is," Jys corrected, "but you do not need her. I am your hunted."

"We will have the girl as well," the Katai leader said.

"Then pray to your god," Jys said. "Though I doubt it will do you any good."

"I should have known you would be a blasphemer in addition to all else," the Katai replied.

"I wonder if you'll not blaspheme when I put this sword in your belly," Jys said, holding up his Slayer brand.

The leader smiled faintly and Jys realized these men were too well trained to be baited. They were not Kraal monks and he would do well to remember that. He had occasion to do so as they dropped free of their saddles and stalked forward in a short skirmish line. Many with lesser training would have come up to the very steps on their horses and found themselves under attack while they tried to dismount.

The leader's eyes flicked upward once as he approached, and Jys knew that Tleeh had been spotted and his arrow would be useless. Yet, he waited until he heard the thrum of the bowstring and the arrow came down to be batted away by a sword. And in the instant the blade was out of the line of the Katai's body, Jys put his own sword right through the man's throat with a straight thrust. The leader barely had time to realize how badly he'd underestimated the ex-Slayer's speed before his heart pumped enough of his blood out into the frosty air to kill him.

Jys withdrew his sword and interposed the brand between his chest and a thrust by a second Katai. The blades rang like bells. Jys's left hand dagger slid out of guard to trick a thrust from yet another enemy, and the Slayer blade sang over and across. The man fell back, screaming, and emptied his bowels as he fumbled with one hand to stuff his intestines back where they belonged.

No more time then for surprise moves or fancy swordsmanship. The Katai bore in and both Seriph and Jys were forced back toward the keep's door. The two enemies left facing Jys were good and quick, and he could do nothing for moments but parry. He heard Seriph grunt and knew his friend had taken a cut. Then Tleeh came roaring out of the door with a short axe to hand.

Seriph yelled for his servant to get back, but the words

fell on dead ears as a Katai avoided the small scout's clumsy slash and sent his blade stabbing through the man's upper chest where the heart would be. The fatal weapon hung in flesh for an instant too long and Seriph killed the killer, but he let his anger get in the way of his defense and his own leg took Katai steel through it. The albino went down, and in desperation Jys hurled his left hand dagger at the foe who stood over his friend. To Jys's surprise, the knife took the man high in the shoulder, and Seriph got his sword in the way as the man fell forward so he could fall upon it.

The blade Jys had been parrying with the dagger nearly opened his face and he barely got his head away in time. He blocked two quick thrusts in what was almost a miracle, and knew he could not keep that up for long. Seriph was out of the fight and the two remaining Katai sensed Jys's desperation. They came in to the attack on left and right, swords and daggers grabbing the light, and Jys caught one weapon on his own blade and slid the other.

Then the attacker on Jys's right suddenly staggered back and went to his knees as something came down from the window above and struck him. A second thrown object caught the fellow in the face, and he screeched as a sharp point took an eye. A larger third object knocked his scream into unconsciousness.

The last Katai standing with a sword knew he was dead when he saw Jys smile. Still, he put up a fanatical resistance for a few more strokes, until Jys caught the man's blade out of line and drove a Slayer's sword through his chest. The silence that followed was welcome.

Jys went to Seriph and helped him sit. The leg wound was deep, but barring an infection his friend would live. That was more than could be said for the Katai. They were dead, save for one who lay unconscious on his back, several small stone objects about his head. When Jys picked one of the objects up, he realized they were some of the smaller statues that Seriph had sculpted and scattered profusely throughout the keep. He looked up and saw Marilan leaning out of a window, weighing another statue in her hand. She smiled.

"I hope I wasn't in your way," she called down.

VIII. EPILOGUE

Jys gazed out the window of the room he'd used in the keep. Marilan stood behind him.

"Then you will go?" she asked.

"Yes," he said.

"And I will stay."

"Yes," he said again, turning to face her. "For one who says he is not a sorcerer, Seriph knows many things. You could find no better teacher."

"I want to learn," Marilan said. "I have always wanted that. But I had thought, perhaps, you might stay as well and we could learn together."

"What I need to know is not in this keep."

"Then I will not say goodbye, for I will see you again."

"I should think perhaps you are right," he said, as he walked up to her. He lifted her chin with a hand and bent down to kiss her on the lips. She opened them for him. When the kiss was ended, both their eyes were wide.

"Stay a bit," she said.

He kissed her again as she pulled him down on the rug covered floor. He kissed her while they made love. And afterwards, he lifted off the mask and kissed her lips and her scars goodbye.

She was smiling a little behind the tears when he rode away.

Just outside the valley, Jys met a jagdyke sitting atop a fallen boulder. It was an albino and wore a silver torc of entwined snakes about its throat. He saluted it with his sword and rode on as its tongue came out in what seemed almost a smile.

From a quarter of a mile higher, the ex-Slayer looked back and saw Seriph limping down the pass into the valley. Not a sorcerer, but cursed by one perhaps, Jys thought. He saluted his friend again, but it was too far to see any response.

Author's Note: *I wrote this piece as a result of a gauntlet thrown down by a member of my 1990s writing group—David Lanoue. He'd written a story in which the members of the group were transported back to Old Japan. He challenged us to write a scene set in the same milieu, and "Of Sake and Swords" is what came out for me. It's as much a prose poem as it is a story.*

OF SAKE AND SWORDS

In the early morning, through the sweated rice fumes of sake, I arose and went down to the nearby lake to bathe my face in cool water. It was only a few paces from where I had slept the night, beneath a cherry tree from which the blossoms had all fallen. Some of those blossoms were wet in the water, and with them swirled the bright ruins of fireworks. I remembered those fireworks, the ephemera of their colors, the clash and wheel and drama of their brief existence, their sound which reminded me so much of war.

Too, I remembered women, geishas whose white faces and brocaded silks seemed designed to torment men such as myself. There had been a pair of them here. But they had left—I think they had left—borne high on covered litters and the arms of eight matched bearers. I could not remember the faces or bodies of the bearers, only the women who had floated like raptures above them.

I wondered why I had not followed those women. But perhaps I had been too full of swords at that moment, too full of the companionship of fellow warriors. Perhaps I had simply been drunk. I knew only that once the women had gone into the village my memories ceased. After that, I recalled only fragments of dreams, strange dreams in which metal insects moved on stone roads, in which buildings of glass rose up to the clouds. It had almost seemed as if I belonged in that place, as if I had been only a quiet little man who liked to spin tales of glory rather than living them.

Such could not be.

I reached down then, touched at my "do" where it was covered with mud from my bed, touched at the white cords that bound my blades. My head was bare and I wondered what I had done with my "kabuto." It shamed me that my armor was dirty, that my helmet was lost, shamed me that the lacquered "same" of my scabbards was stained.

My hand found the cord-wrapped hilt of the "katana" and drew the sword out. The dawn star's rays struck the steel and my shame turned to horror. All along the blade lay the black remnant of blood. In the night I had taken a life. And I did not recall it.

At that moment a high and wavering scream startled morning birds in the village behind me. The voice in that scream ached with loss and I turned and ran toward the sound, hoping it was not my hand which had birthed that shout, hoping I had killed only a peasant or a poet, someone of no importance. I feared such would not be the case, and I found I was right when I reached the place from which the voice had sounded.

In a pile on the ground lay a geisha, her red robes covering what surely was blood. But in the next moment I saw she had risen, with tears streaking the frosted white from her cheeks. And I saw what she had covered with her body, the cold emptiness of a dead man who was neither peasant nor poet.

Her lover!

The woman had to have seen me there, a crimsoned weapon in my fist. But she did not speak, did not look toward me. Instead, she turned and walked slowly away down the street, her kimono touching the dust at her heels.

And I remembered.

A man had stumbled against me and spilled the sake from my hands. Ah, I had hated the man in that moment. Though not a poet, he surely would have had a poet's ways, smooth with the words and the glances women love. Yes, I had hated him, though I did not feel that way anymore.

Later, as I sat on a dark stone by the lake, I saw a piece of rice paper that had washed ashore. It had once borne words—no doubt the worthless scribblings of the local poet who was always sticking haiku into dung heaps around the village—but the water had faded the writing and taken away the meaning. I used the paper to clean the blood from my sword.

In the spring, how I hate the poets.

YOU WERE THERE

Saw the veils of light
in the dawns of a thousand years.
And you were there.

Red hair, dark hair, gold.
Silken gowns or peasant linen.
But always your eyes,
and the lips of memory's desire.

Armored as a gray-irised killer,
carrying the sword of dread gods
or the hammer of bastard war,
astride black horse or afoot,
I came,
to a farm, a village, a town,
in bloody rage, or friendship,
and you were there.

Do you remember the sere grass of
 too many dry summers?

Do you recall the drumming of
 battle-shod hooves?

Do you know how I came home to you
 at winter's end,
 my soul unshriven,

my body weeping wounds,
my eyes red with the smoke
 of bone fires?

How I cried those nights in your arms.
How I loved you in the darkness,
spilled all my fears to your heart.
And you were there.

Always there.

AUTHOR'S NOTE: The following six stories all feature the character Thal Kyrin, and are arranged in roughly chronological order. I didn't write them that way, though, and as you'll see there are a lot of gaps in Thal's life that remain unexplored. I've made some notes at the end of these stories about the gaps, and also about the world where the pieces are set.

Robert E. Howard said of his Conan stories that it felt like Conan were telling him the tales and skipping around in an eventful life to pluck out the most interesting bits. The Thal stories came in much the same way. Maybe someday, Thal will return to fill in the gaps.

DARK WIND

1: Thal Loses His Horse

The wind came up dry and hot from the northwest, pushing dust and a gray rider before it. The rider's name was Thal Kyrin and he had traveled far to this place, from Sagea across the Thorn Desert with little water and little sleep that was not disturbed by questions. A month ago a message had come to him on the talon of a hawk, a message written in a hand both familiar and impossible. He had ridden fast in the wake of that note, and now his strange, dark eyes were red-laced as they watched the evening-haunted walls of a city loom ahead. He was glad the gates were open, for he was thirsty and tired, and sore from long days in the saddle.

The sands around his horse erupted men.

Thal glimpsed bearded faces and the dulled gleam of ash-blackened swords. Then he drove booted feet into his stallion's flanks as he tried to ride through his attackers—or over them. His own sword flashed out, left and right, hacking into a shoulder here, glancing from an iron helm there. In another instant he would have won free, but one foe slashed at the horse rather than the man. Tendons parted beneath steel and the animal collapsed like an arrow-shot bird.

Thal pitched over the beast's head to strike the ground with numbing force. A warrior's instincts bade him roll over, pulled him to his knees with his weapon ready. But his mind tallied a dozen men around him with crossbows locked and loaded. The quarrel tips were discolored red and Thal did not think it was from rust in the dry air. His eyes narrowed; a muscle at his jaw twitched. Thoughts of poison made his skin crawl.

Carefully, Thal pushed to his feet, sword still gripped in his right fist. It seemed his attackers did not wish to kill him for the moment, and he was loath to compel them to try. If need be, he'd wade in among them and take as many as he could to Hell. But better now to wait and see what they might let slip. Or to force it from them.

"All right, dogs," he growled. "Come and let's play if that's what you have in mind. But don't bore me to death waiting for you."

A hulking fellow pushed through the others to face the black-haired young warrior. It was he who had slashed the stallion's legs.

"Do not tempt me, Northlander," the fellow said. He motioned toward Thal's red-clotted blade. "You've already taken the arm from one of my best men. I might take yours in payment if you anger me. The lady who bought our hire said not to kill! She didn't mention hurting."

Thal's fists clenched and he took a step forward, only to halt again as the arms holding the crossbows stiffened with tension. Deliberately, he turned away from the venom-dipped quarrels and strode over to his ruined stallion. The warhorse watched him in almost human agony and Thal felt a white rage caress his thoughts like a whip. He reached to stroke the silk-soft muzzle, then lifted to his full height and with one savage blow of his sword cut through the horse's neck into the sandy soil. He cleaned the blade on a tuft of jitter grass and scabbarded it at his hip. When again he looked up, his black eyes bore directly into the brown ones of his enemy.

"I would know your name," Thal said softly.

"Harik," the man answered proudly. "He who is known as the Reaver."

"Well...Reaver. There'll be a day when poisoned quarrels do not stand between us. But for now I think we should go see this lady who hired you. She owes me a horse."

He turned and stalked toward the city, which was called Toralba. The muscles of his back tensed against the possibility of iron bolts, but none came and after a moment footsteps began to beat against the dust behind him. He let himself breathe again.

2: White Lady of the North

"Dhies! It cannot be you, girl!"

The woman who awaited Thal in a marble-walled villa behind the gates of Toralba waved the hired swords from the room before giving the Sagean a sweet but knowing smile.

"No. You are right, Thal. For I am no more a girl. I am no more the fourteen-year-old Alia who stole kisses from you in the gardens of your father's palace."

"But we thought you killed," Thal protested. "When

our hunting camp was attacked by the snow panther and you were carried off. Kranus and I searched for days among the peaks. Even after your bloodied clothes were found, we searched. And nothing."

"Because I was no longer there to *be* found," Alia said. "By evening of that first day I was on my way south."

"How?" Thal asked. "Why? And why have you never returned home?"

Alia stood up from the brocaded couch that made her seat. "I will show you, Thal. So you can see why I never came back to Sagea. Back to you."

With those words, Alia dropped the silver tissue that gowned her upper body, and for a moment Thal's mind could not interpret what his eyes were telling him. Below the woman's perfect face and slim neck her body was changed. It was as if she wore other clothing beneath her robes, a garment of horror rather than silk. Her breasts and stomach were coated with a hard, shiny chitin that molded itself obscenely against her. Black as slate it was, shot through with yellow streamers, like veins of pus. In places the wet black was ridged and whorled, like ritual scars. But there was no symmetry to these scars, nothing to please the human eye. They entwined the woman's form like the marks of chains and nettles.

Wherever small patches of true skin showed through the awful coating there were blisters and welts, burns that looked as if they were rubbed each day with salt to keep them fresh. Other wounds, older, ran across the flare of the woman's hips and down her legs beneath the amethyst silk that fell from her girdle. This dark sheath could move, Thal realized. And wherever it touched, it left its horrid stain.

Why did that stain seem so familiar?

Only an effort of will tore Thal's gaze from the cruelly used girl with whom he'd shared early explorations.

"What man could have done such a thing?" he asked.

Alia shrugged back into her robe and reseated herself amid the bright pillows that filled her couch.

"It was no man, Thal. Nor yet an animal. The snow panther that took me was not just a beast. Something was...riding it. The animal died once we were away from the camp. And the thing—" She paused. "I thought at first it was the kind of being called 'were-kind.' But it was more. It could take many shapes. Some more pleasing than others."

"A demon then?" Thal inquired, though he wasn't sure he believed in such.

"Not exactly. Though not made of flesh as we understand that word. You remember when we were taught of the Conquered Years? And of the monstrous beings created to rule man in that long ago age? I think this was one such being. Perhaps one of the last of them."

Thal started. *That's* why Alia's scars seemed familiar. The patterns mimicked the runes that Kranus, Thal's older brother, had often pointed out to him in the northern highlands above Sagea. Those runes had been engraved on worked stones dating from the age men called the Conquered Years, when star-beings had owned this world of Thanos. Some believed the runes were left by the aliens themselves and that they held a source of great power if they could be translated. Kranus had certainly thought so, and years ago had left Sagea to find proof of his strange obsession. Thal suddenly began to suspect that his brother had been right.

"You seem to know much about this...thing, girl. How did you escape it?"

Alia leaned forward, lowering her head into her hands. "I didn't," she whispered. "It's here with us now."

3: The Thing of Scars

Thal frowned. Then he saw the woman's garment flutter and lift from an unseen touch. He stepped forward, an oath wrung from tight-pressed lips, his face flushing with blood as Alia's gown was pushed aside by something underneath it. An oil-like darkness uncoiled from around her body and slid down to puddle on the floor, then began to swirl around on itself until it started to thicken and rise up on black legs. A head and arms pushed out from the swelling trunk and a man took shape before Thal. He was not tall, nor muscular, nor remarkable in any way except he had no eyes, only crimson runes that twined like smoke where his sockets should have been.

The being spoke, its voice like the purr of satin over skin. "Sweet Alia is so right," it said. "I do not like to be away from her even for a moment. And it is so much easier to ride than to maintain for long this form you now see."

Thal's eyes raged. Alia had been the first girl he had kissed. In time he would have loved her. And this thing—

"Get away from her," he roared. "I'll not have anything so foul touching her again."

The Sagean drew his sword and leaped forward. The being giggled, and before Thal crossed half the distance between them it melted where it stood and flowed back onto the woman's body. Alia threw up her head and shrieked, and Thal dropped his blade and caught her before she could fall. His hands touched the dark coating, and almost he jerked back from the loathsomeness of that contact. He guided Alia to her divan, then pulled away to wipe sticky palms against his leather breeks. It was a wonder the girl was not mad from the sick caress of the thing.

"Alia," he called. "Alia! Can you hear me?"

The woman's eyes fluttered open. They seemed far gone into a landscape of pain, but after a long moment they cleared and focused.

"Thal!"

She reached toward him but dropped her hand before

he could grasp it, as if sensing his reluctance to touch her. With his skin writhing, Thal forced himself to kneel beside her, to take her hand firmly in his. She began, quietly, to weep.

"Par Dhies, girl! What can I do? How can we get rid of this thing?"

"It— He...has promised to release me. But he wants something from you first. He seems to know much about you; I don't know how. But that's why he had me send a message calling you here."

"And the mercenaries who attacked me outside the gates?"

"His doing. Not mine. Harik the Reaver is becoming *his* creature, though the man thinks himself free. The being wanted to...see you coming. Through Harik's eyes. He wanted to test you."

"For what purpose?"

"I am told little. I know only that there is a place in the Jutari Mountains where you will find an object buried in the ice. That's what he wants. He says I will die unless he gets it."

4: In the Jutari Mountains

Thal stopped where a knob of bare granite thrust from snow drifts to block the wind. He looked over his shoulder at Alia toiling up the mountain behind him, her small, gloved hands on the rope he'd slung between them. Her face lay hidden within the cowl of a great cloak. But Thal could see her breath streaming. Only in the past ahr had she begun to tire, after a trek that would have dropped many men to their knees. Thal wondered if the thing that lived on her was supplying her with some of its own awful strength. Was it tiring as well?

Thal grasped the rope and pulled the girl up beside him. Her eyes sparked with light and her cheeks had crimsoned with the chill. She looked so alive, and Thal knew that below the neck it was as if her body was dead.

"How much farther?" he asked, his voice unintentionally rough.

She leaned toward him, her breath coming in gasps of steam. "Not far. An ahr, maybe. We should find a rock chimney just off the trail. At the top lies the place he seeks."

"You act as if you've been here before."

"Only in dreams. He has been here. Several times, I think."

"Then why hasn't he gotten this thing he wants?"

"I don't know, Thal. He doesn't tell me everything."

"But you believe he's telling you everything when he says he'll let you go after this?"

She looked at him. Her eyelashes were dusted with crystal ice, from frozen tears or wind burn, he couldn't tell. After a moment, her glance dropped.

She whispered: "I *have* to believe."

She started past him and he grabbed her arm. "We'll camp here. It's almost dark."

"But he doesn't want to wait," Alia protested. "I feel him...moving."

Thal hoped it was the setting sun that made the girl's eyes gleam so red. He didn't want her hurt, but he wasn't going the rest of the way up the mountain until the sun was strong again.

"He'll have to if he wants *my* help. I stop here."

He thought she was going to defy him. Her eyes glittered and her lips curved back over clenched teeth. But the emotion passed and Alia's tense body sagged.

"He doesn't...like it," she said. "But he'll accept it."

She turned away as Thal released her arm, moving off the trail toward the mountain's vast edge where the world fell away into white insanity. Shrugging from his pack, Thal set up camp. He scraped away snow and pitched the hide tent he'd brought. With firestones and tinder he built a small flame that readily warmed the tent's interior. Alia joined him for stew. And after a short time of talk, they fell asleep. The fire burned down. Darkness closed in.

5: The Coming of the Dark Man

Thal awoke to find a man standing over him. He filled his hand with a sword as he leaped to his feet and called for Alia. But the cloaked stranger made no overt threat, just stood and loomed, like a massive piece of statuary. For an instant, Thal thought it was Harik the Reaver. But Harik was dead, because of a horse. And though vaguely familiar, the man in this tent seemed even bigger than the Harik Thal had killed just before leaving for the mountains.

Remaining wary, Thal poked the dead fire with his sword, breaking the crust of ashes and letting the dregs of the coals throw up enough light to show the stranger's face. The features were sharp-angled, the bones pressing out against the flesh, the eyes set deep under a broad slice of brow. The skin was black, but not naturally so. It looked as if it had been cooked. And every visible inch was covered by scarred runes that resembled those on Alia's body, the main difference being that *these* runes were not alive.

"Who are you?" Thal demanded.

"I waited," the dark man said, his voice filled with the base throb of thunder's drum. "Your goal is only a little ahead. Why did you stop?"

"I do nothing that smacks of sorcery in the darkness," Thal retorted. "When the sun comes up, we'll go on. Not till then."

After a strained moment, the man nodded, his movements slow and ponderous. "I will wait until first light," he said. He bowed beneath the flap of the tent and moved out into the snow, his last words hanging behind like a threat.

Thal spoke a few comforting words to Alia and lay down to sleep again. He couldn't. He wasn't afraid the other man would try to kill them. Apparently, he and Alia were needed too badly. But he was afraid of something else, something he hadn't seen and hadn't heard—though he should have. The dark man had not been breathing.

6: Buried in the Ice

In a crystal bright but shivery morn, Thal arose stiffly and shook Alia awake. He did not feel rested, and even the rebuilt fire could not warm him. Nor was last night's stew anything more than gruel in his mouth. When they left the tent, the dark man awaited them, standing out in the open. Snow clung on his cheeks and in his hair, snow that had fallen in the night and remained unmelted on what should have been warm flesh.

"Quickly now," the dark man said, and he waited no longer than it took for Thal to pull down the tent and pack it before turning and heading up the mountain. Thal roped Alia to him and followed.

Journey's end wasn't far. Alia had been right. Barely an ahr past the dawn saw them at the foot of the rock chimney she'd described. It took only a few minutes to reach the top. There, cupped between jagged rocks, lay a tiny natural amphitheater filled with ice. It stood out from the mountain like an eye on a stalk, perfectly circular but only twenty feet across. It wasn't natural. Beyond it the mountain fell away; below lay a massive glacier.

The dark man dropped down between the rocks to reach the floor of the small arena, then picked up a cloth sack hidden behind a granite outcropping. He strode to the center of the circle and dumped the sack open. An iron pick fell out to ring like a chime on the ice.

Thal shrugged free of his pack and followed the man

onto the ice. In looking down, he saw a shadow, an imperfection in the frozen layers beneath the pick. Something lay buried there.

"Dig," the dark man said.

"For what?" asked the Sagean. "What is that thing?"

"Dig!"

Thal felt his anger surge and rounded on the man. Thal's father may have been a king, but that king had been born a barbarian and the same blood rushed in the veins of the son.

"I'll dig my sword through your chest if you don't curb your tongue," Thal snapped. I'll know what that thing is before I hack it out. Or perhaps I'll make *you* dig."

"Thal!" It was Alia.

The dark-eyed warrior turned toward the woman, hearing pain in her voice, then seeing it in her face. He moved quickly to help her to a seat amid the rocks.

She spoke, gasping: "I don't...think...he can...dig. The ice is...protected...somehow. Only someone not...of him, can dig."

"Then why me, girl? Why force me here by torturing you? Men are easy enough to hire."

"Maybe for the same reason he chose *me*. Something about us. Some connection. Or something else." She shook her head. "I don't know."

"And he'll free you once I've dug this thing up?"

"Yes. At least, I know he'll leave me."

Thal turned back toward the dark man, walked past him to take up the pick.

"All right," he said. "I'll dig." And he swept the tool over his shoulder to bury its tip deep in the ice. White cracks bloomed away from the impact point, distorting the buried shape even further. But Thal knew it was still there.

The dark man moved into the surrounding rocks, leaving Thal to his work. The Sagean let his anger bleed through into the pick. Ice cracked away in slabs. A hole formed, grew steadily deeper.

The color of the ice changed a few feet down, from translucent to milky. And it was softer, and embedded in places with small sphericals of what looked like glass. Thal saw the dark man climb farther into the rocks, looking agitated; it was the first emotion the man had displayed. But Thal's mind was on the object buried beneath him. It was clearly visible now, a black stone the size of a coffin, with glyphs inscribed thickly over its surface. Those markings were twins to the scars that coated Alia's body.

And they writhed as the Sagean watched.

7: Stone Black as Night

In half an ahr more the stone lay uncovered. Swallowing his revulsion, Thal tossed the pick aside and dropped into the pit he'd dug. He'd excavated deeply around the object's edges and now he locked corded arms around it and with a tremendous jerk tore it loose from a cold bed and heaved it out onto the flat of the ice. He was glad to let it go. Handling it was like touching decayed meat.

"Over here," the dark man ordered.

Thal bristled, but climbed out of the pit and dutifully carried the stone over to the edge of the frozen circle where a layer of snow still clung. He dropped it there, and even as it hit the ice, Alia fainted. Thal started toward her, but stopped as he saw her furs bulge up and flatten again as the scarred thing came off her body to flow down toward the black stone. Thal stepped over that flow, knelt to lift Alia to a sitting position. Her furs fell open for a moment and Thal's eyes widened. Through her linen undergarment he could see her skin, free of blemishes and almost too lovely.

The dark man struck.

Thal was grabbed from behind with a strength that pinioned his arms to his sides. He grunted as his ribs took the strain, then reacted, snapping his head back to impact the dark man's face. It felt like hitting stone. But he did it again.

The dark man growled like an animal, shoved Thal forward against the surrounding rocks. A brutal blow hammered the Sagean to his knees, drawing blood where black nails raked. Thal fell forward onto his hands, kicked back and up with his right leg. The kick connected, staggering the other man, letting Thal pivot onto his feet and launch a savage backhand that rocked the dark man's head on his shoulders.

The strike earned a snarl but little else. The dark man lashed out with both hands, palms open, fingers curved like talons. Thal ducked under the massive arms, came up again with his elbow driving like a blade into the other man's throat. The dark man grunted. His feet slipped and he crashed backward to the ice of the tiny amphitheater. Thal drew his sword, leaped down onto the ice himself. He'd end it now.

From the corner of an eye, Thal saw the black stone awhirl with acid colors. The scarred thing had joined with it; its surface bubbled. But there was the dark man to deal with, and Thal stabbed straight down with his sword to finish that foe. The blow never landed. The other man caught the blade in mid-stroke, caught it with both hands and stopped it cold. Thal shoved his whole weight behind the steel, saw it slice down between the other's fingers and halt again. No blood spurted and Thal's spine shivered. A man should not have been able to do that.

Shocked into stillness, Thal hesitated. The dark man thrust the sword to one side, the point grating on ice, and as Thal fell forward the man brought up a foot to catch the Sagean's weight and lever him up and over. Thal hit near the edge of the ice circlet in a soft explosion of snow; the sword spun away with a clatter. Thal rose, his back in agony, his lungs gasping through the pain for air. The dark man charged.

Thal met the other man on the ice. Their arms locked and strained. Feet slid, then found purchase again as they struggled to throw each other down. Sweat ran beneath Thal's furs, froze when it touched the air. The Sagean cursed; the other fought in silence.

Thal's feet slipped as he was pushed back. He lost six inches, then another six. Then more. Thal had known only one man stronger than himself—his brother Kranus. Now he'd met another. His thighs struck the short wall of rock that ringed the ice circle. The dark man's hands shifted upward, caught at the Sagean's throat. Thal's face suffused with blood as his spine bent backward to touch cold stone.

Thal released the dark man's shoulders and grabbed the other's wrists. Straining every muscle, he twisted those wrists, fingers grinding on bone until the grip on his neck broke and the curled hands were forced back from his flesh. He gained half an inch. Then a little more. His back rose from the stone. And the smashing blow of a forehead pulped his nose and hammered him down. Once again the hands locked around his throat and began to tighten. This time, Thal couldn't get free.

8: One Spine Breaking

Black flakes of snow rose in Thal's eyes, gathered into a blizzard that hid the day. His breath slowed and what little air that entered his lungs burned. He heard Alia screaming but could do nothing. His eyes closed despite the struggle to hold them open. From somewhere a dark wind roared, though he knew it could not truly exist. In that wind, he heard suddenly his brother's voice, in one of their last practice bouts before Kranus had left Sagea to wander.

"Against a stronger opponent, use everything as a

weapon."

Thal's eyes snapped open. The dark man's face was close above him, showing every pocked crater and river line of burnt skin. The eyes glittered huge and without soul. Perhaps this man had once been human. Now he was no more than a disfigured slave for the Thing of Scars.

With a final effort, Thal twisted his body to the side. The hands closed more tightly around his throat but the movement brought the dark man's thumb within reach of Thal's mouth. Thal shifted his head forward and locked his teeth behind the first joint of that thumb. He bit down, felt his teeth grind together through bone and muscle. The dark man was still human enough to shriek in pain, and he jerked away, eyes shocked and suddenly just a little afraid.

Thal stood up, coughing and choking, hands rubbing at his throat while a Stygian ooze spilled from his mouth and slid down his chin. He took a step forward and spat the severed thumb into his enemy's face. The dark man's fear went away and he came rushing again.

Thal held his balance, waiting, then shifted aside at the last instant to avoid the dark man's charge. As the man passed him, Thal stomped hard with a booted foot against the inside of the other's right knee. Bone splintered out through the flesh and the dark man went down like a snapped reed. Somehow, he got his one good knee under him, but as he looked up Thal slashed an open handed blow into his throat.

The Sagean's blunted fingers crushed muscle and ripped through cartilage, pulling away to reveal the open drainage of the neck. An oil-black fluid spilled out but still the dark man wouldn't die. Thal locked his broad hands around the man's head and twisted. For a moment the spine held. Then it cracked and broke across like a tree limb splitting in the cold. Thal let the body fall and this time it didn't move.

The Sagean turned toward Alia, and between him and

the girl there rose from the ice an abomination no god should ever have allowed to exist. The Thing of Scars had completed its joining with the black stone. They were one now.

9: The Strength of Thal

As if sprouted from the frozen ground, the thing stood, on two massive legs and spined feet as large as platters. Its black and white body curved up and forward from the legs, sleek and streamlined and hairless, with a pair of arms to either side. It seemed to have no skin, only muscle and tendon and bone, with spaces between where tissue should have been. Yet, Thal could hear the harsh draw of its breath.

The face was beautiful. And rotted. Thal saw three eyes that were jade, diamond, and ruby, and three pair of ears with each pair more elaborate than the one below it. He saw three mouths with pouting lips, and six slits above that might have been nostrils. Three tentacles whipped from the chest, and six bone tails spread out behind like white snakes. Runes of saffron and cinnabar bloomed over its flesh, expanded and burst and died. Others replaced them.

Worst of all, the thing could talk.

"Come, Thal," it said. "Your blood will smear nicely on this ice."

Thal's chest heaved from his battle with the dark man but he moved forward anyway, scuffing his boots, roughing the slick surface to give himself footing. The other had little need of such. Rows of claws extruded from the sides of its feet and gripped down like bent iron nails. When it took a step, the screech of the claws on ice was enough to jell a demon's blood.

"Why me?" Thal asked.

He suddenly wanted the being to talk. Anything to

give himself time to breathe. But he wanted the answer as well.

The creature took another step toward him. Again its claws screeched.

"Your strength, Thal. I want your strength."

"Want? Or need?"

"They are identical."

Tentacles lashed for Thal's face as the being tried to end the fight before it had begun. Thal leaped back, narrowly avoiding the strike.

"There are many strong men!" he shouted.

The creature grinned, the expression grotesque as it was repeated from three different mouths.

"Not the same, my friend. Not at all the same."

"Then tell me why!"

Again the being moved forward.

"Only at the point of death," it said. "Your death. Then you'll see it all. As the dark man saw it."

The being lunged, tentacles and arms whipping forward. Thal dropped to his hands on the ice and swept out with a booted foot to try and take the creature's legs from beneath it. He missed as the thing leaped into the air and lashed downward with the bony tips of its six tails. The Sagean was already rolling to one side but the tips hit and cut, ripping furrows down his back. In the next instant he had come to his feet, his body streaming blood but his eyes hot and angry. In his hands nestled the sword he'd lost against the dark man.

"Oh ho! You are fast, warrior," the being said. "But only fast for a human."

The next attack came like a blur.

Thal slashed upward with his blade, left hand behind the right to add strength to the blow. One of the being's tentacles was cut through, sent spinning to the ice where it writhed like a worm on blazing stone. But the other tentacles whipped around Thal's wrists, locking his grip on the sword. Four hands seized crushingly at his shoulders and elbows.

The heads of bone tails reared like vipers all around him, scored lines down his chest, then lifted to threaten his eyes. A massive foot came up between them and smashed Thal in the ribs, sent him hurtling to the ground. The sword was torn from his grasp and he went sliding across the ice on his back, leaving streaks of red behind. The creature tossed the sword off the side of the mountain to disappear below. Laughter boomed from three mouths, each venting a different pitch.

Thal climbed to his feet. "Come on then," he said, backing slowly toward the edge of the circular depression. "Finish it. If you can!"

The creature stalked forward. "After I've done with you I'll have the woman beneath me," it said.

"You promised to release her."

The being shrugged, its gesture very human. "I promise whatever I need to."

"Then let me give you a promise I'll keep.

"And what might that be? Warrior?"

"That I'll see you in Hell before you touch Alia again."

The being smiled. "An empty threat from an empty-handed little man."

Thal smiled as well, and the being hesitated for a moment. The Sagean raised his hands, palms open.

"I killed your dark man with these," he said. "Broke his neck like string. I hardly think you'll do better."

The creature's smile stopped. With a snarl, it charged.

Thal had positioned himself near the edge of the ice circle where lay piles of frozen debris from his excavation of the black stone. As the Thing of Scars attacked him, he squatted and raked an armful of broken ice up into the creature's face. The material couldn't truly hurt the thing, but it distracted it. As the being sliced through the debris

cloud, Thal ducked its scissoring limbs and came up behind it.

The thing bounced off rock and started to turn, and
Thal reached with both hands and gathered in its tails. He
heaved backward and up. The creature tried to dig in its
claws but had retracted its nails while running and its feet
were already slipping. It crashed forward, striking the ice
with enough force to send a web of cracks spidering away
from it.

With the creature momentarily stunned, Thal leaped
onto its back and noosed its own tails around its neck. He
snugged them tight and began to twist. The being flailed
on the ice, then came aware to its danger. It bellowed—a
mistake. Thal took up more slack on the tails, constricting
the throat passages through which oxygen moved. Unlike
the dark man, this creature breathed. And he could starve
it of air.

The being tried to lift itself, to push back from the ice,
and Thal stamped down on a bent limb, snapping it just
where bare bone met the muscle of the shoulder. The creature's other limbs were beneath it, though, and it got up on
its twisted knees. Thal locked his left elbow as he strained
to hold the tails around the thing's neck. Tentacles lashed
across his face and the raw bone in his hands cut deeply
through the palms. But he held on and tightened his grip.
And still the thing rose onto its hind limbs beneath him.

Splayed fingers hooked Thal's fur vest and tore it off,
then slipped against the warrior's sweaty skin. Another
long-fingered hand lashed over a shoulder with claws that
could take off his face. Thal ducked his head and wrapped
his legs around the front of the creature's knees, tripping it
and sending them both crashing onto the ice. Again the
thing bellowed, and kept on bellowing as limbs and tentacles churned.

One tail slipped from Thal's grasp and lashed at him,
flaying the skin from a cheek. Thal gave his own bellow—

half scream, half growl—and leaned forward to drive strong white teeth into the monster's neck muscles. He tore loose a tithe of flesh, and in its agony the being flipped itself completely over to land on its back on top of the man.

Thal felt the shock in every tissue of his body but he didn't let go his grip. He wasn't sure he could. The being struggled and writhed above him, still living though it couldn't be truly breathing through the crushed mass of its throat. Its tails fell suddenly limp in Thal's fists and it rolled onto its side, freeing some of the pressure against the man's chest.

A grim smile curved the Sagean's mouth, but fell away again as the creature got hold of rock with its hands and dragged them both toward the edge of the ice circle. Tendons in the monster's great arms swelled and popped. And slowly, ponderously, the being stood up again underneath him. Its legs quivered; but it stood.

Fear began to creep over Thal. He'd used all he had and still the creature lived. Maybe he couldn't kill it! But then the hate climbed back into his head—for what this thing had done to Alia. He felt his own strength rebuilding to meet the challenge, felt the laboring heart grow steady again in his chest. His eyes lit with a dark flame as he released his grip with one hand and raked curved fingers down over the being's face. An eye pulped; soft lips tore. The creature had no wind left to scream but shook its head in agony.

Thal felt no sympathy. He released his grip completely and dropped to his feet on the ice. The creature swung a feeble backhand and Thal caught the wrist and snapped it down across his leg to break the bone. Still holding the shattered wrist, he hammered a boot against its leg, bringing it crashing to its knees. He stood over it then, bare chest heaving in the frigid air. The being tried to get its feet under it and Thal punched an open hand to its face, stepping into the blow to drive its head back against rock. It slumped, its two remaining eyes staring at the Sagean in defeat.

"Your will. Too strong," it said, its ravaged voice like a whisper of gravel over brass. "I would have made you a god. As the dark man was a god. As Alia would have been. Under me." It choked. "We would have ruled Sagea. And then—"

The creature crumpled forward onto its face. The runes that had shifted constantly over its body bloomed suddenly in crimson and then faded for the last time. Thal shook his head at the being's words.

It had wanted Sagea, wanted an empire it hadn't earned. It had wanted to be a god, to rule humans as its kind had once ruled them. The thought sickened Thal and he dead-lifted the being off the ice, took a few steps to the edge of the mountain and threw the body over. He watched it smash on the glacier below and go sliding off to where the whiteness dropped down ten thousand feet onto fangs of granite. It was too far to hear it hit, but he heard Alia when she screamed in a voice that burned his nerves raw.

10: Accursed

Thal spun on his heels to see Alia's eyes wide with horror and her hands ripping away the furs and linen that covered her. Beneath the clothing, her body was no longer the pure, undefiled essence of beauty it had been after the Thing of Scars left her. With the being's death, all the energy leached out of her over years was finally lost. Her loveliness began to shrivel, to wrinkle, to age. In a matter of seconds her breasts withered and fell, her full belly melted back into ribs and gaunt flanks. Sores began to appear, began to weep blood and pus.

Alia looked up; her eyes met those of Thal. Her mouth

worked in silence. The Sagean started to run toward her and she turned and hurled herself over the edge of the rocks.

"No," Thal shouted, as he dove in a desperate effort to catch the woman's leg. His fingers grazed her ankle, slipped off as she went over, and he could only climb to his feet and watch as she slid and slid and then disappeared over the brink of the vast ice falls. His fists clenched until the fingernails embedded themselves in his palms.

"No," he said again, but this time it had no heat. When he turned away at last he saw that the dark man's flesh had shed its master's stain as well. Then he understood the final truth, and in that truth his despair was complete.

11: End of Days

At the glacier's foot, Thal piled stones to build a cairn over two graves, Alia's and the dark man's. In a year's time the ice would cover them both and take them into itself. And it would carry them down the mountain as it advanced. Thal felt a moment's envy. How easy it would be to lie down beside them and freeze, to become part of a world that could feel no pain.

It began to snow, and Thal looked up from where he squatted to watch the white flakes swirl from a gray sky. They fell on his shoulders and hair and melted. He lifted a last stone and placed it atop the cairn as he stood up. In one hand he held a lock of Alia's hair meant for her mother. But of the dark man he had taken nothing. Inside that empty shell there had been nothing left of his brother Kranus he could want.

Thal turned then and began to walk toward home. All around him the dark wind arose from among the rocks, speaking softly in its cold and empty voices.

END NOTES

1: **The Conquered Years / Thanos**. In ages past the Earth was conquered by the Selkrie, a race from outside our galaxy. Eventually, the very name of the planet was forgotten and the world became known as Thanos, which means exile. In destroying human civilization, the Selkrie hurled the moon from its orbit into a closer and swifter partnership with the Earth. The resulting cataclysms led to the formation of Saturn-like rings around the moon.

2: **Ahr**. Because of the war with the Selkrie, the moon is now closer to Earth/Thanos and the resulting gravitational drag has slowed the planet's rotation to about twenty-eight hours. This has forced a change in time reckoning. An ahr consists of about eighty minutes. The word itself seems clearly related to "hour" and no doubt is a corruption of that word. A Thanosean day consists of twenty ahrs.

IN THE MEMORY OF RUINS

Prologue

Among the foothills of the Aritainies, in a long valley filled with evening shadows cast down by granite peaks, the memory of ruins brooded. Little marked their presence except for humps of earth and low piles of stone—that and the pale flowers, which seldom grew wild. Yet, the wind that lived in the valley knew those ruins of old, and it whistled and sang in places where walls had once stood as if they were still there.

The evening grew longer and ran into darkness, hiding the ruins for a while—until the moon came up. Then fairy spires rose from nothingness as ancient laughter cried on the wind. Argent gleams lay where streets had once twisted, danced where fountains had once danced. And the flowers bloomed, their scent drifting in the valley. To that scent came shadow-dancers both dark and pale, the stars shining in their flesh and white frost stitched in their hair. For a moment the ruins seemed to wake, shimmering with torches that were only reflections of the moon, thronged with crowds who were only shadows with phosphor dreams in their eyes. But it was a false awakening, and gone when the moon fell.

Karillon! First of cities to rise after the Conquered Years. Where are your spires now? Where your temples and elder Gods? And Karillon. Where are your armies that once bestrode the world? Let them come and fight the dust and the passing of years. Karillon?

I: On A Cold Ride

In the last cold days of winter, Thal rode north, away from Rhohaan and the dark people there whose hearts were colder than the winter, away from memories and toward the mountains where the loneliness was so sharp it cut like daggers. But it was loneliness he craved now. He found it amid the foothills of the Aritainies, but he could not outride the memories.

Thal had come to Rhohaan aboard a black ship the year before, and he left it now astride a black horse. The city meant nothing to him, though he had spilled blood and sweat there. It was only one more scar on the map of his body and mind. Before Rhohaan there had been many other places, many other scars that stretched behind him all the way to Sagea and his birth. In Sagea he had been a prince, and could have been still had he chosen to return. But Thal knew it was not for him. His roads closed behind him like the sea closes behind the vessel that sails it.

Yet, despite the memories, Thal was still young. There was no silver in his dark hair, no lines in his lean face. There was only a part of him behind the eyes that was very ancient. He touched his sword's hilt, recalling too many times when it had been used, and his gaze was drawn to the milkstones encupped in the quillons of the crossguard. A grayness swirled in their depths, like ashes pearled. He lifted his face once more to the wind and urged the stallion on faster, turning distance behind him as a plough turns the earth.

II: Huntress

The pyrvoll ranged south of her usual haunts, drifting down through an unnamed pass into the lower steps of the

Aritainies. She was battle-marked and old, with white tipping her russet fur, but the black savagery of her eyes was undimmed. Winter had beaten hard on the high slopes this year. She'd been among barren rock and snow for many days and had left her kittens dead behind her. At first it had been the cold that drove her. Now it was the faint images that flickered in her awareness, visions of men and of clubs falling, of red on the snow and on the cooling bodies of her young. The pyrvolls were not truly sentient—not quite—but the images of death built fires behind this one's eyes and left her fangs aching with hatred.

The beat of hooves crossed her awareness and sent her quivering to earth. A hunter's gaze panned the landscape and soon identified the source of the sounds. A lone human rode a dark horse toward her. She did not recognize this one's scent and knew it was not among those who had killed her cubs, but that did not matter. It was human. She drifted into a clump of brush that broke the quilted pattern of her coat, and her tail flicked as she crouched again. The man and horse came on, oblivious.

III: When Predators Stalk Predators

The day had flown swiftly for Thal, eaten away by the steady hooves of his warhorse. The two had been long together and meshed easily; the horse seemed never to tire. And the gray peaks of the Aritainies reached up all around them. Thal had reached his goal, though he had no idea what to do now. The country here was largely unknown, though the capital of an empire greater than Rhohaan was said to have once stood near these mountains. Its exact location was centuries forgotten and only rumors were told of the city, rumors of gold and ghosts. Thal cared little for gold, and enough ghosts already lived in his memories.

To prevent those specters rising again, Thal busied himself watching for a place to camp. A forested knoll to the east looked promising and he turned the stallion toward it. They came onto a shallow slope that led down into the dry bed of a silted up stream, and hesitated for a moment. Thal felt uneasy about riding along that empty concourse, as if a shadow lay there while the sun shone brightly everywhere else. All other paths were choked with brush, however, so he urged the horse down into the streambed, his hand resting lightly on the hilt of his sword.

The horse, too, seemed uneasy, but pranced forward at Thal's urging, weaving daintily between stream-worn boulders. They passed a clump of brush and Thal's glance caught it and passed on, seeing nothing. The stallion did see something and shied violently, backing onto its haunches. Thal palmed his sword as a yellow streak came out of the brush to plaster itself to the stallion's forequarters. The horse screamed and reared as a heavy paw reached out and slapped at Thal. The blow was only a glancing one but it spun the Sagean from the saddle nevertheless.

Thal hit hard but rolled quickly to his feet. The pyrvoll's strike had been meant for the man but the reflexive startle of the warhorse had ruined the animal's aim and the killing blow had fallen short. The black was not so lucky. Frustrated of her intended prey, the pyrvoll buried fangs and claws into the throat and shoulder of the horse and took the stallion down. Thal roared a challenge, hoping to distract the beast, and was met by the sight of a five-hundred pound cat that stood nearly four feet at the shoulder rising from behind the bloody hump of the stallion. Without an answering sound, the pyrvoll charged.

Others might have had the courage but few would have had the skill to stand against that onslaught. Thal had learned the sword while still a youth; the movements were ingrained in his muscles. And he had fought in the arena against beasts before. He held the blade loosely, in the grip favored by Sagean sword-masters, and as the pyrvoll rose onto her hind legs to strike with both paws he spun aside and twisted the sword over his head and down. The pyrvoll was quick as a wind and the blow did not connect as Thal had hoped. Still, the blade's tip sliced across the cat's face, pulping one eye into running gore.

The beast fell back, screeching in agony, but the killing urge was in her now and she came up off the turf and charged again. This time Thal went down under her weight, losing his sword. Fangs glistened as they drove for the man's neck, but Thal got his elbow in the way and slid the thrusting muzzle aside. His hands locked on the animal's throat. Claws scrabbled at his chest, hooking in the mail there, and only the good armor saved him from evisceration. The cat's hind legs were momentarily caught, though, and Thal brought his own legs up between his foe's and shoved the cat up and over his head with a tremendous heave.

The pyrvoll landed heavily amid the stones of the dry streambed. She got up more slowly than before, but she got up all the same. Thal went to one knee, scooping up his fallen sword and lunging forward as the pyrvoll launched herself at him. The cat, too heavy to change directions quickly, impaled herself on the steel and ripped open her lungs. The jolt of contact knocked Thal backwards, the cat on top of him. A massive head twisted savagely as the huntress struck at the man who had just killed her. The fangs slid away from a mailed chest and ripped into the Sagean's thigh, but Thal kicked out with his other leg and knocked the cat's grip loose before it could crack the bone. Then he was out from under the beast and back on his feet.

Ignoring the tearing pain in his leg, Thal drew his dagger. The cat was down, then up. With a foot of steel hanging from her chest and bloody froth pouring from her muzzle, the pyrvoll had still gotten to her feet. The warrior admired her courage even as he hoped she would die. She did, staggering forward only a few steps before collapsing, her eyes glazing over like a skim of ice forming on black water.

Thal's leg gave out and he sat down hard. Quickly, he pulled off his mail and used his knife to open the bite wound further. He bent and sucked at the cut, spitting out salt-sweet blood until it ceased to flow freely. After, he tore his linen undershirt into strips and bound the injury tightly. He wondered if the legends were true, and hoped they weren't. The venom of a pyrvoll's bite was said to drive men mad.

Still holding the dagger, Thal rose and limped over to where his horse lay in a welter of its own blood. He winced at the extent of its wounds. The throat was badly gashed, though the jugular had been missed, but the worst injury was to the shoulder where the joint had been ripped free of the muscle. Jagged ivory pieces stuck up through the flesh.

Even if the horse survived the blood loss, it would never walk again. Thal sat down beside the black, cradling its head in his lap. It did not try to rise and he stroked its tight-fleshed hide until it calmed under his hands. Then he drove the dagger into the socket at the back of the skull. The stallion quivered once and was dead.

Shivering with shock and sick from what he'd just had to do to his horse, Thal pushed himself to his feet. He took his sword back from the sheath of the pyrvoll's chest and gathered up his food and blankets. His water-skin lay crushed beneath the rump of the stallion and he felt a surge of fear, knowing he'd need water when the poison-fever started to ride him. He'd need shelter too, for the evening chill was growing. But neither water nor shelter was anywhere to be seen.

Thal began to walk. To the south lay the cities and the physicians who could help him heal. But they were very far away and he would never live to reach them. He walked north.

IV: Karillon in Ruins

As Thal went on deeper into the mountains, an ooze of blood continued to stain his bandages and he hoped more of the pyrvoll's venom was working its way out. Even if the poison didn't kill him outright, he would surely die here alone if it brought madness. He needed water to cleanse the wound. Already the leg had started to stiffen, and he soon cut a crutch to help him walk.

An ahr passed, and more. Darkness came and still he'd found no water. The leg had swollen and he stopped to loosen the constricting linen. Red streaks pinwheeled out from the gash like a hemorrhaging sun, but Thal could do nothing for that except worry and mutter a prayer to Dhies, though it had been long since he'd asked any God for favor. His head felt light and he recognized the signs of poison fever. Potent stuff, this pyrvoll venom. Even his lips were swollen from the tainted blood he'd sucked from his wound. He stopped to rest where a deadfall blocked the breeze. His eyes closed. For only a moment, he told himself.

Cold woke him. He had fallen over until his head was pillowed on a clump of dried grass. He lay there staring up at the icy stars in the black sky and listening to the wind rush through the trees. A hark owl cried in the forest; a fox barked. Both sights and sounds were distant and doubled. With an act of will, the Sagean climbed to his feet and staggered on. Toward morning, he walked into a valley where odd swirling winds spoke to him in tongues he almost knew. A hump of earth caught his feet and he fell.

Thal found himself sprawled across a low stone wall partially buried in the valley floor. Around him in the gray dawn were other such walls, and knolls of earth that might hide the debris of fallen buildings. He had stumbled into the midst of a sea of ruins, or, rather, the memory of what might once have been ruins. And where people had lived there must have been water.

Thal found signs of that water in the rich lushness of tangled vines growing in clumps around the site of the forgotten city. He climbed to his feet and hobbled toward the nearest such clump, pushing a way through grasping branches to find the remnants of a fountain. He fell to his belly and dunked his head deep into crystal sweetness where liquid still poured out between torn pieces of ancient marble.

After drinking himself full, Thal built a fire and heated water to bathe his lacerations. The wound looked bad when he cut away the bandages, but the warm water helped ease the swelling. The flesh had not yet turned black and he hoped it wouldn't. The only cure for such rot was amputation and he wasn't sure he had the will to cut his own leg off. He doubted he would survive it anyway.

The lessening of Thal's pain and fever eventually brought hunger and the Sagean heated more water to make stew. He added dried beef and corn from his bags, and a thick measure of honey he'd brought along for its sweetness. The mixture went down oddly but it warmed his insides as the fire warmed his skin. He soon felt well enough to sleep, knowing the fever would come back with darkness and he'd be less able to rest then. His last thoughts before slumber claimed him concerned the ruins where he rested. He wondered what they were called.

V: Karillon in Dreams

Sometime after the rising of the moon, Thal came awake to the rhythmic ebb and flow of sound. He sat up, his ears filled with the synchronous murmur of chanting voices. His mind seemed pure and clear, but Thal felt quite sure he was now experiencing the full effects of the pyrvoll's poison. The world had changed while he slept.

Warm and humid air hinted of summer instead of late winter, and there was no sign of the fire Thal had built against a lost chill. Gone, too, were the tangled vines that had made his bed. He sat instead on a carefully clipped sward of scarlet grasses, and the trees around him were lean and healthy, their crowns bending under the pregnant weight of silvered fruit. The spring where he had drunk his fill no longer had to force its way from a mouth of broken marble. It spilled in chinkling waves from the mouth of a jade statue.

The statue was of Zerus, God of streams, and Thal knew from seeing it that he must indeed be mad. Zerus had not been worshipped for centuries. Thal only knew about the God from his studies of history. This image, then, must be from his own mind. He stood—his leg twinged but did not hurt as badly as expected—and limped over to the statue. He stroked its cold shoulder with a finger, then cupped both hands beneath its mouth and raised them filled to his lips. The liquid was delicious and chill. If this were madness then it was a strangely lucid one.

The chanting had not stopped while Thal drank and he set off to find its source. Pushing aside a few limbs soon led him free of the tiny orchard surrounding the spring. At his feet he found a path paved with seashells of many sizes and shapes, and at the end of the path rose a wall that enclosed the garden space where he stood. An iron-barred gate let him look out upon the city beyond.

Thal saw a hundred cylindrical towers soaring into the air, and on top of each burned a flame of a different hue. Strung between the towers were black stone bridges that held ten thousand chanters. The night was alive with their torches and their murmurous sounds, with their flutes and rattles and timpani. Thal could not believe any of it was real.

The sound of weeping seemed much more true when it

came to him. He turned and saw a young woman walking toward him along the shell path. The light of tree-hung lanterns fell upon her, weaving her hair with golden webs. A simple white robe was belted at her waist; around her neck hung a silver torc. Thal cleared his throat.

Startled, the woman looked up. She was beautiful in her tears, but her eyes went wide at sight of him and her mouth opened as if to scream.

"Please," Thal said, holding out his hands so she could see them empty of weapons. "I mean you no harm."

The woman did not scream but *did* take a reflexive step back. She recovered quickly. "Who are you?" she asked. "You are an outsider? How got you into the city?"

Thal found he could understand her. Her language was much like Rhohaan's, though some of her words were ordered strangely.

"I *am* an outsider," he said. "My name is Thal Kyrin. As for how I got here, I'm afraid I can't tell you. I woke up here is all I know."

She stared at him for a moment and Thal wasn't sure she'd understood him until she nodded. He wondered at her quick acceptance of his vague explanation. But perhaps anything was possible in madness.

"How are you called?" he asked her.

"Kamirin."

He was about to ask the city's name when the pounding of booted feet sounded along the shell path. Kamirin glanced behind her, then back to him. Thal was surprised to see fear in her face, not for herself but for an "outsider."

She rushed forward. "Quick," she said. "You must flee. Deshea will be angry if she finds you here."

"Who's Deshea?" Thal asked, as Kamirin grabbed his arm.

"There's no time," she said. "The guards. I hear the guards."

But it was too late to just hear them. They burst into

view even as she spoke, a half dozen men in scarlet and bronze.

Kamirin let go of Thal's arm and stepped in front of him, but the dark warrior grasped her gently and pushed her aside. Clearly, the guards had no intention of allowing explanations, and Thal did not want the unarmed girl in the path of the weapons. He stepped away from her, blade sliding into his fist, and as the first man thrust for his chest Thal spun his sword a hundred and eighty degrees and batted the stroke aside. His riposte was instinctive and the arc of the ripping blade spilled the fellow's throat into the air. Instantly, Thal sidestepped, going right to favor his injured leg, and the movement was enough to make the guards alter their angle of attack.

A spearman stabbed at Thal from a crouch, hoping to slip below the warrior's defense. Thal took the leaf-shaped head off the spear with a flick of his sword, then caught the destroyed lance's shaft in his left hand and jerked the man toward him. As the guard stumbled forward, Thal smashed an iron sword hilt into his jaw and let him fall unconscious across the path of his fellows. One could not stop his rush quite fast enough and tripped over the body. With an economy of effort, Thal killed the off-balance guard and slid aside yet again.

The remainder of Thal's foes hesitated. In a few short moments three of their number had gone down, two of them dead, and the rest had been maneuvered out of position. They were stunned by the change in fortunes, and open to slaughter. Thal chose not to kill them. He had nothing against them. He only wanted to know where he was and how he had gotten here, for the clang of swords had driven thoughts of any madness from his mind. He was about to lower his blade when a voice called out from behind the guards. It was a woman's voice, harsh, commanding.

"Do not kill him, fools," the voice said. "See you not

that he is a stranger?"

Thal did not like the hungry emphasis the speaker put on that last word. Without taking his eyes off his recent attackers, who seemed quite happy not to have to *kill him*, Thal moved to where he could see the woman who gave the orders here. She was like her voice, commanding, with a sharpness etched deeply in the angles of her face. But she was also beautiful, dark of hair and dressed in scarlet.

The harshness went away when she smiled at Thal and spoke: "Forgive my guards," she said. "So few strangers come here. My name is Deshea, Queen of this city. You've already met my sister, Kamirin. Please, come and let me pour you wine and welcome you to Karillon."

Thal saw no anger in the Queen, as Kamirin had prophesied. He saw only the kind of refined beauty he'd known years before at the court of his father. He had not realized how much he missed it.

Yet, Karillon? The name snapped at Thal's memory but it was not until later he recalled the reason. Karillon had fallen half a hundred centuries before. Thal did not ask the Queen to explain. By that time he was lost in the hollows of her eyes, which were wet and full of dancers.

VI: Karillon in Glory

Karillon is full of wines like mists on the throat, full of music like the caress of water over pure silver bells. In that city it is always a beautiful dark and the moon hangs ever in the sky. Even the movements of the people are lovely, as lovely as the whispering of sands in a vast desert. And the time is given over to pleasure.

Thal tasted all the pleasures, with the Queen by his side. In time she even kissed him, and her eyes and lips pledged more, always more. For a while, Thal fought the city's lure. He knew this was no poison dream and there were questions to which he wanted answers. How had he come here? Was this truly Karillon? What did Deshea want with him? But the Queen always evaded replies, filling his mouth with wine and his ears with promises that turned him away from questions.

In a few days the dark-eyed warrior ceased to wonder. He rose when he wished, went to bed when he wished, or when the Queen wished. Many substances besides wine existed in Karillon, and under Deshea's guidance Thal sampled them all.

He swallowed night, a substance as black as its name. He ate the tiny ivory blooms of the tsleetha plant and sniffed crushed powder from the pearls of the kellet. His teas were laced with chirik root and thorn leaves, his food with dream-bird eggs. The Queen's lips were the moistest of drugs. He forgot his worries in them, and only the sight of Kamirin would bring his fears back for a little while. Another cup was always handy, though, if he should need hide a troublesome face.

In truth he was fevered now, if not before. He rode on soporific wings over the city, wafting on delicate thermals over rainbow towers and feathered bridges of amethyst and black. He lay in hard rains, with daggered hail stabbing his body, and the Queen like warm blood in his arms. His feasts, she conjured from the cinnamon air, and they were meats on his tongue and sugars to his teeth, though he wondered why they did not appease his hunger. But mostly his food was the Queen herself, in the guise of a thousand women whose eyes never changed.

The ahrs marched away to be buried.

Thal had no way of measuring how much time had passed when he returned to his quarters one morning to find a dead man at his door, a black-headed crossbow quarrel protruding from his chest. Kamirin stood over the body, the crossbow still in her hands.

Though both Kamirin and Deshea were beautiful, they looked nothing alike. The Queen was dark haired and fleshed, Kamirin blonde and pale. For the first time, Thal realized how truly lovely Kamirin was. And he saw again the look of concern that had crossed her face so often of late. He couldn't quite recall when he'd first seen that look. It had been in a garden, he thought. With guards.

Then he remembered the fight on his first night in Karillon, though it seemed a different man who had beaten those guards. He remembered a pyrvoll bite wound to his leg as well, and his fingers touched the place through the silk robe he wore. The wound had healed, and he forgot about it all as he looked to Kamirin and asked her for wine.

She shook her head. "You need no more wine. Come. We must go."

"Where?" he asked, letting her take his hand, letting her lead him. "I must soon meet the Queen."

Kamirin did not speak, and after a moment Thal pulled away. "What are you doing?" he asked suspiciously. "Where are you taking me?"

She turned on him, snapping at him as if he were a spoiled child. "Are you such a fool that you cannot see what the Queen really is? By Zerus, I thought you were smarter than that. The Queen is using you for her own ends. She cares nothing for you!"

"No! Not true. She has said we will be married!"

Kamirin laughed, the sound jarring Thal with its ugliness. He had heard little laughter, even cruel laughter, in Karillon. Kamirin grabbed Thal's hand and drug him over to the wall, to where hung a burnished shield that boasted of past battles.

"Look at yourself," she said, shoving him forward to face the mirror of the shield. "Look at yourself when the Queen is not there to fill your eyes with mirages. Do you truly think Deshea will marry you?"

Thal looked as he was bid, and what he saw did not seem to be what he was. His face was all lines and hollows, empty of soul. His body lay thin and shrunken beneath sleeping silks stained with wine and drool. A ring on his finger glowed blood red and pulsed to the beat of his heart. The Queen had given it to him at their first feast together, and for the first time he felt its cold, felt it moving on his finger as the skin tried desperately to writhe away from its touch.

It was not enough. He saw the horror of what the Queen had done to him, but it was not enough. Something inside of him wanted it all, until Kamirin opened his palm and placed a fetish within. She bade him look, and Thal looked and saw his sword; how could he have misplaced it? The milkstones in the quillons sparked and glittered with life.

If only he had noticed before. Milkstones were jewels of power, used by sorcerers and against sorcerers. Their gleamings would have told him what the Queen was, if he had not stared into her eyes so much that he forgot to glance down. As the warmth of the stones entered his hand and moved up the arm toward his heart, he swore not to forget again. After a moment, he tore the ruby ring from his finger and hurled it to the floor.

"Now you see," Kamirin said.

"Yes," Thal said. "You are right. We must leave. Only, you must tell me what the Queen wished of me."

There is no time to explain fully now," Kamirin said. "I will tell you that the strength you've lost has fed the Queen, and her city. You are the reason Karillon lives as much as it does. You! And the Queen will drain you to the dregs to keep it so."

Thal nodded, knowing the truth of what Kamirin had said and realizing he could wait to hear the rest. He turned to follow her, and a honeyed voice snared them like rabbits.

"Why don't you tell him all of it *now*, beloved sister? I give you leave."

Thal's eyes cracked with anger as he turned to see Deshea's smirk. He took a step toward her, fist on his sword, and the Queen held up her spread hand so the fingers dripped green and scarlet sparks.

"Tell him, sister," she said. And now no sweet pretense coated her voice.

Kamirin obeyed, her words infected with pain. "On the morrow," she said, "Deshea intends to sacrifice you to Aven the Glorious, Lord of the New Moon."

The Queen smiled into Thal's face as he heard the truth.

"Why?" he asked her. The question was meant for the Queen, but Kamirin answered.

"Because this is Karillon. Karillon, which fell in an earthquake five hundred years ago and did not die. The Queen...." Kamirin looked at her sister with hate. "The Queen would not let it die. She used the power of Aven, the power of sorcery, to chain the shades of Karillon's people to the ruins. And then she waited. We have all waited. Until one would come whose strength she could drain to appease the God. You are that sacrifice. Your death will return this city to its glory, and my sister to the power of a living throne."

Thal's eyes lay very cold upon the Queen when Kamirin had finished. Deshea only laughed. "The two of you are so excellent. Barbarian filth and silly girl child. Aven will enjoy you immensely. As I have done."

Thal laughed too, which turned down the corners of Deshea's lips. He started walking forward, swinging his sword lightly from side to side.

"Guards," the Queen called, and a dozen men stepped from wall openings to interpose themselves between their mistress and the dark warrior who stalked toward her.

"They are not enough," Thal called to her. Then he leaped.

The guards closed ranks, ripping out their own steel.

Thal's whirring blade tore splinters from the defender's shields but his furious attack could not quite break through the line to reach the Queen. In the first lull, the guards were even able to counterattack, forcing the Sagean back under the weight of armor and swords. Luckily for Thal, the hallway where they fought was too narrow for the guards to come at him all at once. He backed slowly away, holding his enemies at bay by skill and the power of anger. It could not last.

They came finally to a place where their hallway was joined by other corridors, and the Queen's men saw their chance at a flanking movement. They circled out around him, moving to come at him from all sides. Thal did not try to retreat further, as they expected. Instead, he saw an opening in their midst and hurled himself forward, hoping to reach the Queen and take her hostage for his and Kamirin's safe passage from the city.

His sword flashed left and right, clearing a path. His shoulder struck a shield, knocking a burly soldier off his feet. Then Thal was free of the crush and reaching for the Queen. She smiled and cast a spell of glittery dust in his eyes. The Sagean stumbled, half blinded, and the guards caught him from behind and drove him to his knees. The hilt of a sword hammered him behind the ear.

"Do not kill him," the Queen commanded. "He must still serve Aven as sacrifice."

Deshea's last words had to fight their way through the bat-wings of unconsciousness that flapped in Thal's head. Behind the Queen's voice he heard Kamirin weeping, but another blow struck even that awareness from him and he slipped to the floor. As he fell, Thal released the catch holding the milkstones to the quillons of the sword. His last waking act was to palm them and command his hand to hold them tightly.

VII: Aven

Beneath a brilliant moon, the arena of Karillon was much the same as that of Rhohaan, or Tanith, or Vendori. Thal recognized the white blood-sands and the rising tiers of seats immediately after coming to. He had fought in such places before, but he was not to fight now apparently. His arms were roped behind him to a massive stake of yew. Kamirin was bound at his back, still unaware.

In front of Thal were the grated tunnels leading to the underground cages where the animals and gladiators would be kept. He wondered if the God Aven was kept in those tunnels. He wondered what Aven was. Thal no longer believed the true Gods took much part in human affairs, but he had seen beings *others* worshipped as Gods. And some of them had been powerful. Things other than human dwelt on Thanos, and who knew what beings might have dwelt in this city of the past, in Karillon of the Empire.

It had not been much before that time when the Selkrie had come from beyond to plough up human civilization. Thal knew from ancient texts and songs that those mysterious beings had tried to make themselves Gods before returning to the stars, and that some of their creatures had continued to try, until humans tore down the last of them. Or thought they had.

Thal had already met at least *one* survivor from that time. Was this Aven another remnant, mired perhaps in the amber realm that was Karillon? Or, maybe it was just such a being that held Karillon here, fallen but undead. To such, five hundred years might seem ephemeral.

Though Thal knew his speculations could be wrong, he also knew enough history and mythology to believe his guesses were not wild ones. The Selkrie *had* been here on Thanos, and had created things of great power and horror.

And, as evidence too, there were the milkstones that he still held in his left hand. Their heat was greater than he'd ever felt it in the presence of a mere human sorcerer.

The stones were a legacy of the Selkrie and not really all that rare; he'd once found dozens of them buried in a field of ice. But few humans could use them to work sorcery. Deshea was probably one such, though Thal had never seen her carrying a stone.

The Sagean was himself no wizard, but he remembered what his brother Kranus had taught him about the Conquered Years, and what he'd learned himself in the time since his brother's death. The milkstones could also be used to nullify magic, even reverse it. It required only the kind of mind discipline innate in the training of a warrior, the ability to block out all pain, all thoughts except the immediacy of parry and riposte. The milkstones could build a wall around such a mind, a perfect reflecting sphere from which sorcery was banished.

Of course, any being left over from the Selkrie's reign would be immensely more powerful than a human thaumaturge, but Thal felt sure the stones would work on it too. After all, the Selkrie were supposed to have used the milkstones to control their own minions.

A moan from Thal's stake companion snapped his mind back to the arena. Kamirin was awake.

"Are you well?" he asked her.

"No! They drugged me! And now my head hurts and I feel sick!"

Thal chuckled at Kamirin's tone but there wasn't much humor in it. "Well, you may not feel sick much longer," he said.

"I wish they would get it over with."

"I'm not anxious to be sacrificed myself."

"I know," Kamirin said. "It's just that the waiting will tear at my courage and I don't want to cry in front of Deshea."

"What's supposed to happen, anyway?" Thal asked.

"Deshea will call Aven to come and take us. I don't think she is in the tiers yet, though. The crowd is too quiet."

"And when she calls on Aven, what will come?" Thal asked.

"I have no answer. I've never seen him, though those who have say he can take many forms, that sometimes he comes as a giant raptor, sometimes as a burning cloud or as a wind."

"But he is real?"

"Quite."

"I do not understand how my sacrifice is to awaken the city?"

"Nor do I, really. That is what Deshea tells the people, and what they believe. She says a spark of your life will be given to every person and Aven will use that spark to heal them of death. I do not know if it is true."

"Why did Aven wait five hundred years? Surely he could have found a living soul before this."

"No. Aven is as bound to Karillon as the city is to him. He had to wait for someone to come. And not just anyone. He needs a special soul. Your soul. I knew it when I saw you, as did Deshea."

Kamirin's words reminded Thal of more legends. The Selkrie were said to have created a race of artificial beings called Tyzinn to serve them. The most powerful were the Nha-Tyzinn, who had been so dangerous even the Selkrie had feared them, and so had chained them by massive sorceries to the place of their creation. It had been the Nha-Tyzinn who ruled humankind during the Conquered Years, when the Selkrie owned Thanos. All were supposed to have been destroyed when the Selkrie left, but the Sagean had begun to believe that Aven might be one that had escaped. If so, Thal had only the milkstones to try and fight it.

A barely restrained roar went up from the crowd, and Thal looked up to see that the Queen had arrived. He watched her, eyes narrowing with remembered use at her hands. She strode like the ruler she was to a platform raised above the other tiers and lifted her arms for silence. The throng gave it to her instantly. A moment later she broke the silence herself, with a chant full of alien words that were ancient when Karillon was young. Thal did not understand them. But they burned.

"*Paar Vaull*, Aven. *Dirkitsch allnen sonne. Komish vor tuan en loas ses-seyno. Paar Vaull. Komish. Yhr ventano ses.*"

Again and again Deshea hurled the words into the sky, and just when Thal thought she would get no answer the sky started to change. Cloudy tears of darkness began to pour from the eyeless face of the moon, and the normal white light of that orb began to shimmer and alter, from pearl, to gray, to bloody red. And when it was all red, the color poured out into the surrounding clouds, igniting crimson lightning that cracked wide the night.

The people in the tiers, the shades of Karillon, gasped and fell to their knees, hiding their faces as their God began to materialize out of the storm. Wings unfolded from tattered cumulus streamers; eyes blinked open with thunder. In another moment, bladed talons extended beneath the mass and the shape of a giant raptor was born. It hung in awesome silence above the arena.

Deshea's chant intensified now. "*Paar Vaull*, Aven. *Durnish nak tarin. Ramen vor en-lish todencril. RAMEN VOR EN-LISH TETHERAMON!*"

Thal sensed the urgency, the exhortation in the Queen's voice. The God heard it too, and came down, dropping straight toward the arena and the stake that held its bound offerings. Thal strained desperately to free himself and the girl, but the ropes held tight as a boulder-sized claw reached out and plucked both prey and stake from the arena sands. The catch of a God's wings on air jerked the two humans upward into the atmosphere. The constriction of the talon sliced through the restraining ropes but then held them even harder, hard enough to cut off their breath. Thal and Kamirin started to die.

Thal closed his eyes and gave every ounce of his strength to the act of loosening the raptor's tightened claw. But in another instant the constriction released on its own and the swift sense of motion through the air ceased. Thal blinked to find himself standing on the dome of a peak in the Aritainies. The sky was dark around him, but the ringed moon overhead was red. Far beneath him, as if through a fog, glimmered the lights of Karillon. Kamirin lay at his feet, breathing but unconscious.

The sound of laughter called on Thal to attend. It was a laughter filled with both sweetness and evil, like rotten honey, and it came from a man who sat before them on a throne of antlers. Well, not a man but a God in the guise of a man perhaps. No man could own such iridescent eyes. They broke light like the mirrored scales of a fish.

"Aven," Thal said.

"Yes."

The milkstones in Thal's palm began to cook like coals, the pain leaping from his hands to his wrists, and from there to his arms. Still, he held the jewels. The intensity of their reaction proved Thal's suspicions right—this had to be a Nha-Tyzinn—and that same intensity promised his only weapon.

"I'm afraid I must resist you," he said to Aven. "Karillon is better dead."

The silvered tarns of the Nha-Tyzinn's eyes widened with surprise. He must have forgotten what humans were like in his long, quiet time. It made him angry.

"You cannot stop me. No human can stop me."

"Yes, I can," Thal said. "I know you are not a true God."

The horn throne where Aven sat began to shiver and shake with the Nha-Tyzinn's growing rage. The skin of the being's fingers split to reveal the wicked curving of dark talons.

"For that, human, I will destroy your soul utterly."

"No," Thal said. "You might kill me but you have no power over my soul. I know who you really are. Not Aven the Glorious but a Nha-Tyzinn with a gift for the theatrical. A thousand years ago the Selkrie, your masters, tried to make themselves Gods of Thanos. As ever, your kind tried to mimic them. Until humans threw you down and you fled back to whence you came."

Thal knew only what he had heard and read about the Nha-Tyzinn, what had been passed down for centuries. It could easily have been distorted beyond all recognition. Yet, it seemed his words sliced close to the target.

"Not all of us were thrown down!" Aven roared. "Not all of us fled! I survived in this wilderness until humans came here to found a city. I made that city an empire." The God's roar softened then. The sparkle in his eyes quieted. "But it began to bore me," he added. "If you know the Nha-Tyzinn then you know I am chained here. But only so long as I inhabit this flesh. In human form I can leave. I killed Karillon myself, because I needed the souls of a million dead to work that sorcery. Now all I need is your body. With it, I rule this world."

"And Karillon?"

"You said it. Karillon is better dead. Its only purpose was to serve as bait."

"I cannot let you do this."

"I'm afraid you must." And Aven reached out his hands to take Thal's life, and Kamirin's death.

Those hands turned into shadow-clouds filled with lightning, hail, and cold oblivion. Thal waited until the dark enveloped him. Then he held up his clenched left fist and opened it outward. On his palm lay the twin ovals of the milkstones. Once ashen and cold, the stones burned like suns now, ignited by the nearness of the Nha-Tyzinn. Thal drew one into either hand and struck them together within the shadows that wreathed him. And he called out a phrase his brother had taught him: *"Jurenda vomikar."*

The shadows recoiled.

For a moment, Thal caught sight of Aven's strange, fish-scale eyes. In the next moment those eyes were gone as red and gold light leaped outward from the stones to hammer against the darkness of a would-be God.

An explosion of steam followed, as of an achingly hot rock dropped into equally cold water. Veils of sparks clashed against each other amid the screaming sizzle of a monstrous griddle. Then the golden light was thrown back and Aven rematerialized. Half his face appeared made out of puddled iron, but his one good eye fixed on Thal with more than human hatred. Thal felt his will weaken as he realized the stones were not going to be enough. Then he heard Kamirin scream Aven's name.

Thal looked down to see something in Kamirin's hand, something she had taken from her dress and held aloft, something that cooked with the same flame as Thal's milkstones.

"Paar Vaull, Aven," she screamed. *"Paar Vaull. Jurendis vomikaris."*

Kamirin knew the *right* words. And she knew the right thing to do. She threw the thing in her hand toward the Nha-Tyzinn. It struck against the creature's wounded face and instantly sucked the remnants of the golden light down around it.

Aven howled, in terror rather than anger, and Thal hurled his own milkstones into the gaping mouth of the figure. The Nha-Tyzinn fell back, screeching with fresh agony and fear, and his limbs began to flail as convulsion after convulsion swept his body. The moon seemed to swell insanely above their heads before it ripped open to spill a hundred thousand burning petals down on the mountain. Where the petals struck there sprouted black flowers that grew to entwine Aven in a thorned embrace.

Aven held his hands to the sky and cried out one word: "*Tetheramon.*" In the next instant, a light bloomed inside his belly, so bright it was clearly visible through his skin. That glow brightened more, and even more, until it dazzled like the corona of a sun. And when it was so bright it could not be looked upon, it imploded and was gone, taking Aven with it.

Thal staggered over to where Kamirin lay on the ground and collapsed to his knees beside her. He lifted her head against his chest and her hands clasped down hard on his. Over her shoulder, down at the foot of the mountain, he could see where the ruins of Karillon stood. Even with Aven gone the phosphor shapes of rock walls and bridges and towers loomed ghost-like beneath a newly sane silver moon. Thal knew it wouldn't last. The coming of dawn would mean the going of Karillon. Forever. And with the city would go Kamirin, whom he was quite sure he loved.

"Yes," she said, as if reading part of his thoughts. "At dawn the city will die a last time. And me with it. Even now the sky is graying."

"You can stop it," Thal said. "I saw you had the power. We can stop it together."

"No. Not this time. I shared some little bit of my sister's power, it is true. I had a milkstone. But now it is gone and my power went with it. Aven and Deshea were warring against time itself to save Karillon. You saw that they lost. With all the power between them, they lost. We would lose too. And I would rather not fight. Let things be as they should."

Tears welled in Thal's eyes and he started to protest. But he did not. He clasped her hands harder and leaned down to kiss her. The sun chose the same moment to kiss the horizon, and a palette of red and gold light began to spill down over the peaks.

Kamirin arched her back off the stone and her eyes went wide. Thal pulled her to him, held her tight while he squeezed his eyes shut against the hard truth of knowing. There came a soft shudder, and a smell like mint crushed in a gauntleted fist. When Thal opened his eyes, Kamirin was lost.

The dark-eyed warrior looked out from the mountain to the valley where the morning light came creeping like a mist. He saw it strike a great shadowy wall, which wavered for a second before disappearing. Then a tower went, and a bridge full of a thousand ghosts. And yet another tower, from which rose a bell-like scream that Thal recognized. Deshea had been touched by the sun.

Ahrs later, Thal walked down among the ruins. He found his sword amid a pile of rubble. The milkstones were missing from the hilt, but the blade was warm to his touch for just a moment and he knew Kamirin was still with him. Perhaps, sometime, he would dream of her.

END NOTES

1: **Milkstones**. The milkstones are so called because of their color, which is generally whitish. In the story "Dark Wind," there's a scene where Thal is digging up the black stone for the "Thing of Scars" and finds a layer in the ice "embedded in places with small sphericals." Although not named in that story, these sphericals were milkstones, and they were what prevented the Thing of Scars or its servants like the dark man from digging the stone up themselves. At some point, Thal seems to have realized this and gathered some of the stones as possible protection against other encounters with the Selkrie's creations.

WINE AND SWORDS

Prologue

The night sands whispered with rain and hooves as shadows moved in the dunes and steel slid softly from leather and silk. Trailing wings of the rare shower lifted equally over the cloth tents and camels of a mendicant's caravan, and over riders with charcoaled faces and blackened swords. Among the tents, they thought all sounds were children of the rain, and they died for that mistake when raiders came from the darkness.

I.

Thal heard a sharp ringing cry and glanced up to see a lammergeier slide out of the pale sun like a nine foot blade and come to earth behind distant sand hills. Others of the bearded vultures circled higher, and Thal knew what he would find beyond the dunes. Death lay under the hot, white sky of morning. He booted Skaal forward, the copper bells on the stallion's reins jingling like ice chimes in the heated breeze, and he loosened the sword scabbarded at his side.

Beneath the spiral of soaring vultures that had guided him, Thal found where a small caravan had dry camped the night before. They had stopped only a day's ride out of the oasis city of Savipoor but they would never reach that goal. Their striped tents lay slashed and burned, their wagons thrown over and ripped apart. A copy of the Ved-Tahr, holy book of the JHestus sect, let its pages ripple in the wind, and a gutted camel nearby had its tongue, liver, and other delicacies cut away. The carrion birds scarcely stirred when Thal rode down among them.

Amid the imbroglio lay a dozen corpses—all males—some in the red robes of JHestus monks, others in the gray and white of drovers. JHestus priests were not celibates and missing women and children meant slavers. Slavers in this land meant Chi'ang. Thal did not even need to see the black arrows standing up from the slain.

Nor would it avail to search the camp for survivors, he thought, until he heard a sound of sliding sand. He spun in the saddle, sword drawn into his fist, and saw nothing except vultures. Yet, that sound had been too heavy for a bird. He dismounted and stalked in search.

In a hollowed place beneath an overturned wagon, he found her. She could have been no more than eleven, with dark eyes and hair, and olive skin. Already sharp cheekbones and large eyes told of the beauty she would have, but for now she was very young, very dirty, and afraid. Thal wondered how the raiders had missed her. Then he saw the sign on her jaw of the horned cross and wondered if that might be the reason. The Chi'ang outlaws were not particularly superstitious, but perhaps even they did not wish to touch a Choizen of JHestus. *Though*, he thought, they would leave her to die.

He reached a hand toward her and she nearly removed it with an owl-swift strike of the dagger she'd concealed in the folds of her crimson robes. Thal jerked away and she came out of the hollow after him. He grabbed at her and she dodged and nearly got the knife into him, but he caught her wrist at the last moment and twisted to make her let go. She did. Then she buried white teeth in his forearm. Thal yelped in pain and surprise, but in a moment he had her down and was sitting astride her. She ceased struggling and lay still.

"Dhies," Thal muttered. "I'm glad you aren't any bigger."

He spoke in Durbin, the language of most tribes in the Kalarg Wastes, and was rewarded with eyes that widened slightly in recognition.

"Now," he continued, "I was not among those who attacked this caravan. I mean you no harm, and if you will allow it I will take you to Savipoor and a place of friends."

She did not speak but he felt the tension go out of her arms and belly, and he released her and stood up. She got up as well, stopping to retrieve her weapon and slide it into a scabbard sewn into the sleeve of her robe. Only then did she brush sand from her hair and clothes.

Thal whistled Skaal over and mounted. She watched with an empty face, but he thought he caught a hint of relief when he offered her a hand and swung her up on the high saddle in front of him. They rode away south.

II.

"Hey, warrior. How muches?"

Thal turned from the merchant's stall where he was purchasing fruit to see a corpulent fellow in the blue and white robes of the slavers standing near the girl. Two others stood behind him, slaver's men by their look. The open gate of Savipoor lay just beyond.

"Goot," the slaver said loudly in heavily accented Savicean, a tongue that people of the Kalarg assumed all northerners spoke. Thal did speak it but did not reply.

"Bet skinny," the man continued, pinching the child's shoulder.

She flinched away from the fellow as Thal strode over.

"Virgin, eh," the man leered, his breath stinking of meat and wine. He tried to elbow Thal, who moved deftly away, lips curling slightly in reply.

The man nodded, half to himself, as he took Thal's response for a smile of assent. "I maybe buys," he said. How muches coin?"

Thal watched the fellow's eyes as he held up a palm with fingers spread.

The man shook his head. "Too muches. I gif three."

Thal did smile then as he closed the open hand into a fist and drove it into the slaver's mouth. The man fell back with a screech, hands at his face where blood poured freely from mangled lips.

"You're a pig, slaver," Thal said in flawless Durbin. "And if I smell you near me or the lady again I'll spread your tripe about for the dogs."

He glanced at the man's guards. One had bent to the downed slaver; the other had his tulwar halfway out of its scabbard.

"Draw it," Thal said conversationally. "I haven't sacrificed to my gods yet today and you'll do as well as any other sheep."

The man hesitated, glancing from Thal, to the slaver, to the girl. There, for a moment, his eyes narrowed, and when he looked back at Thal's size and glittering pupils he slid the blade back into its sheath and left it there. He helped the other guard lift the moaning slaver to his feet and they carried him away between them.

Thal's nostrils flared. He did not like the way the man had backed down. It hadn't been out of fear. He glanced at the girl and frowned; she caught his glance and held it. He handed her the bright yellow Tapazel he had bought and watched her bite into the succulent fruit with ill concealed relish. She was not afraid either, Thal realized, and he wasn't particularly happy about that. He helped her up on Skaal's saddle, pulled up behind her, and they rode on into the city.

"My name is Minay," she said quietly.

Thal smiled again.

III.

The winds of the Kalarg generally blow everything east. Only a few nomad encampments and the city of Savipoor seem to resist their power. And Savipoor is an accident. It lies within a protecting arm of rock where an ancient earthquake once lifted the land. As a result, it is surrounded by broken ravines instead of dunes, and its streets are largely free of sand.

The quake had also provided Savipoor with water, opening channels to the surface from the aquifers that normally lay deep below the desert's skin. Three springs and half a dozen wells dotted the city, providing a richness of life found few places else inside the Kalarg. Trees grew there: dates, olives, a few scrub oaks and thorns. And there was grass. The abundance of water and graze had seduced nomadic herders into a more permanent way of life, and passing caravans had driven the village to grow until it became a city that now held some 12,000 people.

In the year 2117 by the Dhiest calendar, the year 53 after the Prophet's coming by that of the JHestus monks, the Emir Jelikar had built a wall around the city. Now, in the year 2142, the wall still stood but its gates were always open, for the city had outgrown them. Thal and Minay rode through one of those gates.

Thal had been to Savipoor once before, coming up from the south and west as a caravan guard for a man he had met on the Horse Plains. Jhubarr had been the man, a philosopher of sorts, and a merchant when the fancy struck him. Thal had liked him and had learned much from him of the Kalarg and its people. Now, the dark-eyed warrior was back, having come south from Phunom along the Camel Trail. Along the way he'd picked up another traveler, neither philosopher nor merchant.

Minay's caravan had been headed for Savipoor,

though she told Thal their final destination had lain in Phunom, at the northern edge of the Kalarg. They had turned south to Savipoor rather than north along the Camel Trail because the latter road, while fine for horses or camels, was a difficult way for wagons. They had planned to turn north at Savipoor and take the Vikharin Road, which was longer but an easier haul. Thal hoped Jhubarr would know of the caravan, and, maybe, of where the girl's relatives could be found.

Once inside the city, Thal crossed Almener Bridge and turned up Stone Street where it curved north and then east. Along the eastern stretch lay the villas of the wealthier citizens: the merchants and money changers, the nobles, the better of the artisans, the kinsmen of the Emir. There was no dung in the streets there, no rotting fruit with fly speckled skins, no camels or dirty children. Jhubarr lived on that stretch, though he himself was not rich. After the death of his merchant father, Jhubarr had freed the family's slaves and divided most of his wealth among them. He kept only the villa where he had grown to manhood and been happy, surviving on what he made lecturing at the Ceasum, the local academy, and what he picked up on the occasional trading venture.

The merchant's house was much like other nearby villas—adobe and tile—but low bushes hugged the walls and there seemed a thousand birds playing their internal harps nearby. Jhubarr had always been interested in birds and growing things. Thal knew, in a garden at the rear would be flowers.

Thal and Minay dismounted and walked up a narrow stone path to a door of heavy, olive wood. The brass knocker was shaped like a gyre's head and it rang hollowly on the wooden boards. Approaching footsteps soon echoed on the tiles within, and a barred panel slid aside to reveal a black face. The face looked its surprise, and a moment later the door was thrust open and a giant of a man grabbed Thal's arm, a wide smile splitting the huge, square features.

"Yosef," Thal said. "Good to see you once more."

The man nodded, beaming, and then began rapidly finger-speaking.

"Slow, slow," Thal said, holding up his hands and laughing. "It has been a time since I've used that language."

Yosef nodded and made the signs again, slower this time, and Thal was able to catch the meaning. "Good also to see you, Thal. We thought you gone to the east. Come in."

"Almost," Thal signed back as he walked through the door, Minay in tow.

Yosef smiled and bowed to the girl.

Yosef was a castrato and a mute. He could hear and comprehend language, several in fact, but could not speak because his tongue had been removed. Although the black would not hint of it, Jhubarr believed he had served as a sword-slave for someone who thought it important to insure his celibacy and silence with a knife. Jhubarr had purchased and freed him and the big man now served as the philosopher's aide and guard, being well skilled with the lengthy tulwar he carried always over his left shoulder. Just as Thal was friends with Jhubarr, so he had come to befriend Yosef. The three of them were much alike in many ways.

"You seek Jhubarr?" Yosef questioned with quick fingers.

"Yes," Thal said. "Is he about?"

Yosef nodded and motioned them to follow. They found Jhubarr in his garden, kneeling to tend the miniature flowers of which he was so fond, and so absorbed was he that he didn't hear them until Yosef cleared his throat. Then he glanced up in surprise, for his aide and friend seldom made a sound. His eyes widened further when he saw who else was in his house.

"Thal," he said, rising. "I am pleased. And who is the young lady?"

IV.

"So," Jhubarr said, as he poured the last of a bottle of yellow Tra-eala wine into two goblets and passed one to Thal, "you brought the girl with you?"

"There was nothing else to do," Thal answered.

Jhubarr sighed. "You have no idea what you've involved yourself with, my friend."

Thal was not particularly surprised by the comment. Yosef had taken Minay inside for food and a bath, but Thal had seen Jhubarr's look of recognition and shock when he glimpsed the horned cross on the girl's jaw. He'd also noted Jhubarr's smile declining steadily as he told the philosopher about finding the girl.

"You, of course, would have left her on the desert," Thal said.

"No. You did what you had to. But the girl is in much danger. And you with her."

"How so?" Thal asked.

"You suggested the Chi'ang let Minay live because she was a Choizen. Not so. I imagine they attacked the caravan with the very intention of taking her."

"What?"

Jhubarr nodded his head. "That," he said, waving a free hand in the general direction of the house, "is the daughter of Mahmoud, Emir of the Duh-kahari. When his daughter was born with the horned cross on her face the Emir converted to the JHestus sect. You know, of course, that the JHestusians abhor slavery. Since his conversion, Mahmoud has outlawed slavery in his territory, which lies athwart two major caravan arteries running toward the east and the Sunjar Empire. That means the Chi'ang slave columns must go north to Phunom and thence east.

"So?" Thal questioned.

"Mahmoud's daughter was recently betrothed in an arranged marriage to Virsinder, son of Victorios III, ruler of Phunom."

Thal raised an eyebrow. "And, if Minay converts Victorios's son, then the northern routes may eventually be closed to the Chi'ang as well."

"Exactly."

"It is unlike the Chi'ang to think so far ahead," Thal said.

"No," Jhubarr replied, "not like them at all. But then, a man named Kathamoundis has recently come to power among them. He is a thief and slaver like the rest, but more intelligent. It is rumored he is a half-breed Phunomian. Perhaps he knows something the rest of us do not."

"And he would kill the girl to stop the marriage from taking place?"

"Yes, or enslave her. They must have missed her through some quirk. Maybe she was away from the wagons for a moment. But I assure you they will be back for another look when she fails to turn up elsewhere. Did anyone see you with her?"

"Aye. I had a brief run in with a drunken slaver and his guards. I'm not sure if they saw Minay's horn-mark, though."

"Describe this slaver," Jhubarr said, frowning.

Thal did so and saw Jhubarr shake his head. "You do have a penchant, my friend. That was Tarsin. A bought man. Bought by Kathamoundis. If he or his people recognized the girl then they'll be sniffing out your trail even now."

Thal stood. "Then we cannot stay here and endanger you," he said.

Jhubarr waved a hand. "Oh, sit down," he said. "You're right. You can't stay here, but not because of any danger to me. Quite simply, Yosef and myself, even with your blade, could not defend the villa against a determined attack. We'll have to find a place."

"Such as?" Thal inquired.

"Well, I do have an interest in a small inn down in the Warrens."

"The Warrens?"

"Local thieves' quarter."

Thal grinned but said nothing.

"A philosopher has to experience life," Jhubarr protested. "You of all people should know that, Thal."

V.

It was called the White Pearl Inn, though Thal saw nothing of pearls, nor even of white amid the grime. The proprietor was named Stereg, a squat fellow with a blacksmith's build and pale hair cropped close to the skull. He was not of the Kalarg. Nor was he friendly to Thal or Minay, though he spoke to Jhubarr with a whining, submissive tone that grated on the northlander. Thal did not know Jhubarr's connection with the unsavory fellow, and did not ask. He wanted only a room.

Ostensibly, Thal was here as a northern renegade and outlaw; Minay was his slave. Thal had protested the latter but Jhubarr had pointed out that the denizens of the Warrens had seen as bad or worse.

"No one will lift an eyebrow," Jhubarr had said. "Which is exactly the point."

Thal had snorted in disgust but said nothing.

Jhubarr had changed the subject, but in the end Thal had been forced to heed his friend's argument, and Minay stood beside him now in bells and silks and kohled eyes while the philosopher conversed with Stereg about a room. Only when Jhubarr turned to lead the way upstairs did he notice the white knuckles Thal kept wrapped around the hilt of his sword, and he gave thanks to several gods that no one had spoken ill to the girl. The northerner would surely have killed them. Only after the two were safely ensconced in a room on the second floor did Jhubarr relax.

"Take that stuff off and put on your robe," Thal ordered Minay as soon as they were through the door into the room.

The girl moved quickly to obey and Jhubarr hid a smile behind a false yawn.

"I'll leave you now," the philosopher told them. "Yosef will be by in a day or so to collect you. We'll have to figure a way to get you out of the city, but once free you shouldn't have too much trouble making it to Minay's people. Stay inside until then. Stereg is scum, but he's scared scum."

"I thank you for your help," Thal said.

"We are friends," Jhubarr replied. And that was enough.

VI.

Minay slept well that evening; Thal was restless. Just past the twentieth ahr, Stereg brought them cold meat, bread, cheese, and barley beer. Thal awakened Minay and let her eat while he watched. He gnawed on a bread crust spread with cheese, and drank the beer. Surprisingly, it was cold and good.

Minay ate in silence, and when finished she curled up on the bed with her feet hidden beneath her robe. Thal swallowed the last of the beer and sat looking at her.

"You don't speak much," he said finally.

She stared at him blankly for a minute. Then: "Why do you help me?" she asked. "You do not know me. I am not even of your people."

Thal shrugged. "I don't know all the reasons myself," he said. "Maybe I just remember what it was like when I was twelve and got lost in the woods. Or maybe because I never had a sister. Or," he added with a grin, "because you're pretty. I think, mainly though, that it's because I have to live with what I do."

Minay nodded. "The tyranny of kindness my teacher calls such."

"Perhaps," Thal said. "I have not read the Ved-Tahr but have heard similar sentiments expressed elsewhere. There is little new in the world."

"JHestus is new," she said with fervor.

"Then," Thal said, smiling, "perhaps I should read him."

"I will see that you have a book," she said. And then, a moment later: "Do you really think I'm pretty?"

"Yes," Thal said. "And you will be a beautiful woman."

"Beauty is nothing but a random arrangement of sands that does not remain. So says JHestus."

"No," Thal agreed. "But even the memory of beauty gives pleasure."

"Who said that?" Minay inquired.

"I did."

"Perhaps that is what my teacher meant when he said no one dies until the last memory of them is lost."

Thal laughed. "Aye, perhaps it was. But I think philosophy will have to wait until I have slept. Will you keep watch?"

She nodded as she got up from the bed. He touched her on the shoulder as he passed by. "Wake me if there is anything unusual, anything at all."

"All right," she said.

Thal lay down and was soon asleep. And he was awake again in an ahr as Minay's fingers touched his arm. He came up instantly, sword sliding into his hand, and motioned Minay to silence as she started to speak. It was quiet beyond the wood panel of the door, but the emptiness breathed and Thal knew someone stood nearby. He moved toward the corridor and a board creaked slightly under his weight. On that sound, he jerked the door open and leaped out. The hallway was empty.

Minay had followed him into the hall and he looked at her, puzzled.

She shrugged apologetically. "I was sure I heard something," she said.

"I, too, thought there was something," Thal said. "Only shadows I guess. Come on. Let's get back inside before someone sees us."

As he turned to reenter the room, Thal caught a faint odor as bitter as copper. It seemed familiar but he could not place it. With a slight shake of his head, he went in and shut the door.

VII.

Night again, and Thal stalked restlessly, pacing like a caged gyre in the narrow room. Minay sat still. She looked up when he stopped near her.

"I need to use the chamber pot," she said.

Thal blinked. "Uh, of course," he said. "I'll wait outside. Knock on the door when you're finished."

Immediately upon stepping into the hall, Thal felt something was wrong. Again there was the smell of copper, heavier now, and after a moment he recognized it: chirik root—the drug used by gladiators to fuel their rage for battle, the drug used by the poor so they could work for a day with little food, the drug used by paid assassins.

"Minay," he yelled, as he spun toward the room.

The spin saved him as a wheel-dagger flashed by his head and burrowed into the wall at his back. He caught a glimpse of a figure at the end of the hall, but ignored it as a crashing of wooden shutters came from within the room. He smashed back the olive-wood door with a shoulder and leaped in, his sword already cleared. Minay was squatting, her robes pulled up around her waist and a startled look on her face. Behind her, a gray-clad assassin was rising from the wreckage of the broken shutters, the rope he had used to enter the room still looped over the sill.

Thal launched himself. These were Kagarii, from the best of the assassin brotherhoods, and there were two of them, coming at him from different directions. He couldn't deal with them both at once, but he had a few seconds before the one in the hall reached him. He raced across the room, yelling at the top of his lungs in hopes of startling the first killer long enough to get to him. It worked.

The Kagarii slid his long sword out and flicked its tip toward Thal, but the northerner was already past it. Steel whispered against Thal's leather jerkin, and then he'd driven into the assassin and smashed him against the wall. He saw the Kagarii's shocked eyes as his sword tore through the man's sternum, then ripped free to scrawl blood runes across the fellow's gray clothing.

Thal twisted around, letting the first assassin's body fall just as the second killer entered through the door. A flung wheel-dagger clanged off the northerner's raised blade, and then the two warriors engaged. The Kagarii's sword was thinner and lighter than Thal's. That meant it was faster, and for a moment Thal struggled to keep his enemy's point at bay. Then his anger lit and he was pushing the surprised killer back.

As the Kagarii danced lightly away, Minay shoved a chair into his path. The man stumbled and, for an instant, his sword pointed downward. Thal took the opening and buried nearly a foot of his own blade into the man's chest. It came out covered with red shadows.

Footsteps pounded in the hall and Thal glanced once at Minay. "Ready your dagger, girl," he told her, as he moved toward the door.

A half dozen men spilled into the room, all dressed in

the livery of slavers. These were not assassins. They were probably Tarsin's men sent to clean up after the Kagarii, who rarely removed their own bodies. They seemed shocked to see two gray-cloaked corpses on the floor and one tall northlander who was very much alive.

Thal gave them no time to recover from their shock. He attacked. His broadsword sliced downward at an angle to bite through the upper part of one man's shoulder, then continued across to the left to open the throat. Blood spewed in an arc over Thal's blade as it lifted, and the dark-eyed warrior brought up his other hand to grasp the hilt and power the stroke he drove into a second man's face. A scream erupted, and choked off just as quickly as Thal's steel splintered through teeth and into the fellow's mouth. The would-be killers were suddenly falling all over themselves to get out of the room. It wasn't that easy.

As the four remaining slavers turned to the doorway, they ran into a shadow, Yosef with tulwar raised. That heavy blade whistled down to bury itself in a skull, then leaped upward in a spray of wet to deflect a sword stroke before taking another life. The last two slavers stumbled backward into the room to escape Yosef, and found Thal waiting. He killed them quickly.

The short fight over, Yosef grabbed Thal's shoulder and finger-spoke rapidly. "The city guard will be here soon. We must be gone. Or it will go hard with you and the girl."

"Aye," Thal said. "And we'd best hurry. I hear hob-nailed boots now."

Yosef's eyes widened as he, too, caught the sound.

"The window," Thal suggested.

Yosef nodded and crossed to it. The Kagarii's rope still hung over the sill. Yosef tested its strength, then swarmed rapidly up it to the next story. Thal motioned Minay to follow.

"But I wasn't finished," she protested.

Thal grinned, despite their predicament. "You'll have to hold it I'm afraid. Come on."

In another minute, the two had joined Yosef on the third story ledge and Thal hacked away the rope so no one could follow along that path. Then it was only a short pull to the flat, slate roof of the inn. Thal carried Minay on his back as they leaped across to the next building, and the next. They were soon blocks away and Yosef came to the ground, the other two with him.

"Where now?" Thal questioned his friend.

"Out," Yosef finger-spoke back. "All is prepared."

"Good," Thal said.

VIII.

The three of them moved silently through the Warrens. No one paid them heed. Thal was lost after a few back-alley turns but Yosef seemed to know where they were going. Before long they came to the city wall.

Once, there had been a space between the inside of the wall and the nearest buildings to aid in bringing up reinforcements and supplies in case of siege. That siege had never materialized and various structures had long since expanded to fill the available space. The three entered one such structure, a den where ninjam addicts lay enveloped in smoke and dreams. Yosef passed them by without a glance and led the way up a set of narrow stairs at the side.

They entered an empty room on the third floor where a burning candle indicated they had been expected. The room's single window opened directly onto the city wall. All they had to do was step out. Yosef stripped a knotted rope from around his waist and slung it out and over, anchoring it to a merlon that tested solid. They were soon on the ground outside the city.

The ringed moon had not yet risen but Yosef seemed unperturbed by the darkness. He led the way west until they entered a narrow, snake-like ravine. At the far end they found Thal's horse, Skaal, and a camel loaded with supplies.

"I leave you here, Thal," Yosef signed. "Jhubarr will have need of me. The tracks, I will cover. They should not know how you have gone."

"I thank you, old friend," Thal said, resting a hand on the mute's shoulder. "Tell Jhubarr I'll remember him."

Yosef nodded, grasping Thal's arm in turn. In the next instant, he was gone.

Thal moved to lift Minay into Skaal's saddle and saw that her face was screwed up as if in pain. Quickly, he bent to her.

"Are you hurt?" he asked.

"No," she said. "But can I go now?"

It was all Thal could do to keep from laughing.

Minutes later, they were mounted and forging away through the darkness.

IX.

Thal and Minay were a week out of Savipoor, traveling north to skirt the waterless heat of the Zubola depression, when a Nyk-quall attacked their camel. The big orange and yellow lizards were rare and Thal cursed the luck that had let this one find them. It must have been coming up out of the Zubola, and it must have been very hungry to attack a beast twice its size. Thal blinded it with arrows and drove it off, but not before it had fatally wounded the pack camel.

The beast of burden was not yet dead when Thal dismounted beside it. But it soon would be. For now it was suffering. Thal drew his knife and knelt to cut its throat. The animal died quickly but Thal still felt sick. Then he felt something else where his knees touched sand. Bending further, he placed an ear to the ground and heard vibrations that rocked through the earth. Not far away, horses ran, a great number of them. It could only be the Chi'ang.

Thal glanced about desperately for an escape but saw none. There was no cover, not even a ravine. He could run for it but Skaal was already weary from carrying the girl's extra weight. And putting Minay on the horse alone would not work. Skaal had never known another master and Thal didn't think the stallion would go far. The Chi'ang would find him.

Thal reached again for the camel.

When the horsemen, Chi'ang as he had expected, came over the nearby rise and rode down toward him, Thal was sitting with his back to the dead camel munching on a piece of raw, bloody liver. He did not particularly care for liver, especially uncooked liver, but the Chi'ang, to whom it was a delicacy, did not know that. He took another bite as they rode up, pretending to do so with relish.

Thal looked up at the Chi'ang; they looked down on him. The leader, a pale-eyed, gaunt-looking killer with graying hair at the temples, urged his silver bedecked stallion forward.

"What is your name, barbar?" he asked Thal.

Thal took a last bite of liver and moved up to the camel's head where he deftly removed the tongue. "Thal," he said. "And you—outlaw?"

The man smiled at the thinly veiled insult. "Kathamoundis," he said. "Perhaps you've heard of me?"

Thal shrugged. "It would seem you flatter yourself," he said.

The man's lips thinned. He gestured with a finger and fifty hornbows were strung and loaded and pointed at Thal's chest.

"I'll have the girl now," Kathamoundis said.

Thal looked pointedly around. "What girl? I see no girl."

"Where have you hidden her? We've seen her tracks at

your camps."

"Ah, that girl! I sold her at Two Wells."

"I think not," the outlaw leader snapped.

"Think as you choose," Thal said. "But you're calling me a liar. Perhaps you'd like to reconsider."

"Perhaps you'd like to die," Kathamoundis stated.

Thal shrugged again. "That was not particularly high on the list of things I had planned for the day."

"Your plans have just been altered."

Thal stood and began to walk toward the horsemen. He lifted his hands for binding.

"I always try to be accommodating," he said.

X.

"Will it be wine or swords?" Kathamoundis asked, holding up a flagon of dark yellow Tra-eala with one hand and stroking the pommel of his sword with the other.

Thal looked up from where he sat bound to a thick pole thrust deep into the sandy soil of the Chi'ang camp.

"Wine," he said. "For now."

"Release him," Kathamoundis ordered the guards.

The ropes were untied and Thal stood. He waited until the circulation started back into his wrists and arms, then followed the outlaw leader into a nearby tent that loomed larger than the rest.

Kathamoundis sat down behind a table with a kyrellian board carved into the surface; Thal sat on a stool opposite him. The Chi'ang leader took a small, hand-held crossbow from a drawer in front of him and cradled it in his left fist. He then motioned the two guards who stood near the entrance to depart.

"This crossbow has a short range," the pale-eyed outlaw said, "no more than fifteen feet."

"But the quarrel is poisoned," Thal said.

Kathamoundis inclined his head slightly. "A dishonorable weapon, to be sure. But effective."

Thal smiled. "You mentioned, I believe, wine."

"Ah, yes. Tra-eala," the outlaw said, as he drew two leaded crystal goblets from a second drawer in the desk. He poured each glass half full and pushed one over to Thal.

Thal took it and drank. "I don't imagine the wine is poisoned," he said, as he lowered the glass again.

"That would defeat the purpose for which I brought you here."

"So I surmised."

Kathamoundis took a sip of his own wine, then waved the goblet around the room. "What do you see here, Thal?" he asked.

The northerner glanced about at the purple dyed silk of the tent, half covered with lavish arras, at the woven rugs threaded with gold webs from Bir-Noir, at the goblet inlaid with silver that he held.

"Wealth," he said.

"Just so."

"Slaving must be good," Thal said.

"It is, and, though I do have other interests, it is very important to me that the slave routes stay open."

"I do not care much for the company of slavers, myself," Thal said.

"Nor do I generally, but of course you see why I must have the girl."

"You plan ahead," Thal said. "It will be years before Minay's betrothed becomes king of Phunom. Even then she may not convert him."

"It may not be so long. Besides, she is a Choizen. It is said they are birthed with certain powers."

"I would not have thought you one to believe such tales."

"I don't," the outlaw replied, "but others do. And belief is itself a strong power."

"Aye," Thal said. "I suppose it is."

"So you will give me the girl?"

"No."

Kathamoundis seemed unperturbed by the answer. He offered Thal more wine, and when the warrior refused he poured himself another goblet and sat back in his chair. "There is more wealth in the desert," he said.

"And you would, of course, make me your lieutenant."

"Why not?" Kathamoundis asked. "*I'm* an outlander. The Chi'ang are often happy to accept such. But they are still a clannish bunch at times. I could use a man such as you. And I know you can use a sword. I saw the remains of the Kagarii."

Thal shrugged. "And if I refuse?" he asked.

"I will torture you. You will not break and will eventually die. The girl will have eluded me temporarily, but I'll find her eventually. She will not then have you to intervene.

"But," the outlaw said, leaning forward, "if you give her to me then I will promise not to kill her. She must not marry her prince but that can be as well served by selling her south to the Stone Cities. She'll live, and I will tell you I did not wish to kill her anyway."

"She'll live as a slave," Thal stated.

"True," the Chi'ang outlaw agreed. "But we are all slaves of one sort or another."

"Perhaps," Thal agreed.

"Then you will help me?"

"Perhaps I have a counter proposal to make."

"Then make it."

"The Dance of Thorns."

Kathamoundis did not speak for a moment. "You know much of us it seems," he said at last.

"One hears things."

"The Dance of Thorns is not to be taken lightly. It is more than a test of strength, more than a contest to see whom the gods favor. If you win, then you will *be* Chi'ang."

"If I win I will leave here and take the girl to her place. You will have to risk that she will not convert her future husband."

"And if *I* win?" Kathamoundis questioned.

"Then I myself will take the girl away. I swear she will never return to the Kalarg and never marry Virsinder."

"You will sell her?"

"I will take her to another place, to my land. She will not return."

"How do I know I can trust you?"

"You cannot know. No more than I can be sure of you. However, I think you have honor. I do not believe you will go back on your word. Neither will I."

"Would we fight for death or blood?"

"Blood," Thal said. "I do not wish to kill you."

Kathamoundis smiled. "I have never lost at Thorns," he said.

"I didn't think you had," Thal said. "But then," he continued as he rose from the stool where he had been sitting, "you've never fought me."

Kathamoundis also stood and tossed the crossbow aside. "A place will be provided for you," he said. "We fight on the morrow."

"Tonight," Thal said.

"You fear for the girl?"

"Yes."

"Very well. I do not know why I grant you this, but we will fight tonight. In two ahr the moon will rise. I will meet you then."

"Accepted."

XI.

Dust hung in the torchlight, raised by striding feet and

the dance of hooves. Thal ignored both dust and light, sitting alone in a chiaroscuro of stillness before a small tent where steam rose. Only moments before he had been immersed in the tent's heat. His seconds, men appointed by Kathamoundis, had come periodically with fire-heated stones and cold water to pour over them. Now, purified, Thal sat beyond the tent in the warm wind. It fell cool on his sweaty skin.

Before Thal lay a circular area of raked sand some twenty-five feet across. Beyond it sat Kathamoundis, who was clad like Thal in a loincloth and nothing else. The bright torches threw the arena into relief; the people beyond were in shadow.

Thal rose to the sound of a horn and strode onto the sand. A lance of wine-red wood was handed him. Sharpened stakes attached at various points to the wood turned the lance into a ten foot thorn.

The Dance of Thorns is an ancient custom among the desert tribes, who have long known of a poison distilled from the thorn trees that proliferate in damper areas of the Kalarg. High doses of the poison kill; smaller amounts merely paralyze. The tribes sometimes use the poison on their hunting arrows or to aid in capturing wild camels. They also use it in the Dance of Thorns, coating the lance tips with it.

The Dance serves two purposes for the tribes. It is occasionally used to determine chieftainship, as when a challenge has been made to a leader's courage and strength. More commonly, it is used to settle disputes between warriors when no amount of arbitration can do so, such disputes as those over women or horses. Battles for succession are to the death; battles to decide disputes are not. In the latter type of contest, which would characterize the fight between Thal and Kathamoundis, the fighters continue until one is incapacitated by thorn poison.

Fatal thrusts are forbidden, as are deliberate strikes at

eyes or genitals. A triumvirate of tribal elders sits in judgment, and theirs is the final decision. Should they decide the winner fought dishonorably, then they might well give advantage of the bout to the loser.

Thal expected Kathamoundis to fight honorably, even though as leader he could probably escape the consequences of mild cheating. Though Thal didn't like slavers, he respected something in Kathamoundis. The man was ruthless, but Thal sensed a latent decency in him. The northerner lifted his lance and saluted the outlaw.

Again the horn sounded. Thal crouched where he stood. Kathamoundis raised his lance and shook it at the crowd. They cheered, and the outlaw leader smiled at Thal. The smile became a blood snarl as he came trotting across the sand. He stopped six feet from the northerner, balancing on the balls of his feet, then thrust out high, and low. Thal parried.

Kathamoundis flicked his point at Thal's face, and when Thal blocked with his own lance the outlaw spun his weapon through a half circle and lunged in. Thal turned the thrust aside into the sand, then leaped his own thorn toward the Chi'ang's shoulder. Kathamoundis danced away and a returning backhand slash missed Thal's bare stomach by an inch.

Thal closed and they met lance to lance, chest to chest. Thal realized he was the stronger. Kathamoundis reached the same conclusion and abruptly fell back onto his haunches, leaving Thal staggering forward, overbalanced at the sudden loss of resistance. Twisting desperately to one side, Thal tried to avoid the strike he knew was coming and Kathamoundis's thorn scored only lightly along his ribs. It could have been much worse. Still, the touch arched along the northerner's nerves like the stroke of a whip.

Pressing his advantage, Kathamoundis sprang to his feet and whipped his lance around at Thal's unprotected shoulder. The dark-eyed warrior avoided the stroke only by throwing himself forward onto the ground, and as the outlaw came in Thal rolled to the side and snapped a kick that caught Kathamoundis in the thigh and drove him reeling back.

Using his lance, Thal levered himself to his feet and crouched, ready for the next attack. But Kathamoundis closed in slowly, fencing with the poisoned tip of his thorn. Thal blocked, and blocked, then leaped in with a riposte that Kathamoundis easily avoided. Quickly, the outlaw returned to the offensive, tapping and tapping against Thal's guard, trying to slip in another thrust to the northerner's ribs.

Fortunately, the scratch Thal had taken had bled only a little and not much poison had worked into the bloodstream, certainly not enough to incapacitate him. Still, he was backing up, and he kept on retreating until Kathamoundis changed tactics and stomped into his ankle with the bladed side of a foot.

Thal grunted in pain and went to one knee. Kathamoundis struck downward from his greater height, but misjudged Thal's speed as the northerner swayed aside. The outlaw's blow missed and it was the opening Thal needed. He stabbed upward from his knees, the tip of his lance scoring an angry red gash across the outlaw's chest. The Chi'ang leaped back and Thal could see his surprise. He must seldom have been struck at Thorns.

Thal charged up from his knees and smashed Kathamoundis back. The outlaw jabbed at an arm but the northerner was too close and the blow missed. Thal's strike did not, and the tip of his lance daggered deeply into the Chi'ang's thigh. Kathamoundis grunted and staggered. The wounded leg betrayed him and he fell. Thal came in swiftly, but somehow the outlaw managed to get his lance in the way for a parry. Thal's strike went into the sand, and in an instant the Chi'ang leader was on his feet.

Both men hesitated for a moment, breathing hard and covered in sweat. The crowd had long since been forgotten. Then Thal came forward and began testing Kathamoundis's defense with repeated jabs. The outlaw's thigh wound was bad, the leg weakened and probably already starting to stiffen. Thal had the advantage now.

Kathamoundis was not stupid. He knew whose side time was on, and he wasted none of his own precious moments. He came in, scorpion swift, and Thal had to dance to stay away. Only the outlaw's weakened leg kept his point from finding the northerner's flesh.

The exchange ended and Kathamoundis moved back, the heavy poison dew breaking out on his brow and will alone keeping his leg working. Though Thal felt mercy, he showed none of it. Too much was at stake and he bored in to the attack. A high thrust was parried and Thal spun, kicking out his right foot to sweep the Chi'ang's wounded leg from beneath him. The outlaw fell heavily and lost his lance. Thal leaped to stand over him, his weapon pointed at a bare throat. Kathamoundis made no move.

"I'll be free to go now," Thal stated.

"So it was agreed," Kathamoundis said.

Thal lowered the lance and reached a hand to pull the outlaw to his feet. Kathamoundis winced as weight fell on his wounded leg.

"You're good," he told the northerner. "Too good. If you reconsidered you could probably take my place as head of the Chi'ang."

"And spend my time looking over my shoulder?" Thal asked.

The outlaw snorted, shaking his head. "Yes... Well, perhaps I should join you instead."

"If you wish."

"Nay. Not for me, I'm afraid. As I promised, your horse and weapons are returned. Go to your girl. She is probably quite afraid by now."

Thal tossed down his thorn and strode away.

Epilogue

It was just after dawn when Thal topped a rise and found again his dead camel. He could smell the animal's stench, though it was not yet strong, and it was hard to believe less than one full day had passed since he had been taken by the Chi'ang from this spot. He was just about to call out when he heard the shout of hooves behind him. He twisted in the saddle, rapidly pulling, stringing, and arming the hornbow at his side. And he cursed himself for a fool as a rider on a Chi'ang horse came over the rise behind him. It was Kathamoundis, but he seemed alone.

The outlaw leader pulled his dun stallion to a halt several yards away. He looked wan and haggard and Thal knew what it must have cost him to sit a horse so soon after his encounter with thorn poison. The gash on his chest had still not closed, and it stood out purple and angry against the tanned skin.

"So," Thal said, "you have no honor after all."

"I came alone," Kathamoundis replied.

Thal let his eyes roam the nearby dunes and saw nothing. He listened, and heard nothing.

"Am I to believe you?" he asked.

"If that arrow is for me, then kill me. Else believe me."

"Then why did you follow me?"

"I am filled with curiosity," Kathamoundis said. "I would know where you hid the girl."

"And you intend her no harm?"

"I gave my word."

"Then," Thal said, as he turned toward the dead camel. "Minay," he called. "It's Thal. Come out, girl."

The camel seemed to quiver and a moment later a hand and head poked out of its belly. Shortly, a bedraggled Minay had squirmed her way free and stood beside Thal. She looked warily at Kathamoundis but said nothing.

"I hope you haven't been in there since yesterday," Thal said.

"No," she said. "But I heard someone coming and was afraid."

"That was wise," Thal said.

Thal looked back at Kathamoundis, who was staring with wide eyes. Suddenly, the Chi'ang outlaw burst out laughing. "In a swiving camel," he said. "Right in front of us the whole time."

"Curb your tongue," Thal said. "There is a lady present."

Kathamoundis stopped laughing and looked at the two before him. He bowed to Minay. "I beg your pardon, lady. I fear my manners are a bit crude."

"Yes," Minay said. "I fear you are right."

Kathamoundis laughed again. "So," he said to Thal. "I take it you will be escorting the princess home now?"

"Aye."

"Then I'll let you be on your way. Perhaps we'll see each other again."

"Yes," Thal said. "I'll be watching when they hang you."

"I can promise a good show," Kathamoundis said. He turned and rode away.

Thal reached down and pulled Minay up on the saddle before him, lifting a sand veil to cover his nose. "We have got to find a place for you to take a bath," he told her.

Minay laughed and kicked her heels into Skaal's flanks. The stallion started, ears laid back in surprise, but he was soon trotting his way west toward the girl's home. The dust they raised quickly settled again.

END NOTES

1: **JHestus / Ved-Tahr**. The similarities between the JHestus religious sect and Christianity seem too close to be accidental, particularly with the name JHestus being nearly identical with Jesus. It seems most likely the sect is a "rediscovered" religion from the past, and that at least parts of the Ved-Tahr holy book have been taken from the New Testament Bible. Either that, or Jesus was born once again on Thanos.

2: **Chirik root**. Chirik is a common plant whose root contains a powerful stimulant. In low doses it is used to lace coffee and teas, much like caffeine. In higher doses it is used to enhance aggression, or as an intoxicant to induce a kind of euphoria.

3. **Gyre**. Mentioned a couple of times in the story, a gyre is a type of predator that resembles a mix between a wolf and a panther. It may not be native to Earth/Thanos, but might have been imported during the Conquered Years.

4. **Nyk-Quall**. As described by Thal here, it appears to be type of Gila monster grown to gigantic size.

COIN AND STEEL

The empire of Evranoire died at Bloody
Ground and Raven's Forest, at Swept Plain
and Axe Hill. It died under the iron hooves of
the Dayne riders. And its ashes were scattered
on the wind, never to return.
—Maritos, *History of the Dayne Wars*

Prologue

The evening sun hung crucified, bleeding into the surrounding sky. And on the earth below, a thousand warriors
readied to die.

"They'll call this place, Bloody Ground," Thal Kyrin
said, and his horsemen nodded and seated their lances for
the charge. In another moment the battle-horns sounded
and the men moved forward in answer, hawk pennons
snapping silver and black, dirt rising under the hooves of
their war-horses. Thal Kyrin led them, from a walk, to a
trot, to a gallop, and they were five hundred Iron Riders
when they struck the enemy lines, bowed them in, and
rolled them back. And like a tide behind, the Dayne pha-
lanxes came. The left wing of the Evranoire army ceased
to be.

The center of the battle line was a clotted mass of the
dead and dying, piled too high with bodies to ride over or
through, and Thal took his gore-bedecked warriors around
the chaos to strike hard into Evranoire's right wing. It

held.

Few in that wing had been birthed in Evranoire. They were mercenaries mostly, men whose lives were given to coin and steel, but they stood while others ran. They stood beneath the onslaught of the best army on Thanos, and for a time turned them back. Only with the fall of night did the mercenaries disengage and slip away. They were not pursued. Even the Daynes were sated with slaughter.

"Well done," Thal Kyrin said, when word was brought of the condottiere's escape. "Would that I could meet the commander of those troops. By Suva, but he is a man."

I.

Where olive groves overlooked the Ysaye River, the band of travelers stopped to rest their horses. There was grass for the animals and the groves lay on a hill that provided an excellent view all around. The view was especially important. There might be pursuit. But that worry would disappear when they crossed the river below and reached Verhtai, a week's ride to the southeast. Between them and safety lay Ott's Ferry, with its few unpainted hovels and the ferry for which it was named.

The leader of the travelers was called Rhing, and he stood at the edge of the trees looking down at the river village and the plain beyond. He wondered what reception might await them in Verhtai. Probably a good one, considering the rulers of that city would be looking for soldiers as they stewed over what the Dayne hordes might do when they finished ripping up Evranoire.

Not that there was much left to rip, Rhing mused. The eighty men who lay exhausted beneath the shading trees behind him had once been part of the army of Evranoire, and they might well be the largest body of organized troops left from that army. All had been in the ranks of the thousand Rhing had captained at the battle of Bloody

Ground, where they'd managed to hold the line against an enemy three times their number.

They had been only five hundred in the fighting later at Axe Hill, and still they'd held the earthworks for four days against the Dayne Second Army while they bled the enemy's First Phalanx nearly white. Only the Iron Riders, the elite heavy cavalry of the Daynes, had been able to break their line, and then only after three costly charges.

None of it had mattered, though. Axe Hill was three months gone and the hooves of Dayne war-horses echoed in the streets of Evranoire's capital now. Those who had fought on the losing side were running for their lives. It wasn't a good idea to resist the Dayne Empire.

Rhing shrugged. This war was over. There would be others, perhaps in Verhtai. First, though, they had to cross a river. The young commander took out the far-seeing scope that was his mother's only legacy and studied the ferry. Smoke rose from a few chimneys and half a dozen horses stood tied to hitching rails along the dirt path that served as a street. He saw only one man, who came from the nearest building to spit and return.

The word "building" was, perhaps, too kind for the wooden shacks making up most of the town. There was only one stone structure, a square two-story that anchored the ferry's west end and undoubtedly served as a ware-house in more prosperous times. The flag of Evranoire should have flown over that building but the gold and midnight blue of the Evraneese had been replaced by the rust-brown war-flag of the Daynes, and by another banner of silver and black. It was the latter that stroked memories from Rhing, memories he didn't care for. He lowered the glass.

"Geisic," he called. "Let me borrow your eyes for a moment."

The youth who joined Rhing was tall and thin, with brown hair spun to straw by the hot southern sun. Geisic was youngest of the condottiere, probably no more than seventeen, though he claimed older. War-daughter's luck didn't care about age, though, as long as you could wield a sword or draw a bow. Rhing himself was barely twenty-two, and most of the rest, though veterans, were scarcely older. Geisic could shoot the eyes out of snake at 100 paces with a bow, and his own eyes were acknowledged best in the company. No one joked about his beardless-ness.

The boy accepted the glass Rhing handed him and looked where his Captain pointed. "Tell me the device on that dark flag, my friend. It might be important."

Geisic stared for a moment, rubbed his eyes, then looked again. "A hawk," he said. "A sword in its talons." He handed the scope back to Rhing.

"A hawk, eh?" Rhing asked.

"Yes."

"*Verdi*," Rhing cursed.

"You recognize it?" Geisic asked.

"Maybe. Remember the company of Iron Riders who cracked our lines at Axe Hill?"

"Not likely I'd forget those bastards."

"Well, I got a pretty good look at their commander, a big brute on a black horse."

"And the banner he rode under was a silver hawk on a sable field," Geisic interrupted.

"Aye."

"*Verdi!*"

"It'd be our luck," Rhing added.

"I'm not gonna like going up against that bloody bunch again."

"Nor any of us."

"Can we ride around?"

Rhing shook his head. "The skirrit are spawning in the river and those devil fish will eat a horse right from under you. The next closest ferry is at Harissport, but the Evraneese always kept a garrison there so I expect the Daynes to be present in force."

"Then the question is, how many men are down there and can we ride over them?"

Rhing looked back toward the river, and the sky did not seem as bright as it had moments earlier. "I'll scout tonight," he said. "Though I begrudge the lost time."

"Maybe we won't have to wait that long," Geisic said.

"Wha—?"

Geisic pointed and this time *Rhing*'s gaze followed the *other*'s finger. A spike of dust rose from the town, coming their way. Rhing raised his scope and found himself staring at two figures, one riding an onager while the other led on foot.

"Could be the War-daughters have smiled," he said, lowering the glass so a stray reflection wouldn't catch any eyes below. "Let's get the men behind the trees and have someone brush out the tracks we've made. Our visitors look young and I don't want to spook them. They've not likely seen much good from roving bands of men during recent months."

II.

Kerrin jerked the donkey's lead-rope, hoping to make it move. It didn't. The beast had halted just short of Olive Ridge and would go no further. Kerrin jerked again, as hard as she could, and the donkey brayed but did not budge.

"Kick it, Mais," Kerrin called to her younger brother, who sat astride the stubborn creature. "Do something!"

"Jaak take it!" the boy exclaimed. "I been kickin' the damn thing but it don't pay no mind."

"Then get off and push," his sister replied. "And watch your mouth. You know what Ma would give you if she heard you talking that way."

The boy slid obediently off the donkey's back and went around behind to push. He was still muttering curses, though none loud enough for his sister to hear, when the donkey suddenly started forward, leaving him to fall on his face in the dust. He got up mad, his fists clenched, but Kerrin and the offending brute had already disappeared over the lip of the rise where they'd come to pick olives. He stomped up the trail behind them to come in under the cool shade of the groves.

Kerrin untied the baskets from the ass and handed one to her brother. Mais took it reluctantly. He'd rather have been fishing for skirrit but his mother had caught him for chores before he could get away.

"There ain't even many ripe ones," he complained.

"There's enough. You'd think you'd stop griping about putting food in your mouth. Come on!"

Wiping sweat from her brow with the back of a hand, thirteen year old Kerrin walked around the donkey and came face to face with half a dozen men who stepped from the trees. Their clothes were coated with dust and they looked to have ridden far. Their weapons seemed well cared for, however. And Kerrin had seen enough weapons to know.

The girl froze and Mais bumped into her as he came around the donkey to join her. "What the—?" the boy started, and stopped as he saw the strangers.

One of the men, whom both Kerrin and Mais took to be the leader, had dark, shoulder-length hair and green eyes of a phosphorous hue neither child had ever seen before. He seemed careful not to make any threatening gestures, but still Kerrin slid a hand into the pocket of her skirt where her olive knife lay. The blade was only for comfort. She didn't think it would be much use against an adult male.

"I'm Rhing," the leader said. His voice was soft. "We won't harm you. We just want to ask a few questions."

Kerrin relaxed slightly. "What kind of questions?"

"I'm curious about those who ride under the silver hawk banner. How long ago did they come here?"

"I'm not sure I should tell you," Kerrin said.

The man smiled. "What can it hurt? I doubt they're your friends."

Kerrin thought about that, and finally shrugged. "Three days ago," she said.

"How many were they?"

"Many tens. Perhaps as many as the fingers and toes of my brother and I."

Nearly four hundred men, Rhing thought. But to the girl, he said: "There isn't room to quarter that many at the ferry. Where are they now?"

"Why do you want to know?" Kerrin asked. "They haven't harmed us. Perhaps you will."

Rhing looked at her for a moment, then took a deep breath and let it out. "Let me speak truthfully," he said. "Those men may not have harmed *you,* but they'll harm *us* if they find us. We've fought them before. But now, we only want to cross the river. And I don't think they'll let us just because we ask. I want to know whether we have the strength to force them. I intend to talk first. But it may come to a fight."

It was Kerrin's turn to pause, but after a moment: "I know truth when I hear it," she said. "I'll give you truth back. Many tens rode in. But most went on across the river, leaving only five tens behind."

Rhing considered. Four hundred had ridden in; fifty remained. Beyond the river was the state of Jakoor. South of there lay Verhtai. What could the Daynes want over there unless they were trying to start another war? Rhing doubted that. Even the Daynes would want a break after the hard campaign against Evranoire.

Kerrin spoke again and Rhing stopped his thoughts to listen.

"The man who first led them may have listened to your talk. But he crossed the river and the one who commands now will not, I think. I believe he likes to fight. I do not care for him"

"The first leader," Rhing said. "Was he a big man on a black mount?"

"Yes. He looked like you, though his eyes were black as his horse."

Rhing smiled. Men in armor often looked alike to children.

"How long ago did he leave?" Rhing asked. "And did he say if he'd return?"

"It was two days ago. He said he would come back. I did not hear when."

"Then we'll have to be gone before he does. But first we have to repay you for your help. Carik," he called to his second in command. "Get the men up. Time to pick some olives."

III.

An ahr later, the mercenaries-without-hire rode down toward Ott's Ferry with swords and lances at the ready. Above them flapped a blue flag with an uprooted oak standing dark in its center. Behind them on the hill sat Kerrin and her brother, baskets of olives piled high around them. They had perfect seats to watch what would come.

The Dayne garrison saw the dust and rode to meet it. It might have been wiser to lay in wait with archers in the houses, but such was not the Dayne way. They were new to civilization and had not yet learned subterfuge. But they knew how to fight.

The two groups met before the village, on a plain of sparse grass ideal for the movement of cavalry. Rhing brought his men to a halt some two hundred yards from the enemy and held up his sword for a parley. The Dayne commander answered with his own sword and they rode out to meet.

"You've come to surrender," the Dayne said. "Good."

Rhing could not help but smile at the arrogant words. He had to admit, though, the Daynes were often good enough to warrant such talk. But not against *his* men.

"Not at all," Rhing said. "I merely wish to inquire about passage aboard the ferry."

The Dayne smiled in return. "I'm afraid the price may be too high for you."

"Such as?"

"Your lives."

"Out of the question," Rhing said. "I was thinking of something much cheaper. Like the lives of yourself and *your* men."

The Dayne's grin widened. "Then," he said, "it looks like we fight."

"So it would appear," Rhing said. "Are you sure you won't reconsider? We outnumber you."

The Dayne's grin turned to a snarl. "I liked you for a moment, Southlander. But I'll not allow myself and my men to be insulted. You can use the ferry when we're all dead."

Inwardly, Rhing sighed. Outwardly, he pointed his sword toward the other and said only: "Let the Gods decide."

The Dayne tapped his steel against Rhing's. "Let the Gods keep out of the way," he replied, before turning and riding back to his men.

IV.

From among the olives, Kerrin and Mais watched the struggle begin. They saw the lines spur together and heard the impact, heard the full voiced war-shouts of men and the shrieks of injured horses. They saw the first men fall to be trampled under hooves. Then Kerrin dragged her brother away with tears in her eyes. She may have seen weapons before; it was the first time she'd seen war.

From where Rhing forced his war-horse into the middle of the maelstrom, the battle was a roar of crimson blades limned by dust and dull light. The Daynes were outnumbered but were also rested and heavily armored while Rhing's men had ridden far and been forced to discard much of their armor to avoid killing their overburdened mounts.

Rhing cut through an attack by two men and spurred his horse at the Dayne commander. Weapons clanged as the warriors met. The Dayne fought with a heated snarl, Rhing with a cold burn deep in his phosphorescent eyes. The cold won. A slash from Rhing's sword opened the man's belly, sent him reeling away.

Rhing stood in his stirrups. "Kare-on-dall!" he screamed.

Instantly, the left and right sides of the mercenary line disengaged and fell back toward the mount of olives. The Daynes did not understand Rhing's word, or the maneuver it called for. They thought their enemies were retreating and came crashing in pursuit, shredding their unit's cohesiveness. Perhaps the barbarians' commander might have figure out what was coming, but his guts were painting his horse's saddle as he died.

The center of the mercenary line formed on Rhing, and that core cut through the weakened Dayne defense like a flood through dust before swinging right to take the enemy's left flank from the rear. At the same time, the apparently retreating mercenaries turned again to the attack. Many men died in the next moments. Most were Daynes, who fell almost to the man. Only four survived, all wounded. Seventeen of Rhing's men were killed, ten others hurt.

Rhing ached to be away but allowed time for the dead

on both sides to be gathered in an abandoned house that was put to the torch. Neither the Daynes nor the mercenaries commonly buried their fallen. The four wounded Daynes were left in a cool spot with food and water in reach. If their curses were any indication, Rhing thought they'd all live.

Though the fired building was of dry wood, a dangerous smoke still rose and Rhing hurried his men to the ferry. There was only one barge, however, and it could haul no more than fifteen men and horses at a time. Rhing waited with the wounded to join the final party, but before he could board the ferry himself a rising dust to the east caught his eye. Praying it was the wind, he raised the far-seeing scope, squinting against shimmering heat waves. In a moment he saw a glint within the dust, as of sunlight on metal. He cursed as others of his men began to look and point.

V.

Rhing leaped quickly from the barge when it touched land on the river's far shore. His orders snapped out. "Keep the wounded where they are on the barge. That damn dust fills the horizon. No way we could outrun it with our injured. We'll stand. See what happens. If they offer terms we may have to surrender. If not, we fight."

And so the mercenaries were ready when the dust came upon them and they saw the three hundred and fifty Iron Riders who followed a man on a charcoal-colored horse. Above that captain flew a silver hawk banner, and Rhing knew this was the same man he and his band had fought twice before, and lost to.

The Daynes drew to a stop several hundred yards away and it was the warrior on the black horse who raised his sword for a parley. Rhing rode to meet him, and was startled to see that little Kerrin had been right. Except for the eyes, there was a faint resemblance between he and this stranger.

The other also seemed to notice it. "How are you called?" he asked.

"Rhing des Valeen. And you?"

Thal. Only Thal."

"It is odd to see Daynes on this side of the river," Rhing remarked."

Thal shrugged. "Know your enemy," he said. "And those who might become enemies."

"And I am such an enemy."

"You were. The war is over."

"Your men beyond the river did not think thus."

"You killed them all?"

"All but four. Those are wounded and we left them in the shade with food and water."

"How did the rest die," Thal asked.

"We outnumbered them. I offered to pass in peace but they refused. They died with honor."

Thal's smile was wolfish. "As I assume would you and yours, should I unleash my hounds."

Rhing shrugged. "This is as good a day as any. And as good a place. I ask only that you treat my wounded as I dealt with yours."

Thal eyed him further for a minute, then changed the subject so abruptly that Rhing was startled.

"You are not really a Southerner, are you? In what country were you born?"

"In a land five hundred leagues north of Standor. I believe it is marked on Dayne maps as Gorzia."

"And your mother?"

"Her name was Yvonne Valeen."

"A beautiful name."

"She was a beautiful woman, I am told. She died a few days after my birth."

Rhing heard then a strange noise from the dark-haired

captain, and he saw the man's knuckles whiten on the horn of his saddle.

"Why so curious," the mercenary asked suspiciously.

"I'd like to know more about those who fought the Iron Riders to a standstill at Bloody Ground and Axe Hill."

"We held you a while at Bloody Ground, but you over-ran us at Axe Hill."

"I made your position untenable by superior numbers, and that is not the same thing."

"Perhaps."

"And what of your father?" Thal asked, again changing the subject. "You do not carry his name? Lives he still?"

"He left before I was born."

"You must hate him for that?"

"No. The monks who raised me spoke of him, and of her. She never told the man she was carrying me."

"Why?"

"Rhing shrugged. "The reasons died with her. As for the man, it's been over twenty years. He is most likely long dead, too."

"And if he lives and you saw him, would you know him?

"I doubt it. But what matter? My family is here." He gestured toward his men.

"I would like to speak with you further," Thal said. "But though the war is over, the fighting continues."

"We will not make it easy for you."

"No?" Thal smiled. "Well, I had hoped. But," he sighed rather dramatically, "if your men are not off the barge and out of our way in fifteen minutes we shall ride over you."

"What?"

"You were mercenaries for Evranoire. I assume that service is at an end?"

"Aye. In fact, we haven't been paid in months."

"Then the Daynes have no more quarrel with you."

Rhing smiled then, and saluted the dark-eyed commander with his sword before turning and riding back to his troop. Within minutes, the mercenaries formed into columns and headed out. Rhing stopped again near where the Dayne commander sat his black horse, but he did not know what to say.

It was Thal who spoke. "I, too, am a mercenary. And my hire nears its end. Were I to come to Jakoor seeking employment, might I find you there?"

"Not in Jakoor, but in Verhtai perhaps. Come if you will."

Epilogue I.

"Forgive me, Commander Thal," a Dayne warrior said. "But why let them pass? The emperor will not like it."

"Two reasons," Thal said. "First, the war is over and I see no reason to sacrifice men."

"And the second?" the soldier asked.

"Second. That warrior is my son."

Epilogue II.

Rhing did not look back as he rode with his men away from the ferry, but he wondered how long it would take his father to find him in Verhtai.

Author's Note: I almost didn't include "Coin and Steel" in this collection. It has not been previously published and Thal Kyrin appears primarily as a peripheral character. I also think the ending is somewhat anticlimactic. It does fill in a gap in Thal's history, though, and in rereading these stories for the anthology I noticed something else, that the theme of lost fathers and sons runs throughout much of the

Thal series. That theme is almost certainly related to the fact I lost my own father when I was thirteen. In the end, I decided to include the story; I hope you found it of interest.

THE EVENING RIDER

Prologue

*Soon the civilization of humans will pass and
their world will become the abode of demons,
and perhaps of gods.*

Silence shattered. Darkness was rent. On an escarp-
ment jutting from the peak known as Serpent's Tongue,
which rises from the Waste of Dead Stones as part of the
vastness of the Scarn Uplands, a figure stood, night drawing a veil about its features. The figure's arms were extended above the Waste as if in benediction, and a high-
pitched keening, like the ululation of demon grief, bubbled
from lips drawn back in a rictus of hate.

In a face half human flesh, half silver metal cast in the
guise of a skull, a jeweled eye gleamed milkily. Abruptly,
the eye's gleam increased, then struck outward like lightning to splash amid dust and the broken stone of fallen
statues. Patches of hoarfrost turned to glittering gemstones
in the sorcerous light. In the lees of boulders, drifts of dirty
snow began to blow away on the wizard's wind.

The sorcerer's body tensed in agony while his jeweled
eye lashed the night with white fire. And beyond him the
shadows gathered, flowing inkily toward the light, painting a chiaroscuro in the wasteland beneath the ringed
moon of Thanos. The crystalline lance of flame intensified. The shadow sea rippled, shuddered, and broke apart.

Dark limbs sprouted as beings of ebony clawed their way up boulders to stand on legs of night. In a moment, the wasteland was no longer empty.

The wizard closed his eye. The light winked out, flooding the world in jet. The master spoke, and in the darkness and wind his ancient servants answered in a voice no human should hear and live. Yet the sorcerer lived, and his voice grew stronger.

"I am the Evening Rider," he shouted. "Come, my angels. Let us feed."

Gliding like storm clouds over the ruined earth they had once ruled, the Shadow-Ones moved, turning south toward the distant lanterns of Destandina and the warm flesh of men.

I: The War in Memory

Wind daggers whipped crystals of ice off the tourmaline peaks of the Scarn Mountains and sent them skittering southward into the face of the oncoming train of wagons. Thal pulled his stallion to a halt as icy fingers plucked at his cloak and found a hole through which to suck greedily at the warmth of his body. He tucked the cloak back beneath the broad leather belt cinching his waist, then looked over his shoulder to where the wagons toiled up the long road from the capital city of Destandina to Krell Crest. A figure on horseback, leading the caravan, raised an arm. Thal returned the gesture, smiling.

The man below—General Aron Corth—seemed in a good mood, as he well deserved after the long campaigns in the south that had seen the fall of Laestrunie and Evranoire. The fortunes of the Dayne Emperor had been much increased, and the general who increased them had received his gratitude and the use of the royal manor at Krell Crest for a long postponed rest. True, it did get the most popular commander in the history of the Dayne Empire out of the capital until the first flush of victory was past, but only a cynic would believe the Emperor feared the popularity of the leader of his legions. Thal smiled cynically to himself and shrugged his horse into motion, musing on the habitual suspicion of tyrants—most probably adaptive considering the usual fate of such creatures.

As he crested the knoll up which he had been riding, Thal caught sight of the manor house and its surrounding wall of granite blocks. The trail curved left around a copse of pines to run along the base of peaks that towered like fangs into the leaden clouds. As if in truth the peaks were fangs and had ripped the sky, a few flakes of snow began to swirl downward. They clung to the cold ground.

Somewhere, snow slid in the mountains, the sound like the pounding hooves of steel-shod cavalry. For a moment, Thal saw the peaceful valley replaced by a battlefield. The distant rumble of snow slide became the thunder of armored horsemen spurring their mounts together, to meet with splintering lances and the screams of men and beasts.

Again, Thal saw the dust rising. Again he heard the crack of pennons and the discordant clash of steel on steel. And he remembered the hooves that never stopped pounding, the iron hooves of the mailed riders of Destandina, which had shattered the enemy at Swept Plain, Raven's Forest, and Bloody Earth, and which rang so hollowly in the abandoned streets of Evranoire. Thal shook his head and the breeze took his thoughts away. The valley echoed only to a faint mistral.

Thal knew the memories would fade in time. But three years of war take a long while to forget. General Corth, a man Thal respected, had made the cavalry his chief weapon in the war against Evranoire, and Thal, the outlander mercenary with the strange dark eyes, had been the fist wielding that weapon—the iron riders as their enemies called them. He was tired, as the General was tired, as most of those with the column—veterans of the southern campaigns—were tired. They would rest and nurse the mental wounds of war, which remain long after most of the physical have healed. Thal felt this valley, with its isolation and tall pines that seemed to whisper welcome, would be a salve for them all. He rode up to the tall gates of the manor and dismounted to unlock them.

II: The Rider Revisited

Quantus Yorl, the Evening Rider, came down off the Serpent's Tongue into one of the many nameless valleys that exist unexplored in the depths of the Scarn range. Around him the night seethed, as if alive. Campfires lay sprinkled like burning rubies across the narrow strath ahead of him, and beside those fires an army ate, or drank, or slept—an army of thieves and outlaws. It was the Rider's army, with which he planned to overthrow an empire.

Yorl—he seldom thought of himself by that name anymore—intended to destroy the Dayne Empire. Utterly. Once, he had ruled in that realm's name as administrator of the city of Turl, until he was accused of treason by the jealousy of his enemies. It was a crime of which he was innocent. The Emperor's men had not bothered with the truth, however. Tortured, unable to withstand the pain that turned men into puling animals, Yorl admitted his guilt. It had not contented his tormentors. They had taken half his face and in the end stole from him that which makes one a man. His screams had only brought laughter.

He was broken, or so they thought, but just before his impalement he managed to escape with the help of a few loyal retainers. Northeast he had gone, into the hollow lands. There he found a smith to fashion a mask for the ruined half of his face, and in time he discovered a temple for his hate, a temple where he had worshiped alone for the last ten years. Now he had finished with worship and was ready for sacrifice.

Yorl had sorcery as his weapon, and hatred to discipline him in pursuit of his goal. But an army of outlaws seldom has such discipline. For them he needed more. He needed something to make them fear him worse than they feared the blades of the Daynes. He had entered the wastes alone. He returned, not unaccompanied, coming into firelight from shadow, startling the men and the not-men who squatted in the light of the flames.

"I see your guards have grown lax again, Armin," Yorl said. "Can I not trust you to obey the simplest of my orders?" He addressed a tall warrior with straw-blond hair who held a wine skin in a calloused and scarred hand.

The man rose, seemingly indifferent. His eyes were cold blue and mocking, and he stood with legs slightly apart and one hand on his sword. There was the look of a reiver and a killer about him, for that's what he was. He had never been anything else. Nor did he wish to be.

"What need have we of guards, Rider?" he asked. "There's scarcely a force in these Suvan forsaken hills that would dare attack us."

"And what of the beasts?" Yorl asked. "What of the Reti? True, many of them serve with us. But what of those who did not answer my call?"

"Hell, wizard, no pack of wild beasts is going to attack three thousand men. Besides, if there were wild ones around the horses would have smelled them. You know how the things stink."

Laughter came from some of the men. The others, who squatted on clawed feet away from the yellow flame of the campfires, looked up at the sound. A few of them snarled, not understanding the words but not liking the tone of the laughter.

"I'd speak softly were I you, Armin," the Rider told him. "Perhaps they know more than you think."

"Well *I* know you better start paying off on some of

the promises you fed us," Armin stated flatly. "We've been hiding in these hills for months now, waiting until you tell us the time is right and your power is strong. None of us want to wait longer. And as for your power. Well, we've seen little enough of that as well. A couple hundred filthy beasts," he waved his hands at the Reti to be met by more snarls, "aren't gonna do much against Dayne steel. The Daynes ain't gonna roll over for you, Rider. They'll chew up your little army and still be hungry. And I for one don't plan to wear a cross because you didn't like the way some pretty faced nobles treated you. So like they say in Destandina, let's see the color of your steel or we all go home."

"Are you through?" the Rider asked. A stillness to his voice should have been a warning, but Armin had said too much to take back.

"I've said what I intended to," he replied, as murmurs of open assent begin to rise from the camp.

"Very well then," the Rider said. "I'll show you power."

The jewel in the Rider's left eye began to gleam, dripping milky light into the fire-haunted darkness. Men stirred and moved away. Only Armin stood his ground, but the fist that gripped his sword was white-knuckled.

The power Armin had wanted to see began to show itself. So softly at first as to be almost undetectable, a faint susurration began to build on the wind, as if a demon whispered obscenities out of the earth. The whispering grew louder, began to grate on Armin's nerves like steel scraping on stone.

Then the whole army heard the sound and the blood turned to chill wine in every man's veins. Harsh shrieks and cackles exploded from all sides of the camp, and below that threnody still lay the faint murmur of evil that made warriors' skins into living, twitching creatures. Even the Reti were on their feet, but silent in their fear as the night in which they were so much at home turned suddenly into an enemy.

All eyes looked to the Rider. The human half of his face was split in a smile. Some eyes beheld the wizard with loathing, others with a faint tinge of lust as they realized the power of the being they had allied themselves with. Armin looked with terror on his death.

A shadow moved for the outlaw, drifting like blown leaves across the camp. The blond mercenary struggled to regain his courage and at the last minute, with the creature nearly to him, tore his blade from its sheath with a yell and slashed madly at a ghost of darkness. The thing never stopped its curious gliding. Slipping aside to avoid the clumsy slash, it took Armin's head in its hands. The other men saw Armin's face go slack and none ever forgot the look of utter despair that came into the outlaw's blue eyes, the eyes they had once thought so cold. None ever forgot, or ceased wondering what Armin had seen in his last seconds. The creature tugged, and, with little effort it seemed, ripped the man's head from his shoulders.

The outlaw's body stood for a moment before twisting slowly to one side as if in grotesque search for its lost part. Then it fell to lie quivering on the earth. A shadow carrying Armin's head faded into the night, taking with it other shadows surrounding the camp. Only the sound of retching could be heard above the great silence.

III: At Night, Even the Sounds Are Cold

The night was an animal, its roar the wind that hammered the manor with icy breath. Thal came out of a dream with sleet rattling like crossbow quarrels on the wooden shutters. His sudden movement brought Cynthe near the surface of sleep, and he held himself still until her breathing steadied and she slid back beneath the velvet curtain of slumber. He stroked her blonde hair lightly, thinking of the love she'd given him and remembering the first time they'd met. She had been one of the many widows of Laestrunie, the wife of a noble who died in battle against the Dayne invaders, for whom Thal had fought.

Her husband's manor had been taken by the dark-haired warrior as a command post. She'd accepted it with resignation, but for days she had spoken to no one under Thal's command and her hatred was plain in her eyes. How had love developed out of hatred? Perhaps it had been the small kindnesses Thal had shown her in the aftermath of her loss, or maybe she had finally realized he was only a man and did not enjoy killing. Perhaps it was the icy cold of winter that drove them together, or the loneliness both knew only too well. The how did not matter. The love was there and Thal did not question. He brushed her lips lightly with his own, watching her wrinkle her nose as his hair tickled her face. She did not awaken.

A faint sound drew Thal's mind to the north. Curious, he shoved away the sleeping furs and went to the window. The freezing wind trickled through the shutters, raising gooseflesh across his chest. With his ear against the wood, he listened to that wind, and heard something else. Scattered by gusts, faint, but clear even over the gale, came the sound of howling. And there was a strangeness in those distant voices, almost a note of fear. That was odd. Anything that could live and move in that cauldron of snow should have nothing to be afraid of.

The sound grew steadily louder, and soon not all the gooseflesh on Thal's body arose from the cold. He took up his sword and went below.

IV: Shadows and Storms

To the north moved the Rider's army, marching in long columns with torches gleaming. Yorl rode at their head, only distantly aware of the howling that blew away from him toward the south. He was more concerned with controlling the sound's cause, the Shadow-Ones, who drove the wild Reti before them like fires before wind. The few beasts that turned to fight had been ripped to tatters. The rest fled.

The Rider's own Reti flanked him, staying close to the man whose demons hunted their brethren. Above lay a clear black sky that stank of sorcery, while to the south a wizard's storm raged, hurling sleet and ice onto the foothills and swirling even now about the towers of Destandina. The Rider was powerful but even he was beginning to tire from the effort he was expending. The tiredness didn't matter to him, though. Now was his moment of vengeance, and he would last long enough. What matter if he died later, as long as he died feeding on Daynish hearts.

V: A Night's Sleep Disturbed

Between the wizard's army and the Dayne capital of Destandina lay the royal manor. The people were awake there, watching closely as an unnatural storm began to fade into an icy and still morning. Torches dripped fire over the gray walls and the dying wind battered fitfully at the flames to send shadows swaying in obscene dance across the stones. Then the last of the storm fled, leaving behind a silence broken only occasionally by the approaching howling. It was as if the things making the sound were saving their breath to run.

Thal Kyrin stood on the manor walls with other Dayne warriors, holding a place near the gate while he sipped a cup of tea laced with chirik root. General Aron Corth stood to the right, leaning on his broadsword. To Thal's left was the General's nephew, Lokeen, who voiced a concern of them all.

"If those things are half as bad as they sound, I'm

really going to hate meeting whatever is chasing them."

"Perhaps they're only coming to welcome us into their mountains," Thal said. "You shouldn't be such a pessimist, Lokeen."

Lokeen grinned, his teeth even and white against his deeply tanned skin. "Uhm...maybe you're right, Thal. Of course, you won't mind being first to grip their hands, or paws, or whatever then will you?"

"I'd thought to save that honor for you, my friend," Thal jested. "After all, you are highborn. I'm just a soldier."

The General joined in the laughter, knowing his nephew and the commander of his cavalry were close friends, their bond hammered out on the anvil of war. And he was pleased. Aron Corth was vastly fond of his nephew, who had proven himself a highly capable officer in the south, and Thal was the only man whose strategic judgment he trusted as well as his own. He had seen the two's byplay release tensions in the men before and suspected their current jesting was not totally spontaneous.

An abrupt rise in the pitch of the approaching howling drove such thoughts from the General's mind. The change meant the creatures had reached the top of the narrow valley just north of the manor, and he warned the men to be ready, noting as he did so the sweat that had started on his palms despite the morning chill. He smiled, knowing the fear as an old friend who would help him stay alive. His sword was another such friend, and he hefted it easily.

General Corth did not realize it, but it was *his* presence on the walls that truly filled his men with courage. The General was tall, as were all the Daynes. His hair, once as brown as any of his warriors, had gone gray with the strain of past battles. But over fifty years of life had not sapped his vigor.

Soldiers habitually curse their leaders, who are seldom found when blood is being spilled, but no such curses had ever been hurled at Aron Corth. His men had seen him in the thick of fighting and knew he did not shirk from dirtying his hands like a common trooper. Now, his men saw him again at the front, his body tall and lean and his flag whipping at his shoulder, and they all stood up straighter and prepared to do whatever he asked of them.

Dawn was still bleeding over the green basaltic peaks that towered above the manor when the howlers came into view, a ragged line of vaguely human shaped figures that quickly resolved itself into a running mass of beasts. Many went by to the east and west but others came directly on, never stopping. They passed swiftly across the open space before the walls. The archers fired and left gaps in the mass, but other beasts reached the manor and scrabbled up the granite.

A fanged face appeared through a crenel before Thal and he smashed at it with his shield. The creature fell back, leaving scratches on the hard metal, and as it staggered to its feet beneath the wall Thal hurled the lance he carried into its chest. The heavy shaft burst forth in a shower of red froth from the thing's back. Thal drew his sword and blooded it quickly as a new foe climbed to the attack and died on the wall.

To the outlander's left, Lokeen split the skull of yet another beast, splattering gray and scarlet matter across the stone. The General, too, made his kill, then rushed to his right where a beast had gained the wall and stood tearing out a man's throat. His heavy sword took off the thing's head and the short battle was over.

The remnant of the howling faded away to the south, toward Destandina. Silence fell on the manor, save for the curses of the injured. Only one man had been killed. Perhaps two dozen beasts—Reti, Thal saw—lay scattered at the foot of the wall. A few more lay farther out where they had been struck by arrows.

The Reti had been intent on fleeing. Only panic had

driven them against the manor. What chased them, Thal wondered? He looked to the north where scarlet dawn was turning to lemon morning. He could see nothing but he knew something was there. He had a feeling they would soon find out what.

VI: Toward Evening

Nothing further came out of the north that day, not even the wind. A storm still swirled around Destandina to the south but the sun had risen over the manor and the heavy snow of the night before had begun to melt. Toward evening, Thal, Lokeen, and two soldiers rode out to the north. An ahr passed swiftly as the sun dropped into the horizon, and they were just about to turn back when they came upon a tiny rill valley where a thin mist of water cascaded over a ridge.

At the base of that linn they found strange rounded depressions in the snow. Nearby lay the savagely mauled body of a Reti. There was no sign of its attacker except, perhaps, the round depressions. All four men felt a chill at sight of those "tracks," as if some residual evil clung to the ground there.

At last, Thal forced down his revulsion and dismounted for a closer look. "Whatever it is, it's not much bigger than a Reti," he said. "But it must be a hell of a lot meaner to do what it did to that poor beast. Looks like it turned back north here but the tracks just fade into slush."

"How long?" Lokeen asked.

"Probably late last night. It's hard to be sure. The thing could still be around, though. Keep an eye out."

Thal's last comment was unneeded. The men were alert, perhaps more than alert. This valley seemed a good place for an ambush and the fear sweat stood out on their faces. They were all men who had faced the charges of enemy cavalry and had seen comrades die many times on the field of battle. But here was no enemy they could fight. Something unnatural stirred in these hills, and its brooding presence seemed to spark cool lightning up and down their spines.

Thal looked at the darkening sky, then at his men. "Drusik, you and Rolfe return to the manor. Tell them what we've found. Lokeen and I will scout a little farther north and return when we have more to report."

The men grumbled a protest but turned their horses' heads toward home gratefully enough. Thal watched them go, and shivered a bit in the deep shadow of the waterfall.

"I take it you sent them home for a better reason than you gave them," Lokeen said.

"Yeah," Thal replied. "They both have young ones to feed. Come on, let's see if we can find more of these tracks."

But no tracks revealed themselves beyond the little valley. The two men circled in hopes of picking up more sign, but found nothing. Finally, Thal signaled Lokeen and they rode north in the direction from which every danger seemed to be coming. No need existed between them for speech.

VII: The Watcher

In a wider valley not far from Thal and Lokeen lay the encampment of the Rider's army. The Shadow-Ones had no power while the sun ruled and so Quantus Yorl remained cloistered in his tent during the day, part of his mind hurling winter at Destandina while another part watched the progress of the scouting party through images that danced in the very air before him. Yorl saw the two strangers approaching and quickly gave orders to the guards near him. They rode out immediately, while the wizard continued to watch his visions and smile.

VIII: Taken!

The strike was subtle and swift. Thal and Lokeen had no time to react as crossbow quarrels flashed out of the snow and struck their horses. Stallions and men both went down, and the ambushers attacked out of the drifts where they had hidden. Thal rolled and came to his feet, the shield he habitually carried over his left shoulder slung down to protect his chest.

The first attacker side-armed his axe at Thal and the dark-eyed warrior caught it on his shield before striking back hard, his sword biting into armor. The man leaped away with a curse. Thal looked about wildly for Lokeen and saw him just beginning to rise from the snow. Pain from an injured leg twisted his friend's face, but Lokeen's saber was in one fist and with it he drew a guard of steel about himself in the dimming light. Thal stepped right to stand at his friend's shoulder. His sword parried a thrust, then batted away a spear that struck at Lokeen's side. The younger man's own blade licked out and across beneath the spearman's helmet, opening the throat.

A dozen ambushers made too many for Thal and Lokeen to handle alone. And even now some of the attackers circled to outflank them. Lokeen twisted to his right to block a spearman dodging in, but his injured leg turned traitor and he fell, involuntarily crying out. He still managed to shunt the enemy's spear aside.

Thal smashed his shield into his own opponent, knocking the man down, then leaped to stand over Lokeen. The spearman who had attacked his friend tried to jump back but was much too slow and Thal's brand sliced off an arm below the elbow. Warm blood spattered the combatants.

For a moment more Thal held out, striking savagely in all directions at the surrounding foes. But no man could keep up such effort for long, certainly not in armor. The outlander's guard weakened and the first blade slid through to score his shoulder. The wound was not serious but it would soon be followed by worse. Just as Thal prepared to rush his attackers in hopes of breaking through their line and drawing their attention from Lokeen, a voice called out and the enemy fell back.

"I said take them alive, you fools."

Thal looked up, breathing heavily. The man who had spoken was mounted on an ash-gray horse liberally decorated with silver and gems. He was clearly a sorcerer. Only half his face was flesh. The other half was metal, engraved with images that writhed like smoke. The eye that glared from behind the mask was of stone, white and milky and running with small flickers of light. Thal knew the power of such stones. Milkstones they were called. Two tiny ones were embedded in the quillons of his sword.

Inwardly, Thal shuddered, but his face did not reflect it. He raised his fist and saluted the victor. He knew they were beaten, for a dozen crossbowmen surrounded the leader, each with a quarrel loaded. Still, he clung to his sword and shield a bit longer, unwilling to part with them until no alternative remained.

Lokeen struggled to rise and Thal leaned down to offer a shoulder. The younger man, too, retained his weapon, though his lips were drawn thin with hurt.

"I am the Evening Rider," the wizard said. "Why do you search for me?"

"I was not aware we were," Thal replied.

"Ah…then it is most unfortunate you have found me. You are now my prisoners. Bind them," the Rider commanded his men. "I shall welcome them properly later. It nears dusk and we must be moving."

The two friends dropped their weapons beneath the threat of the crossbows, but Thal did one other thing first. He slipped a metal catch holding one of the gray-white milkstones captive in his sword's quillons and palmed the miniature jewel. An instant later, before his hands could be bound, he covered his mouth for a cough and slipped the stone into his cheek. Yes, he knew the power of milk-stones. He had seen them used before and had used them himself, and even though he was no wizard he feared the time might be coming to use one again.

The Rider watched them being bound and then turned his horse away.

"Wait!" Thal shouted. "My friend needs help. He can barely walk."

"Then carry him," the sorcerer replied. "Anything else?"

"Yes," Lokeen said. "What do you plan for us?"

"You fight for the Daynes do you not?"

There was no denying it, for their armor and weapons clearly bore the Daynish crests and the seal of the House of Corth. Thal nodded his head.

"Then I shall kill you. But before your death I will allow you to watch the start of my vengeance. I think, perhaps, I will begin at the royal manor. I hope there is no one for whom you would mourn within it."

The wizard laughed at the two's horrified faces, and the sound of his laughter started a miniature wind that blew cold around them.

IX: Berserker

Darkness spread swiftly when dusk came, and the Rider's army stirred to life. Torches were fired and the outlaws, who were unaccustomed to military discipline, managed to form ragged columns that moved unsteadily down out of the hills. At the head of those columns pranced the Rider's horse, with Thal and Lokeen struggling along in its wake as bound and leashed prisoners. Lokeen's ankle, though badly swollen, was not broken, and with Thal's help the nobleman was able to keep up with the slow moving army.

Despite their pace, however, the outlaw force came upon the manor only a short time after dark. Thal saw the General's flag whipping smartly over the stone walls and knew hope that the manor could resist this wizard and his army. He didn't yet understand the Rider's power.

The prisoners watched as a blaze of flame lanced from the sorcerer's jeweled eye and struck the darkness around them. As if from the ground, beings that looked like black coagulated blood rose, their inhuman calls twisting Thal's insides. The creatures went ahead of the army, moving like some kind of viscous fluid over the cleared earth before the manor. Arrows sleeted from the positions of the General's men but provided no obstacle to the shadow things. Nor did the walls. The beings went over them easily and the screaming began.

Thal stepped back to gain some slack on his leash, then hurled himself toward the Rider's back. Nearly, he reached the wizard before he was brought up short and beaten down beneath the mailed fists of his captors. From there he climbed back to his knees, and finally to his feet. He tongued the milkstone in his mouth, shifting it between his teeth. He knew then that he *had* to use it.

The outlaws had already formed skirmish lines to advance on the manor, but still Thal waited just a moment longer, terrified at what he was about to do. Thal understood the power of milkstones. He understood that the Rider's stone was eating the sorcerer up from the inside and he didn't want to use one himself, or let it use him. But he had no choice now if he were to save any of his friends. He gathered all the strength of his jaws to crunch down on the crystal in his mouth, feeling both milkstone and teeth shatter. A spurt of acid-like heat was released on his tongue and his body twitched and jerked as the splintery mass slid down his throat.

"Rider," he called, his voice a harsh croaking.

The wizard turned. He looked into Thal's eyes, and even he looked away from the hatred he saw there.

"You're dead, Rider," Thal said. "I swear you are dead."

The Rider tried to laugh but it came out hollow and sounded like fear. For a moment, Yorl wondered if he had gone too far. Then he snarled to himself and slashed Thal across the face with the cords of his whip.

"Kill them," he ordered a guard, "slowly."

The guard stepped forward, grinning in anticipation, then going still with horror.

Thal began to moan. The eyes rolled back in his head until only the whites showed, and the flesh began to writhe and jerk across his body. Sharp teeth ripped at his lips until blood mixed with the pale froth that foamed from his snarling mouth. The Rider looked around, then yelled frantically for the guard to strike as he realized what was occurring.

Thal opened his eyes. They flamed red with the dying light of the fires and nothing of humanity remained in them, only savagery and hate. Thal grunted like a beast and flexed his wrists. The ropes binding him snapped, like wires drawn impossibly tight. Blood sprayed as his flesh tore along with his bonds, but one outward flailing hand, curled into a raptor's claw, struck the soldier in front of him and ripped off his face. The man screeched and swung his blade wildly; Thal jerked it from his hands and broke it in his own fists. The guard, blinded, was struck casually aside. He was not the prey Thal sought.

The Rider was shouting in a strange tongue as Thal leaped forward, feral as a tiger. The wizard's horse reared. Thal stabbed it behind the ear with the broken prong of the sword and it collapsed on top of the sorcerer, its jugular severed. A bone snapped in Thal's hand but the pain did not even slow the warrior. The outlander had turned berserker now. He was no longer human to such things as pain. He leaped into the air and came down with both feet on the Rider's chest. Again bones snapped, but this time it was the Rider's ribs that cracked.

The wizard cried out in agony and the silver light building in his false eye died away into panic. He lay on his back, legs trapped under his horse, and looked up at the man/beast standing over him. He screamed as Thal reached down with clawed fingers that smashed through his shattered sternum and into his chest. He screamed as Thal brought his hand out; it made a small sucking sound as it came loose from mangled tissue. The Rider screamed a last time as he saw what the berserker held in his grip. Thal's hand dripped hot blood as he pulped the wizard's heart in his fist.

Thal had been moving so swiftly that no one had a chance to stop him. Now came a moment to react and the world exploded into pandemonium, aborting the outlaw attack. The Reti, who had been held only by the Rider's power, turned on the humans near them and began to reap red harvest. The Shadow-Ones flowed up out of the ground and began to feed. The Rider's men fought fiercely for a moment, then tried to flee and failed. Death ran blood red down toward the manor, eating rivulets in the cold ground.

Lokeen used the confusion surrounding the wizard's death as a screen for freeing himself. Hands loose, he found a sword easily enough. And he used it against all comers to protect Thal, who had collapsed after taking the Rider's life. He was lucky only men and Reti came against him, and he still stood when the battle moved away and silence blew down on the scene.

The Reti fled back to their wastelands. The others, sated on flesh, turned into shadows and ran away over the ground. To the south, a storm broke and a thaw began.

X: Endings

Though General Aron Corth was dead on the wall, there were survivors in the manor. Cynthe was among them. She came out after the violence was over, in wonder at the attack's sudden end. Only two living figures remained on the battlefield outside the ravaged manor. Cynthe knelt beside them, beside Lokeen where he nestled the head of his friend in his arms. Her tears joined his as she saw Thal's face and the red eyes that looked far away into insanity.

END NOTES

1: **Shadow-Ones**. Some legends say the Shadow-Ones are actually mutated descendents of the Selkrie, descendents that have lost their intelligence and been left with nothing but hunger.

2: **Krell**. The Krell is a flying reptile with an average wingspan of ten feet. They are carnivorous but are rarely seen in civilized areas and generally do not attack humans. Their hides provide durable leather.

3: **Suvan**. Suva is the main goddess in Destandina and is popular throughout the Dayne Empire. This reflects a common pattern on Thanos, where male dominated barbarian societies often have a female deity at the top of their pantheon.

4: **Reti**. The Reti are an alien species brought to Thanos by the Selkrie. They are sentient, but just barely. They exhibit characteristics of both reptiles and mammals. They are hairless, with thick skins and heavily clawed hands and feet. Their mouths are large and fanged and are set at the bottom of a nose-less face. The eyes are at the sides of the head. They are carnivorous, bear live young, and the females possess a marsupial pouch. Little is known about their social habits, though they seem to travel in small packs and are cooperative hunters.

5: Some careful readers may have noted that Thal used both the milkstones from his sword's quillons in an earlier story in this collection called "In the Ruins of Memory." It would appear he later replaced these. At least that's my explanation, and I'm sticking to it!

6: "The Evening Rider" also seems to break continuity with the previous story, "Coin and Steel." In that tale, Thal was about to finish his term as a mercenary for the Daynes and ride off to find his son, Rhing. Perhaps something happened between the stories that hasn't been recorded. Or maybe it has something to do with the woman, Cynthe.

SWORD OF DREAMS

I suppose no man can forget what he now is when he speaks of what he once was. He can only hope to remember what were for many of us, freer days, softer times, when moments without hardness were like leaves on the trees.

—Thal Kyrin

Prologue

Thal Kyrin rode west from distant Kaminor in response to a summons and a fear, both of which came to him in a dream.

Your slave is dead. I have your son. Come, or he joins her.

The words of loss could mean only one woman, blonde Sooh-nhi of the Horse Plains, who had been a slave when Thal met her. But that was nine years past and Thal had no son.

Yet, he rode, east to those same Plains at first to see what truth there might be in dreams. He found it a hard truth, one that led him farther, on a cold trail to the North.

The North: First Dream

In a rain-sweetened dawn, Thal dreamed. His visions were of the harvest, of barefoot children reaping grain for the winter bread, the pollen from their work lying in golden mantles on their shoulders. He squatted amid the stubble after the children had passed and pulled up a handful of shorn stems. The roots were brown with clumps of good soil. He smiled faintly and tossed the stems aside, licking his fingers clean of sap. One child looked back, he with hair and eyes the same color as the soil. A scythe curved over one thin shoulder. And the wind began to blow up a darkness behind Thal's eyes.

Thal awoke to the lambent touch of mist on his face, and though it was still early the dream had finished his sleep. He rose and stirred the ashes of his fire to life to heat water for a cup of spiced tea. The liquid soon began to boil and Thal emptied the contents of a small leather bag into the roiling waters. The blade of a dagger served to stir, and in a moment the morning knew the glory in the smell of tea.

Skaal, the coal-dark stallion tethered nearby, nickered faintly as the smell brought him to full wakefulness. Thal poured grain into a feedbag and soaked it with a dollop of tea before tying it over the stallion's muzzle. He then returned to his cup, adding a bit of bread and a rind of cheese to make a short breakfast. Within a handful of minutes he had saddled Skaal and was riding out to the north. Behind him lay the Horse Plains, thick with the shades of memory. Ahead lay the mountains. He was needed there.

Second Dream

In a chill wind at the foot of a fog-shrouded gorge—restless—Thal dreamed. He saw once more the streets of Sagea, his boyhood home, and in his dreams he ran ahead of his father to the place of minstrels. There a woman sang with a scarred voice of pain, her stroking fingers knotted on the seven strings of the Kalina. Her words came from - *The Felad*, the story of the Conquered Years, when star-beings had ruled the earth and humanity had wandered like children alone. The words ripped him and Thal wept, until a hand turned him into the heavy coat of his father and his weeping was soothed. Not everyone *has* such a father, the dream seemed to say.

Thal awoke to find his cheeks wet and his mouth bitter as steel. He wiped his face and rose. Around him stood the lowest foothills of the Thakar Mountains. The gorge where he had camped cut a straight line toward the heart of that range. He ate quickly and headed out. The gorge ended after a while and he rode once more on empty stone where the wind swept like a cold broom. Memories rode with him, thorns for his thoughts.

Sooh-nhi had been a slave of the Horse nomads when Thal first saw her. He had come to the nomads for a purpose, and the woman had no part in that. Yet, he had grown to love her. His love had freed her and given her a home among the Horse peoples. But in the end he had gone from her. He did not know if it would have made a difference, but she had not told him of the babe she carried. Only a few days ago had he learned of that reality, after the passage of nine years.

Your slave is dead. I have your son. Come....

Those words had brought him again to the Horse Plains. He had not really believed that *sending*, until he found the slaughtered village of the nomads. Only one hut remained standing. In it were the bones of a woman his love remembered well, and one thing more, a charcoaled sketch made by a mother's hand. It showed a lad of four or five—though he would be older now—with large brown eyes and hair curling at his neck. The cheeks were faintly shaded by the bite of hunger. Thal had cursed himself.

I have your son!

Thal knew the author of those words. *Nictyris!* A year ago he had gone to the woman in search of knowledge, only to find she had nothing he wanted to learn. He had

something she wanted, though, something he was not prepared to give. She wanted his love, though incapable of
that emotion herself. In an unguarded moment, Thal had
told her of Sooh-nhi and of what they'd been like together.
Perhaps he wanted to give Nictyris an example of love. If
so, he had failed. And Nictyris was not as forgiving of his
failures as Sooh-nhi had been. But then, Nictyris was a
sorceress, and insane.

With fear as a goad, Thal urged Skaal on faster and
faster. And the animal responded with its own strengths,
striding on into winter while its rider's face was wreathed
in vapor and pain. The mountains grew up around them as
the days passed.

Third Dream

In the bitter twilight of frost-rimmed peaks, Thal
dreamed, the visions crimson with gore. War-horses
frothed at their bits, eyes rolling like bloody pearls. Men in
bruised armor and torn silks of umber and white hacked
each other into ragged scarecrows. Arrows sleeted the sky
like sharpened flakes of ice. When it was over the ravens
gathered, scarcely moving as Thal rode among them
searching. He found his son's head on a stake.

Thal awoke on horseback, a taste of bile in his throat.
It took him a moment to realize Skaal had stopped, a moment more to realize why. They were deep in the Thakar
range, seemingly alone amid vast greenish crags that
forged through the air like plunder-laden galleons. Then
Skaal snorted and Thal realized they were not alone.
Above him on a mountain ledge lay a white temple with
glacier-bright walls. A shudder passed through the warrior
at sight of those walls. Was it only his imagination that
saw them scrawled with the carmine oils of sacrifice?

What he saw did not matter, though. This was not the
ancient ruin where he and Nictyris had first come together,

but it was the place to which his dreams had led. Now, he needed one more dream before he entered there. He fed the stallion and ate heartily of his own supplies. Then he found a hollow out of the sharp wind and rolled up in his furs. He was asleep in moments.

Fourth Dream

Twisting in a flesh-scented breeze, Thal dreamed all in black and white, chest heaving as the fingers of fear tucked stitches into his skin. Dark snow littered a crematorium where he walked. And women were dancing there in the dappled moonlight, shedding the pelts of wolves, their porcelain faces spilling foul tears and their tongues writhing red from pus-colored lips.

In the center of the dance stood a haggard Sooh-nhi, whipping the flesh from a brown-eyed child who looked too much like someone she hated. Thal screamed it a lie as the dream tried to throw him off into wakefulness. For an instant more he held the image, reaching out his hand and touching the shoulder that raised the whip. Sooh-nhi looked around to him, then fell to her knees and gathered up her son. Somewhere, a voice screamed in frustration.

Thal's eyes snapped open as if the lids had been torn off. The sleeping furs were hot on his sweat and he shoved them away and came to his feet. Above him lay the white, cathedral home of Nictyris. He plucked up his sword and his courage and prepared to assault it, while Skaal stayed behind with an open bag of grain and loosened reins in case his rider never returned.

The cliff face below the temple ledge was cracked from years of freezing and thawing and made for easy climbing. In a few moments Thal stood at the door to Nictyris's abode. She had been expecting him and the door was open. He went in with his sword drawn, and just inside he found a symmetrical array of corridors. He smiled bleakly.

Nictyris often used the form of the mandala for occult purposes, Thal remembered. She would be at the center of this giant one, at the point of reintegration where her power was strongest. But it had been a mistake to use the mandala against Thal. He had seen hundreds of them in her old lairs and knew his way through them. He began to run, moving left and then right in what was almost a patterned dance, spinning against a wall and away, using hands and feet and sword against lines of force that sparked and glittered like rainbow eyes. Any one of those lines could have destroyed him had he touched them wrong. He didn't.

Beyond the last corridor stood an indigo door with runic symbols embedded in its depths. Thal traced the largest with the edge of his blade, watched it glow red for a moment before the door faded to an ashen gray and opened. On the other side was a throne room draped in black. Nictyris was there, in glimmering white silks and dark hair. At her feet, with chains reaching from their necks to the throne itself, sprawled half a dozen creatures that could never have been human, and behind her stood a captive youth who certainly was. Thal knew him.

"Son," he said.

"Father?" the boy asked.

"No," shouted Nictyris, as she loosed the creatures at her feet and screamed them to the attack.

Thal had never seen such beings before, though he had seen things nearly their equal in grotesqueness. These had no heads, only slits in their torsos that might have been mouths or eyes or gills, or all three. And they flailed when they moved, as if their limbs were put together all wrong. Still, they came swiftly, and Thal met them with a rage ignited by the sight of his child imprisoned. The monsters stood no chance against that rage. They died in pieces.

Nictyris did not seem disturbed when Thal hacked

through the last of her minions and strode toward her with his sword dripping. She reached out for the boy and drew him close. A knife slid into her hand and planted itself at the youth's throat.

"I'd come no farther," she said to Thal.

The man stopped. "Why, Nictyris? You sent for me, after all."

"But you're still alive. I wanted you dead after what you did to me."

"I did nothing. I told you from the first I could never love you."

"Liar!" shouted Nictyris. Her grip on the boy tightened and Thal saw a spot of blood appear on the tanned throat where the knife's edge touched. "You could have loved me. You didn't even try. Now you'll wish you had."

Thal watched the boy. The lad was clearly afraid but did not whimper. He was like his mother, Thal saw.

"Release my son, Nictyris. And I will spare you."

"Release him! I'll release his *soul*! Just before I release yours and eat them both."

"Then die, witch."

Thal closed his eyes and began to dream while awake. The sword fell from his fist and the pupils began to dart back and forth beneath his shuttered lids. He heard Nictyris shriek as she realized what he was doing, but by that time her mind was locked with his and her hand could not move on the knife to drive it into a child's throat.

Weeks ago she had started invading Thal's dreams, started filling him with images of terror and despair. She'd wanted to weaken him, to make him suffer. But what she had really done was train his mind to understand exactly how hers worked. Now the two of them were mind-locked together and Thal began pouring the violence in his soul down the open channel between them.

The bar of that hate momentarily united them so that Thal saw what Nictyris saw, heard what Nictyris heard.

She had never known the power inside of Thal, never thought on the forces that had sculpted him over an odd and turbulent life. Now she was feeling the stroke of those forces, and of something much worse that was shadowy and vast with an old anger. It battered and tore to escape Thal's hold, roiling and splintering until even its struggles set Nictyris's brain gonging inside her skull.

Thal felt the last barrier of his will start to fall. He felt the killing blackness hurl itself outward to rip the woman apart, and he howled "No" and turned the blackness aside to send something else, something that had lived with him for nine years.

Thwarted, the presence inside him imploded, driving the dark warrior to his knees. Nictyris was down as well, on her belly with her hands over her face. She would not die, but her sorcery was gone forever. It had been…replaced.

The only one left standing in the room was the boy. With bound hands, he picked up the knife Nictyris had dropped and sawed his way free. Then he walked over and dropped to one knee beside the man who had come to save him.

Final Dream

On the long way south, the boy and his father shared peaceful dreams. The woman who rode with them shared as well. She had the dark hair of Nictyris but called herself Sooh-nhi.

END NOTES

1: This is the last of the Thal Kyrin stories and certainly leaves many questions. How did Thal recover from the insanity he experienced at the end of "The Evening Rider?" Did the "presence inside him" mentioned in

"Sword of Dreams" come about from that time? Was something "alien" released inside him when he crushed that milkstone in his mouth to use it against the Rider? And what happened to the rendezvous he intended to keep with his son Rhing? And now we find he had *another* son by a woman who didn't tell him she was pregnant. Is that likely? Or, could it be that Thal never *did* recover from his insanity? After all, the story is called "Sword of *Dreams*." I don't know myself, and I won't until Thal returns from wherever he's gone to tell me.

SMOKE IN THE BLOOD

Milk scent on the wind
and a spill of salt,
a table is set for wayfarers.

Welcoming torches are fogged by rain,
pipes skirl a summons in the ear.
A rider is coming far to this place,
black wings of a cloak around him.

But there is evil here,
in the twist of vines made for a crown,
in the chalice carvings of bulls and grapes.
The rider wears armor and does not fear;
he has a sword to stroke with scarred fingers.

A curule chair beckons;
the rider pulls to a halt.
There are white faces at the table,
bodies that silk loves.
The rider is young and has blue eyes,
shaded now with the cross of need.
He comes off his horse and sits,
wine like smoke in his blood,
meat like the sweetest air.

A drowsiness begins to settle,
and the others close in with razor looks,

with thoughts of foulest food.
The rider lifts his head to see his death,
but smiles instead,
as he raises his own pipes to blow,
and plays a different summons.

WORMS IN THE EARTH:
BARBARIAN'S BANE

Author's Note: The next three stories are different from other tales in this collection in two ways. First, all are meant to be humorous rather than serious, and I hope they accomplish that goal. Second, "Worms in the Earth" and "Slugger's Holiday" have particular connections to Robert E. Howard. For "Worms," I borrowed—and distorted—a Howard title. He wrote a very fine serious story called "Worms of *the Earth." "Slugger's Holiday" is a pastiche that uses characters and situations created by Howard, who wrote many Sailor Steve Costigan tales. My Costigan piece may not be as good as Howard's, but I've tried to stay true to his voice in those tales. I did add a supernatural element, which Howard didn't normally use with Costigan.*

> In those days there were Worms in the Earth. Big worms. Gigantic! Worms so mighty that the earth shook with their writhings. And one day those worms came forth and attacked the shining cities of man. The destruction was really bad.
>
> *—The Book of "Hopefully" Lost Tales*

The barbarians were gone now, but that did little to cool the fevered hate Farthane the necromancer felt for them. That hate was a black and coiling thing, with smidgens of rust and verdigris in the gruelish mix. He was sick...to death, of barbarians and all their ilk—of nomads, Neanderthals, and Nazis, of savage tribes, troglodytes, and yuppies, of anyone who would drink red wine with fish.

"Why me?" Farthane remonstrated to the foul and brooding sky that roiled like an ulcerated stomach over his nighted castle.

(It was a good question, and one any being, corporeal or otherwise, who happened to gaze upon Farthane at that moment might well have echoed. 'Tis fortunate then, for those of us who *are* gazing upon the necromancer at this moment, that Farthane did not leave the question merely rhetorical. Let's listen in.)

"Why did they have to pick my haunted forest to traipse through? And why did they have to kill my Ogres and Trolls, my Will-o'-the-Wisps and Drachen, my Poltersprites and Skogsnufvas, my Shopiltees and Callicantzarois, my mantichore for Crom's sake? What need was there to eat my cannibal trees and pluck the wings from my pegasi? And why," he gestured at the cloud-bruised sky, which declined to answer but instead spat a dollop of drizzle down his neck, "why did they have to trample my ghoulish gray garden of grim geraniums?"

Farthane sighed as he gazed down then in tormented sadness at his ruined flower beds, and upon the scorch marks that had taken the clear-coat right off the obsidian walls of his keep. Why, the "animals" had besieged him—besieged HIM!—and had nearly burned him out before he'd managed to raise a bevy of Babylonian bimbos from the dead and send them out through his secret underground exit (formerly called his sewer) as a distraction to the besiegers. (He was aware the only thing barbarians like more than looting and pillaging is sex. Just look at how many of them there are.)

Now, after the lust-addled barbs had been enticed off to the south by the alluring mummies, where they would almost certainly lose track of their former purpose of battering down Farthane's walls and doing harm to his actual person, the necromancer was free to ask the gods his "whys," though he did not truly expect a response from the putrid heavens. Besides, he knew the answer to all his questions anyway.

"Because they are barbarians," he muttered to himself. "That is the only reason they need for destroying the livelihood of an honest sorcerer-in-good-standing such as myself."

The spade-shaped beard on Farthane's chin, replete with newly silvered hairs, quivered with agitation. His pale and usually languid fingers curled around his arcane staff with a grip that threatened to crush the delicately filigreed jade-work with which the stave was adorned.

He pondered...and pondered some more...with narrow eyes narrowed in a narrow face.

"I must have my revenge," he muttered with magnificent malevolence. "It must be a big revenge. One that every future barbarian child will learn at the knee of every future barbarian unwed mother. (Which he imagined them all to be.)

"These filth must be taught that they cannot with impunity impugn my power and leave their muddy boot prints and discarded cockatrice bones on my flying carpets. They *must* suffer."

He stamped his silken-soled sandal on the smoke-stained stone of his sadly-soiled balcony.

"Must, must, must!" he ejaculated. And, turning with an intent resolve, he made his way through the piles of spent arrows, death's-head daggers, throwing axes, and razor-embedded Frisbees that littered his battlements to enter his castle of stark renown.

Deep into his palace Farthane stalked, making his way to what he called his "black" room (though a visiting imp had once been heard to remark, "why doesn't he call it his 'blacker' room since his whole castle is most wholesomely black?"). Drawing from his fastidiously immaculate shelves his most ancient and potent grimoire—the Necronudicon (older than the Necronomicon and with better pictures besides)—he turned the laminated bat-wing pages until he found the one spell he sought, the one cantrip he had never used in his rather short long life.

"The Worms in the Earth," he breathed, as he scanned the words scrawled on the vellum sheets with the blood of hundred-year-old virgins. And he cackled most appropriately.

The spell was short (how many hundred-year-old virgins do you think there are anyway?), but the words were filled with a puissance that drummed in the walls as he spoke them. At the first word, his vengeance began. So, of course, he spoke the second as well. And the third he scrawled in the air with a fingernail that blazed with lavender and mauve light.

A fourth and fifth word followed, and the world of his castle trembled, dust puffing up from the closely set Acme bricks of the floor. At the sixth word a spider sitting irritated in a corner of the ceiling changed her web-board from "felicitations" to "shut the Hell up."

But now Farthane spoke the seventh and final word. And he watched in the room's enchanted mirror as the earth of his desecrated garden zippered open, and the night crawlers of his calling crawled forth, dripping with mucous, moist with glabrous slime.

"The Worms!" he shrieked. "The Worms in the Earth!"

With segmented heads questing like pseudopods, the creatures reared up from the soil that had birthed them as if to seek the sorcerer who had called them from their nocturnal domain.

Farthane frowned as he noted that those rearing heads lifted only a scant inch or two above the ground, and that in length the longest of the worms would barely outstretch the penile bone of a male highland gorilla (about two inches). Somehow, he had thought the "Worms in the Earth" would be...bigger.

Quickly checking his spell, the necromancer could find nothing wrong with his casting. Every word had been spoken correctly, with just the right sibilant hiss, with all the required umlauts and glottal stops. Every motion of his hands had been choreographed with precisely the right air of languid languor. Shrugging, a bit nonplussed yet determined to carry through with the program, Farthane replaced the book in its niche and, leaning close to his enchanted mirror, shouted through it to the beings he had raised to do his bidding.

"Go forth!" he ordered. "Go and lay waste to those who would dare abuse, profane and/or desecrate my palace and myself. Destroy themmmmmm! Utterly!"

Again our necromancer cackled (a necessary skill for such as he, and one at which Farthane was quite proficient). And the worms obeyed, jerking, sliding, writhing away to the south in pursuit of the barbarian horde. And as they jerked, slid, and writhed, a most wickedly wondrous thing happened (from Farthane's point of view). In their thousands, the worms began to flow together, began to... melt into each other, slimy flesh melding to slimy flesh like plastic soldiers tossed together into a fire. These new worms began to fuse together in turn, growing larger and larger and larger and larger and larger and larger and larger—until they formed one Worm, a truly gigantic Worm, a gargantuan, monstrous, humongous, Brobdingnagian Worm.

Farthane stood frozen in awe as he watched that incredible "joining," and soon his feet started to tap, started to dance, started to soft-shoe—until he was capering about in his black room, holding up his black robes with their stitches of silver and the phrases of power sewn upon the front ("Loud chants save lives") and back ("If you can read this the witch fell off"). He was suddenly in rare good humor.

As he gazed into his occult mirror and began to imagine the delicious revenge that should be his once the Worm fell upon the barbarians like an avenging angel (a rather appearance-challenged and "mucousy" angel, it is to be admitted), Farthane shivered in almost orgasmic pleasure, and his good humor grew more good.

"I shall see their wagons and belongings crushed like flour tortillas," he intoned. "I shall see the barbarians and their infernal dogs rolled like enchiladas in the felt of their own yurts. And though a thousand plus a thousand warriors attack my Worm with axes and swords and lances and horned helmets, they shall only be...squished. Each and every one of them. Like fresh cow pies between the toes of a barefoot boy.

"Ah, too soon it will be over. And across that crimson sward of carnage, only the lonely wind will murmur, and the only living thing will be MY titanic Wurmmmmmm! I shall be called Mighty Slayer, Foe Destroyer, Barbarian's Bane."

Farthane giggled within his castle of bleak resolve. He chuckled, chortled, and chirruped. But then the necromancer's laughter went chill and hollow, and faintly nasal, and his capering slowed to a mere shuffling of sandaled feet.

Through the miracle of his wizard's glass, Farthane observed a single, bored-looking shamaness of the barbarians stalking out from her roisterous encampment to face the Worm. She appeared to be drinking the kind of beer not served with a slice of lime, and was wearing a T-shirt that read: "Yes, I'm magic. No, you can't touch my dark cauldron."

But it was neither the drink nor the shirt that had seized Farthane's horrified attention. It was the small, rust-flecked amulet the woman held pinched between her thumb and forefinger.

When the Worm saw that amulet it paused, quivering along the entire length of its jello-like bulk. Its upper body lifted, thinning at the neck, whipping back and forth in agitation as if some ancestral memory strove to break through into its dim awareness.

In that instant, Farthane's sorcerously enhanced senses connected with the microcephalic brain of his monster, who had once, if you recall, been billions of much tinier worms. And in that instant of oneness with his creation, Farthane remembered: the squelch of boots in fresh mud, the biting grate of a spade stabbing into earth, and the terror of being jerked into the air from his bed of rich soil to writhe in the hands of men going...fishing.

The shamaness tossed her amulet down in front of the Worm, then turned to re-enter her camp. Farthane was hurled from the mind of his creature to stand shivering, gasping, moaning within his castle of lorn longing. He shut his eyes, knowing what was coming, knowing the results for his palace, gardens, and menagerie would be far worse than anything done by a few noxious, noisome, flea-bitten, scraggly, stinky, smelly, wretched, filth-encrusted, lice-ridden, scab-picking, snot-eating barbarians.

No, Farthane didn't want to see, but after a bit he could not help but open his eyes again. It was as he had thought. The amulet, a steel fishhook, lay on the ground where the barbarian witch had thrown it.

And the Worm? Well, the Worm had turned.

MIRTHGAR

In the 313th year of the reign of Queen Mastiffa, a Pale fell upon the realm of Mirthgar. It was a whiter shade of Pale, and it came as a mist with a late spring frost that coated the fabled land with a cloth of rime.

Mirthgar had not seen a Pale since ancient days, and this one was as harsh as any in the historical record. Day and night the thick fog leashed and lashed the land. And the white did not fade with the rising sun, or, indeed, the rising summer. It lingered into the days of the long grass, and so the grass did not grow long with only a watery yellow orb to feed it. Nor did the Candy Corn yield well, nor the Sweet Wheat or the Honey Bunches of Oats. The harvests that year were meager. The unicorns and goattles and ox-deer grew thin and lost their normally luscious fur coats. And the ruddy-faced, good-hearted people of the land grew short tempered and lost their smiles and the delicate blushes of color that normally rouged their rounded cheeks.

Even the coming of autumn winds did not break the Pale. Instead it thickened, like a python swallowing a bull beefaraffe. Ill omens abounded. A question mark was found crop-circled into a farmer's lotus field in Mirthdale, while in Mirthhedge an albino Irish setter was born to a pair of blue tick coon hounds. In the very halls of the Queen's palace, the infamous ghost of King Hornrey the First was seen to slip on an ectoplasmic banana peel and do the splits with an expression of considerable pain. The habitual hilarity had already fled from the people of Mirthgar, and now hope joined hilarity in exile.

But it was in the first days of iron winter that the worst news came. A ravening band of Oinks was seen in the northern mountains and as far south as Mirthwood. Outlying farmsteads were deliberately infected by the Oinks with voracious termites, and settlements along the Mirth River stirred uneasily behind their wooden walls. At night, the winds snuffled blackly outside the doors of men, and in the cold skies were heard the howls of Wereagons and their Hobblen riders.

In Mirthton, Queen Mastiffa's great crystalline capital of culture, commerce, and casual concupiscence, nearly forgotten armories were broached only to find most of the swords and axes turned to verdigris and rust. And no one seemed to quite remember who was in command of the single platoon of imperial guards that remained in active service. Perhaps it was because most said guards were well beyond their 105th year.

The Queen ordered fresh weapons to be manufactured, and more soldiers to be trained. But the process was agonizingly slow for a people who had been at peace for near on a thousand years. Setbacks were numerous, as when the first new arrows came off the assembly lines with shafts made from the flimsy Yuck tree instead of the sturdy Yew, and with heads of porcelain rather than steel.

In the meantime, the Oinks and Hobblens were not idle and evil stalked the land. Roadways were potholed, cattle were tipped. Dogs were shaved and made to walk backwards. And wells were contaminated with the anti-aphrodisiac saltpeter, which further strained the mood of the stressed-out populace.

At last, in a desperate search for guidance, the Queen left Mirthton and traveled south to the edge of the Great Mirth Valley to consult the Oracle of Alphi who dwelt there. The Oracle was on the port-a-potty when the Queen arrived, but soon finished her morning constitutional and rushed to her post, pulling up her lacey drawers as she ran.

Crawling quickly through the dim tunnel beneath the oracular temple, the fifteen-year-old girl named Mimsy, who had become the Oracle on her twelfth birthday when her womanhood had abruptly visited her uninvited in the night, climbed through the trapdoor and up into the giant statue that stood at the temple's heart. She nestled comfortably down behind the flaring golden nostrils of the idol and awaited the Queen's question, signaling her readiness by a small clearing of the throat, which—magnified by the hollow head around her—sounded like the angry hooting of a herd of river hippopotami.

The Queen bowed humbly and rather ponderously before the knocked-knees of the golden statue, and her words were clear: "How am I to remove the Pale that whitens the world, and defeat the evil creatures who threaten the land at every turn?"

Mimsy took up in her long-fingered hands the "tool" of her trade, around which the great golden statue had been built, and which few people knew of outside the small circle of the Oracle's servants. This device was rumored to have fallen amid a rain of firefly lights from the sky five thousand years before, and it rested on a linen doily on a velvet pillow on a stone doughnut within the statue's head. It resembled nothing so much as a large black egg with a polished clear window on one side. Mimsy sometimes called it the "Magic Egg-Ball," but only when she knew she would not be overheard.

Mimsy shook the Egg-Ball. Once. Twice. Thrice. She memorized the symbols that surfaced each time within the window, then consulted the Codex Histrionica and the twice ancient Scrolls of Pythagarostotleocrates for the proper interpretations. At last, she whispered Queen Mastiffa's answer through the nostrils of the statue.

"Victory will come only with laughter, Oh Queen. So says the Oracle of Alphi."

The Queen raised her humbly bowed head and arched a delicately bushy eyebrow.

"This poses a bit of a problem," she responded to the Oracle. "Humor is hard to come by in Mirthgar these days. How might I find this laughter of which you speak?"

No protocol existed in the oracular bylaws for answering a *second* question. It simply was not done. But these were unusual times and so, again, Mimsy shook the Egg-Ball and noted the symbols.

"Your lucky number is three, Oh Queen," she whispered from the statue. "This, too, is the word of Alphi."

Mastiffa sighed. She wondered why she had expected anything more. Oracles were notoriously unclear. Worse than consultants, practically. Or even math teachers.

The journey back to Mirthton was a sad and worrisome one for the Queen. The Pale had strengthened further and visibility stood at mere yards. Winter had tightened its bare-knuckled grip as well, and Mastiffa's caravan struggled through drizzles of sleet while being constantly harassed by Walgrogs and Boogalins throwing snowballs into which rocks had been packed. It was an exhausted company that finally made its way through the gates and back behind the relative safety of the city's translucent walls.

The Queen immediately retreated to her throne room and ordered that she be left alone to contemplate the words of the Oracle and the horrors now stalking her once placid land. Her chin sank upon her fist in classic "Thinker" pose as tall, yellow candles of Beetle wax cast light upon her troubled brow ridge.

"Laughter," she remonstrated to the portraits that adorned her walls, each a caricature of one of the great kings or queens who had ruled in Mirthgar from ancient days to the present. "How can I find laughter in these fell times?"

But they say hope springs eternal in the human breast, and Mastiffa had three breasts, two of them quite large. So she called to her side all the clowns, mountebanks, buffoons, mimes, harlequins, jesters and academics in the city, and she bade them amuse her. Outside the walls, a horde of Oinks and the dreaded Uber-Hobblens descended from the mountains to lay siege to the gates. Many were mounted on Snarlosaurs, and the stench was as thick and abominable as Troll Toe-Cheese, both from the unwashed Oinks and Hobblens, and from the chronic flatulence of the Snarlosaurs, who are known to be overly fond of baked beans.

The people of Mirthton began to panic, but the Queen remained upon her cotton candy throne and strove to find…laughter. Joy buzzers buzzed. Pratfalls ensued. Clowns sprayed mimes in the face with squirt flowers and mimes doused clowns with tin buckets of colored confetti. Buffoons were pied; Dwarves were juggled. Academics tried to agree on…well, anything.

Throughout it all, the Queen did not crack a smile. Nor did the barest chuckle escape her crimson lips. At last, in anguish, she sent everyone away and brooded upon her candy cane throne. A thought struck her, and for a moment hope flickered. She called upon the most puissant sorcerers in the city, even though they had not been quite puissant enough to abolish the Pale or even chase off the standard issue Hobblens, and she ordered them to cast a spell upon Mirthgar to compel everyone to laugh.

Many noxious vapors were released then, from blackened cauldrons in which ambergris, and linalool, and lavender, and bergamot, and oakmoss, and patchouli, and rotgut Aqua Velva boiled and bubbled. Cantrips were chanted in sing-song voices, and sigils were stamped and restamped with every increasing flourishes. Again nothing worked. Again the Queen ordered those who had failed from her sight.

At last, Mastiffa arose from her cane sugar throne and bade her squires bring armor and weapons. She dressed in purple greaves with pthalo blue cross-stitching, and in a breastplate of polished gizzard stone taken from the massive Roc her long-deceased father had barbecued for her sweet sixteenth birthday party. She took up her great sword, Scold, and went forth among her people to give them courage for the battle that neared.

The walls were already under siege by the evil tide from beyond when the Queen arrived, but she saw that her newly trained soldiers remained firm, if somewhat nervous. And their spines stiffened a bit more when Mastiffa came among them and stood large and proud upon the battlements in her bright, amethyst helm.

So far, only lances and arrows and lotus-soaked spitballs had been used against the battlements by the enemy army. The losses had been minor. A few of the Queen's men had been sent from the walls to have their injuries tended. Other's slept peacefully out of the way until the lotus juice that drugged them wore off. But, Mastiffa knew it would get worse. Already she could see that siege engines were being prepared, and catapults and trebuchets were being erected to pound Mirthton into submission with their giant stone balls.

"We must burn the infernal machines!" the Queen shouted to her soldiers, and she herself took up a longbow and strung it. Fire pots were set between the crenels of the wall and Mastiffa lit the first arrow and fired into the ranks of the enemy. Her bolt struck a catapult and set it aflame, but most of her men could not shoot so far and their arrows fell short. And the enemy quickly grew wise and began to wrap their devices with water soaked wallaby hides to protect them from fire.

Despair raised its ugly head among Mirthton's defenders. One enemy siege engine was completed. And then another. The Queen saw Oinks and Hobblens race aboard, and Snarlosaurs were hitched to the big towers to haul them up against the city walls. In another moment those towers would top those same walls and the foe would spill out onto the battlements like the muttering magpies of mayhem they were.

Mastiffa fired shaft after shaft, only to have their fire sputter out against the towers' protective hides. At last she was down to one arrow, and she paused before using it. From nowhere it seemed, the words of the Oracle of Alphi came to her. "Your lucky number is three, Oh Queen."

On sudden impulse, Mastiffa bussed her last arrow with three quick kisses from her scarlet lips and then sent it on the wing. This time she aimed low, hoping the foul ones had left a weak spot at the base of their towers. It turns out they had, but not in the way she'd imagined.

The Queen had forgotten that Snarlosaurs are notoriously...gassy. Mastiffa's arrow, fired low as it was, passed beneath the tail of one of the giant marsupial lizard-pigs just as the creature vented a rather dainty poot. The methane of that poot ignited, setting off a fireball that shattered the nearby siege engine and sent Oinks and Hobblens flying. The Snarlosaur vented a high-pitched shriek from its other end and proceeded to trundle away at high speed directly through the enemy ranks, bowling them over like nine-pins.

For a moment on the battlements, silence fell. The Queen's eyes bulged. Then her luxurious frame gave a sort of shudder, and a burst of laughter exploded from her throat that dwarfed the Snarlosaur's fireball. Other voices joined hers, until hilarity tore through the ranks of Mirthton's defenders.

"Fire for their arses, lads!" Mastiffa managed to shout, setting off gales of fresh guffaws.

More arrows were rushed forward, and one might say then that the enemy were...lit up. All over the battlefield, Snarlosaur farts were ignited, with disastrous consequences for evil. Within minutes the dark foes had fled, spanked from the field by the sound of laughter.

Then a great snap, crackle and pop was heard overhead, and when the people of Mirthton looked up they saw the Pale split wide open and the sun pierce down to burn off the mist that had tasked their land for nearly a year. Laughter and cheers rose together in that moment, and the Pale rapidly dissipated on a fresh incoming breeze that carried with it all the good natured thoughts that had once been, and had become again, the lifeblood of the city.

An attempt was made to hoist Mastiffa onto the shoulders of her men, but at last they all settled for shouting her name as the Queen returned triumphantly to her sugar plum throne. She reigned for many years after that, and never again did a Pale lighten her rule. And never again did a day pass in her world without laughter, as befitted the magical land known as Mirthgar.

SLUGGER'S HOLIDAY

I had ne'er been to Hawaii before. Me and Mike, which is my white bulldog and my best friend, is used to knocking around Cape Town and Hong Kong and Shanghai and those sort of low down, no account, stinking dives what ain't fit for civilized folk such as ourselves. But what I saw coming down the gangplank of the tramp steamer Hyacinth on the Big Island of Hawaii was pure de heaven. The sky was as blue as fancy Sunday dinner plates and there weren't but a nostril full of ile and soot in the air even down along the wharfs.

"Mike," said I, as we started along the dock. "Mike, ol' boy. This is the first blamed vacation we've had in a season of disasters and I aim to enjoy it. I'm goin' lay back and soak up the atmosphere. Why, I ain't even gonna sling a fist whilst I'm here. It's too purty. I swear off fightin' for the duration or I ain't Steve Costigan, A.B. mariner and champion mauler of the *Sea Girl*, the toughest ship afloat." And I patted the fat poke under my shirt that carried all the dough I'd need to keep my oath for the next two weeks of peace and quiet and restpose.

About then, a big stevedore came tearing along the dock at a hard clip carrying an expensive trunk on one hulking shoulder, and he knocked right into us, nearly percipitating me into the unforgiving waters of the Pacific Ocean.

"Watch it you big lummox," I growled perlitely.

To which he gave a smirk and proceeded to blankety

blank myself and my entire ancestry, of which he clearly didn't know the half. I could see as he needed some lessons in cussing so I gave him back his own words with some apostrophes and exclamation points throwed in. But he wasn't in an appreciative mood, it seemed.

"Why you!" he said. "Iffen I wasn't on an important mission I'd flat-mouth your ugly mug right here and now."

"Grrrr," Mike said, ready to go for him. But I recalled me the oath I'd just swore.

"Ah, let it pass," I said kindly to the stevedore. "I ain't in the fightin' mood at the nonce."

"Ha," he says. "'Twouldn't be no fight. I'd hit you and you'd hit the floor. But iffen yore scared..."

I felt my fists clench at the uncalled for insult, but then something he'd said wormed its way into my brain.

"You mean," said I, "it ain't a fight lessen both men throws a punch?"

"I'm here to tell you that's what it means," he snarled, and he reached to give me a shove with one ham-handed fist.

So, to protect him from Mike, who was about to turn his legs into strip bacon, I went and exploded my right fist just at the point of his chin where a few crumbs of old food dotted his wire brush beard, and he went back and out from under his trunk and landed four square on the dock. His eyes was blue and open but he was out cold. It was only one punch so my oath was saved. I saved the trunk as well, catching it afore it hit the ground and setting it gently down on the planks.

"Oh my! Oh my!" came a pair of feminine voices what made me look up.

I thought for a moment the stevedore must a knocked me out, too, 'cause I was seeing a vision of angels at the pearly gates. There was two women there, blonde curls all a frothing around their winsome cheeks. And both of them dressed in soft, flowing white.

I snatched off my sailor's cap and busted my most endearing smile all over my face, and I reckon the smile put them at ease 'cause they stumbled back only a little and didn't hardly grab onto each other at all.

"That...that was our chosen...fellow," one of them said.

All of a sudden I felt blamed lousy. Their "fellow" wasn't likely to come to anytime soon and I purely did dislike to upset a lady. Much less two of 'em.

"I'm rightly sorry," I said, wringing my cap in my hands. "But I was afeared he'd provoke me into a fight and I done swore an oath."

"He was carrying our trunk for us," the second blonde said, as if she hadn't heard me. "And we're in an all fired hurry."

"Well that's simple then," I said, smiling at them again. "I'll carry yore trunk. Ain't nothin' but a lil handful anyway." I hoisted the thing up on my shoulder with a muffled "umph" and wondered what caliber of iron boulders they had in it to weigh so much. "Just you ladies tell me where I'm carrying it to."

The two of 'em looked at each other, and at the stevedore snoring loudly on the ground, and then at me. Finally, they shrugged two pair of delicate shoulders and pointed off in a direction that leaned to the right of where I'd been headed.

"That's our hotel," they said, both of them speaking at the same time and indicating a large building of tan stone with a golden onion dome on its roof that stood about half a mile distant. That hotel looked pretty much like a church to me, but I'd not had much experience with high falutin' sleeping establishments. So I just shouldered the trunk up high and started off.

It weren't but a few minutes to the hotel and I was a step or two or three ahead of the lady folks when I arrived, having had a hard time amblin' along slow enough for them to keep up. They certainly didn't seem to be in the hurry they'd claimed to be in. But it wasn't my place to question. I was still feeling kicky about knocking out their "fellow." I truly hates to see a woman put out in any way.

Up close, the hotel looked even more like a church. Or maybe like one of those moscues you see among the Mussulmans. It had marble steps leading up to great bronze doors with symbols Xed all over them. But there was a doorman of sorts. Or two of 'em rather. One was a shade shy of my own six feet and kind of ugly and oily like an Eyetalian. The other was bigger and looked to be a mix of Chinese and African, and either a Britisher or a gorilla.

I found myself wonderin' why the doormen of this fancy hotel both carried twelve inches of cold steel pig-sticker thrust through crimson sashes throwed around their waists. But like I said, I'd never been to Hawaii before, much less to a high tone hotel with a golden roof. I don't argue nobody's customs.

Neither of the doormen seemed to like my looks any.

"Ver do ze tink you art gohink?" the oily one asked in a squeaky kind of voice.

Mike didn't care much for the line of questioning, or maybe the voice, and he gave a snarl that would have been a warning to a Texas wild cat. But then, Mike just ain't as tolerant as I am.

"I'm carrying this trunk for two angels," I growled, starting up the steps. "And I aim to deliver it to this here hotel like they asked me to. So step aside the both of you and I won't have to rooin you for havin' children."

Now hadn't I explained myself perfectly reasonable? I knowed I had. But these fellows didn't seem to have a lick of understanding betwixt them. They each gritted out some half strangled curse and whipped out a pig-sticker and came a lunging.

Mike leaped like a whirlwind for one man's chest, but, in an effort to keep the bulldog from tearing out the feller's vitals and at the same time avoid breaking my oath about fighting, I swung around with the trunk and accidentally clipped one doorman on the left side of the head and the other on the right. Oak met skull and oak won. They both went crashing past me down the steps into the street, and all was quiet until just then the lady folks what owned the trunk showed up.

"Oh my! Oh my!" they both said. And that left me feeling plumb awful again.

I hastened down the marble stairs and kicked the two unconscious gentlemen out of the way, then rushed back up and opened the great brass doors for the ladies. They gave me a wide berth going through, but I followed 'em in and I swear the innards of that there hotel drew a little gasp out of me.

The place was all one room, with a long central walkway spread with a crimson carpet, and with dark benches of fine wood in even rows to either side. I guess those benches was where folks slept, though there was no one in 'em now. They looked pretty comfortable and I wondered how much dough it would take to get one for the night. They was likely a sight more expensive than what I was used to, but I was on vacation, after all.

But it weren't just the excellent sleeping accommodations that made me gasp. It was mostly the golden idol what stood at the far end of the hotel with six arms and six hands and in each hand a flaming candle drippin' with tallow. In front of the idol, which was a bit over man- sized but definitely of the feminine persuasion, was a rectangular black stone that looked pert near like an altar, and the rich light pouring down through the nearly translucent golden dome painted both the altar and the statue with a faint but fiery glow.

I started to put down the trunk and one of the blondes said, "You," which I took to mean me since I was the only one there. "Put the trunk on the altar and be quick about it."

The both of them had straightened up and I saw they were taller than they'd seemed at first, and I coulda sworn, though maybe it was a trick of the sunlight streaming in through the onion dome, that their eyes was suddenly all a glitter.

Whatever the change in their appearance, the two ladies sure had altered their tone since arriving at the hotel. But I guessed they had the right to order me around after all the inconvenience I'd caused 'em.

I took the trunk down and set it up on the altar beneath that huge golden statue with the candles all alight in its mitts. And when I turned around the women folk were right there behind me. One of them had taken a pin from her golden curls and she poked me in the shoulder with it.

"Now why in a Texas feud did you do that for?" I bellowed, rubbing my shoulder where the pin had stabbed. "I ain't done nuttin but accidentally knock out a couple of yore...." The world spun dizzily around me. "Yore...." I saw suddenly that dozens of other folks had come into the room behind me and they was all women of various shapes and sizes. "Yore fe...ll...o...."

About that time, Mike went for them and one of them blew a handful of twinkling dust in my old bulldog's face and he crashed to the floor like he'd been cold cocked with a holystone.

"Why you!" I extrapolated. "You ain't no decent women to do such to a dog." But I was staggering and staggering, and falling to one knee.

Then the other blonde poked me with a hair pin. Twice. And I cashed out of daylight into a darkness that roared.

* * * * * * *

I woke up to the sound of Mike growling. And I found the both of us was chained to stone columns in a big round room lit only by torches that smoked and stank.

I got to my feet and stood there swaying with the irons hanging off me like the tatters of an old shirt. My head felt like an aig some lousy cook had half boiled and then decided to scramble instead. I'd been doped enough times to recognize the ache.

"Mike," I said. "Don't I know better than to go in some rich folk's hotel? We two ain't wicked enough for the politer kinds of places. From now on it's the waterfront for us, pardner."

Mike grrrred his agreement.

"You pig," a new voice said, the words at odds with the refined air of the voice that delivered them.

I drew myself up, all six feet and 190 pounds of me. "Are you addressing me?" I asked of the statuesque redhead who'd made her way out from behind some hangin' curtains and stood before me in a golden robe with a scarlet and black dragon embroidered upon it.

"Yes, I'm addressing you. First you knock the stuffing out of our intended sacrifice. Then you manhandle two of our eunuch servants. You have disrupted a ceremony for which we have been preparing for years. And for that you are most certainly a pig."

"I don't know what no 'eunuch' is," I said, "though I'm guessin' it's some furren word for doorman. But 'pig' I understands, and I know what 'sacrifice' means. And I don't much care for those two words gettin' used so close together while I'm chained up to a fancy column of marble."

She sneered, and you ain't never seen a truly good sneer until you seen it on the face of a beautiful woman who has just used the words "pig" and "sacrifice" like they was poetry to her ears.

"You'll soon like things even less," she snapped. "When Khamsin comes for your immortal soul."

"You is very dramatic," I said. "Not to mention

beootefull. But supposin' you take these chains off me and Mike here. Or maybe just take 'em off me and I'll take 'em off Mike so he doesn't go all bulldog on you. And then I'll go on out of here and continue my vacation. You see, the Old Man of the *Sea Girl*. The *Sea Girl* is my ship, that is. And the "Old Man" is the cap'n. Well, the Old Man had a good year this un. Or maybe he just went wobbly. But he gave us sailors bonuses and I ain't never been to Hawaii before so I—"

"Shut up!" the redhead shouted, imperlitely interrupting one of my better speeches of all time. And she pointed her finger at me like it was the finger of sweet Beelzebub himself. And she said with an even sneerier sneer on her face. "You are going to dieeee!"

She clapped her hands three times then and out from the draped velvet curtains at the back of the room came the two blonde angels who I'd first gotten into this mess with. Between them came the hotel doormen. And those eunuchs was carrying the self same trunk I'd hauled here on my own shoulder. The eunuchs sat the trunk down on the polished floor, which was lightly sanded like some fightin' pits I'd seen, and quickly left after a bow to the redhead, who seemed to be in charge of things.

Lady Red went to stand over the trunk and the two blondes knelt beside it and opened it. Red reached in and drew out a ruby statue about a foot high and lifted it up in the air, and I guess it was the whirl of smoke from the torches that made the thing shimmer like the sea when she's all painted from the sunset.

Except for the ruby color, this statue looked exactly like the big statue I'd seen in the parlor of the hotel. It had six arms and hair all braided up in spikes, and it was clearly a woman with jeweled breastplates a coverin' its jeweled chest.

The redhead held the statue aloft while the blondes drug away the empty trunk and then drew a broad circle around the other woman with silver dust that they lit on fire. With the spurt of the flames came a spurt of words from Red's mouth, furren words along the lines of "doorman" and "blimey" and such.

I was getting a mite uncomfortable with this show, and it didn't help none when a whole passel of women, all of them blonde as corn silk, came pushing out from behind the room's billowing curtains and linked hands outside the burning circle. Their voices joined the chant of the redhead, and the ruby statue seemed to like the result because it began to drip with bloody light.

About then came a rattle from overhead and I looked up to see that cracks had appeared in the ceiling, and a big round piece of marble roof was slowly sinking down toward us supported by gleaming chains. On that slab of marble sat the big seven foot golden idol and the black altar I'd seen when first entering the hotel. We was underground, I realized.

The idol and altar came to rest facing me on the sanded floor; the supporting chains dropped away with a clatter. The chant of the women stopped all of a sudden, and though I hadn't liked that sound much I sorta missed it now it was gone. The silence gave me an even worse feeling.

The red headed gal came around the big statue to stand in front of the altar. She carried the little statue with her and it pulsed in her hand like the throb of some devil's heart. I might have thought that pulsing was still the Mickey Finn working in me but Mike saw it too. I could tell by the mix of growls and howls that spilled from his mouth as his feet scrabbled at the floor in order to get at the thing. His chains prevented him.

Red ignored Mike and focused the full intensity of her stare on me, and I say I've seen friendlier faces on sharks and lawyers. Even the Old Man never looked so hateful when he was a cursin' my soul to black damnation.

"Since it was you who took away our intended meat, YOU will be our sacrifice instead," Red gloated, stabbing an elegant finger in my direction. "Khamsin," and she raised her free hand to indicate the golden idol, "will beat the life from you with her own fists and redistribute it to us, her chosen, so we may live forever."

I had an inkling that maybe this wasn't the first time the redhead and the blondes had pulled such a dirty trick on someone. But I couldn't make out exactly what they planned on happening here. I'd been walloped on by bruisers from Cape Horn to Calcutta but nary a statue had ever laid a glove on me.

"I don't spect that hunk of gold there is going to do much mauling," I called out calmly. "Now about these chains—"

"Behold!" Red shouted, not listening a lick to me. She turned to the big statue and opened a panel on the front I hadn't noticed before, and into the hollow behind that panel she thrust the small ruby statue she was still carrying. Closing up the little idol inside the big un, she twisted around to give me a look to scorch Lucifer on his throne.

"Behold," she said again, quietly, and I knew then the drugs the blondes had stabbed into me with those hair pins must a still been boiling in my brain because the big statue suddenly dropped the candles it was holding and moved with a creak and crack of golden limbs. And its eyes popped open, all tiger-yaller and alive.

"Jerusha!" I sputtered.

I could feel my eyes buggin' out, and when I spared a quick glance at Mike he showed the same expression. Not even a growl curved his chops, so deep was his surprise.

"Steel springs and whalebone, Boy," I said to him. "Vacations ain't for the faint of heart, is they?"

All the blondes began to chant again then, in low, mellifluous voices. "Khamsin, Khamsin. Goddess of eternal life. Goddess of eternal death. Take up your sacrifice.

Show us your abiding love."

Red did not chant with the others but came over and thrust a golden key into one of my bound hands. She stepped back quickly as I worked free of my manacles and gave her a glare that would have scored a layer of steel off a battleship.

"I don't reckon you're much of a lady," I said to her, rubbing my wrists to get some feeling back.

She sneered, which was perdictable.

"But you're a man," she gave me back. "And as a man you will be crushed beneath the fists of the great Khamsin. Try to defend yourself. You will die anyway."

I shook my head at her and stalked toward Mike. "I appreciate the offer," I said. "But I done swore off fightin' whilst on holiday. Besides, I don't hit women. And seven foot gold statue or not, Khamsin shorely does look like a woman."

I stuck the key Red had given me into the lock for Mike's chains. It didn't fit, and when I turned back to palaver with the female she was lookin' at me with the glory of religion etched all over her face.

"Khamsin is not woman. She is...God! And if you do not fight, both you and your beast will die horribly."

I frowned. "Well, I guess that God part might change things a bit. But that don't confront the oath I swore. I—"

This time it was the statue that interrupted my speechifying. It leapt clear across the makeshift ring and punched me in the chest with all three fists on its right side. I went caroming around the pillar, flew about ten yards, and slammed down into a face first slide on the sanded marble that took off half a dozen important layers of hide.

Mike set up a racket to shame a herd of catamounts and went to tuggin' at his chains hard enough to drag dust out of the marble column where he was bound. He still wasn't getting free, and Khamsin was coming for me.

I riz with a roar and am ashamed to say that in the

swelter of the moment I clean forgot my oath about not fightin'. As the idol came swooping, I threw my right fist from down near my shin and placed it smack dab in the middle of the thing's ugly face.

Whatever this Khamsin was, it wasn't made of gold metal. Flesh gave under my punch and I heard the crack of knuckles against jawbone. The statue staggered back as if in surprise, putting up one of its three left hands to brush across its thin-lipped mouth. That hand came down to fling golden blood at my eyes, but I was already charging in close and started whamming lefts and rights into the thing's midsection.

The idol gave a high pitched yowl and jerked me up and threw me into a wall, but I came sliding down on my feet and gave it the rush. I wasn't good and truly mad yet but it was working in me.

Mike was howlin', and the women were screamin', and I put my head into Khamsin's belly, wrapped my hands around its waist, and picked it up and drove it into one of the many stone columns dotting our arena. Marble cracked. Dust flew. I let go of the statue's legs and hooked a looping right into its ribs. But then, Wham, Wham, Wham! Three fists hit me and I went flailing back. I didn't go down, though. My fightin' will was startin' to exert itself.

A second leap by the idol brought it down upon me. I blocked some punches, took some others and traded them back. The thing's fists were like mattocks when they got through, clouting and cutting at the same time. One blow shifted my nose an inch to the right. The next shifted it back left and set the claret to flowin'. My cauliflowers were both swelling.

But the thing had no science about it and couldn't stop my jabs and body blows. After a tithe of that it pushed me away and stepped back its ownself. I grinned to show it hadn't hurt me none.

Maybe my punches had learned it some caution, but the idol came in circling me now, crouched in a stance like you see some Chinee fighters use. I wasn't havin' none of that. I just came walkin' forward, poking with my left to test the waters.

I hadn't wanted to fight but now I was in it. My oath was already broke and I could feel by the way this Khamsin slung a fist it weren't no female, despite what it might have looked like. I wasn't gonna let it pound on me without it paying the price. There might not be handlers in this match, no referee or bells to signal the rounds. But a fight is a fight is a fight. And the fact I was battlin' a living statue with a passel of women screamin' for my head in the wings didn't make no never mind.

I threw a haymaker right and had it blocked, then blocked a return right that came back at me from somewhere beyond the sunrise. But I only stopped the uppermost of three rights and the other two crunched into my ribs so hard I could hear the bones protest the treatment and threaten to walk off the job of protecting my innards.

Now, most brawlers will expect you to step back after they hit you a good hard un, so I ordered my ribs to shut up the clamor and rushed forward instead. The idol's arms were a lot longer than mine and it went to tattooing me all over with blows as I came charging. An uppercut straightened some teeth I'd had crooked in a previous brawl. A couple of knuckles cut my face over the cheekbone and sent droplets of gore spraying. But at least I managed to get in one good slam to the body before I got picked up and throwed again. That was gettin' old.

I riz, spittin' blood and sand, and flicked a flap of torn skin that used to be part of my forehead outa my eye. Khamsin was circling me again, but in the process got a little too close to good ol' Mike. The bulldog lunged far enough against his chains to sink a wicked set of chompers into the back of the statue's right leg. The thing yowled and danced around and went to swatting at Mike with all six of its hands.

No single blow would ever have broken the hold of Mike's jaws, but the combination of flying fists must of surprised him and as he went to shift his teeth for a better grip a rattlin' wallop sent him flying into the marble column where he was chained. I heard his broken yelp and saw red rise up outa the floor to cover my eyes. With a howl of fury I launched myself at Khamsin, fists up and head up so I could see where I was hittin'.

The idol swung down and across at me with all its anvil-headed fists, right ones first and then the lefts. But I ducked under the blows and came up inside, hooking punches like avalanches into the thing's solar plexus. I was mad clean through now.

Blows fell on me like hailstones from above, but they only landed against the top of my head and my shoulders and there ain't nothing much to hurt in those places. In the meantime, I hammered and tore at the idol's midsection, and each punch seemed to dent the golden flesh a little more.

A sudden uppercut sent the idol reeling and I followed with an overhand left that caught the thing flush on the cheek and turned it halfway around. That turn exposed its kidneys—iffen it had such—and I pounded a mallet-like fist right there into its lower back. It gave a little scream and slapped at me. I took those blows and smashed a good left into its chest just where the red headed woman had stuck that little ruby statue. The whole idol quivered and I saw the yaller go bleeding from its eyes.

I hit it in the same place again.

The statue twitched and jerked like it had the ague, and a low keening moan purled from its throat. It grabbed at me, trying for a clinch, but I batted some of its mitts off and the others slid on my sweat-slick hide. All the while I was hittin' and hittin' it, lefts to the chest over the small ruby statue, rights to the midriff like I was notching a big oak for cuttin' into firewood.

Screaming came from all around us now but I could barely hear it over the grunts of blows given and taken. Khamsin went to clinch with me again but I shoved it away and hit it solid with a straight right to the chest. It cried out some gibberish that sounded like a Swede speakin' Frenchy, and then grabbed me and tried to throw me. I hooked my leg behind its knee and together we crashed down with a thump that shook dust from the walls.

Up I bounced, and Khamsin kicked me in the wind, nearly taking it all out of me as I doubled over. A second golden foot whanged me in the chin and I went back and down, my head hitting the marble floor with the sound of a melon splatting on a boardwalk. Stars burst before my eyes as thick as ticks on a bloodhound, but through the pinwheel of colors I saw the idol come scuttling toward me on all eights like some big ugly spider.

I lashed out with a kick of my own, catching one of the thing's arms solidly and hearing the limb snap. Suddenly unbalanced, Khamsin crashed down with a squall of pain, but then rolled over and got to its feet again. I riz myself, and I could see the arm I'd kicked hung useless at the idol's side. Its eyes blinked and there weren't much tiger-ishness left in 'em now. I thought I could read doubt in those yaller orbs.

When there's doubt in a foe you gotta go wadin' in, and so I went, snapping jabs, snapping jabs. None of them had dynamite in 'em but all together they was like a ball-peen hammer pecking away at granite.

The statue backed up, slapping at me to keep me off. But by a gorilla's hairy bottom it couldn't do it. It weren't really no boxer after all. Full of hit for sure, it was. Big and ugly and muscled like an ox. But I'd fit men in and out of rings all over the world who coulda beat it with gloves or bare knuckles. It didn't know the first thing about throwing a fist so as the body's whole weight was behind it, and where I was just gettin' my blood up after taking a hunnerd or so punches, Khamsin had taken less than that and didn't seem to have any desire to take no more.

Knowing it was about beat, the idol tore down a purple drapery and threw it at me. I was tangled in velvet for an instant before I got the fabric throwed aside, but the momentary lull was all Khamsin had been hopin' for. The wall behind the tore down curtain was hung with weapons, with swords and javelins and axes and knives. Khamsin filled all five of its workable hands with blades and came calling for to finish me.

Now, I'm a tolerant man, as anyone who knows me will attest. But one thing I can't abide is a cheat. And bringing cold steel to a fist fight is cheatin' if I ever seen it.

The drape I'd hurled aside had landed on one of the torches and burst into flame, adding more smoke and fury to air already so dense you could cut it with a fork and spread it on a biscuit. Through that smoke Khamsin came hurtling, steel a glittering and a winking in its mitts. I let it get close, and just as it started a downward swing with all its blades flashing as one I dove beneath its reach and unloaded a cocked right hand into its middle like old Andrew Jackson unloaded cannon into the Redcoats at the battle of New Orleans.

Something cracked in the big statue's chest and the panel behind which rested the littler ruby statue popped open so the crimson idol came spilling out and shattered into bits on the floor. Khamsin seemed to sigh and then folded up like you'd fold a losin' hand of cards. Daggers and swords went tumbling, nary a one touching me, and the big statue toppled sideways to the earth and moved no more.

Abruptly aware of the whickering sounds of fire all

around me, I glanced up to see that the flames from the one velvet drape had spread to the others and the whole place was going up like tinder. Womenfolk were running everywhere, with a white bulldog snapping at slim legs left and right but not having much luck catching any.

"Mike!" I yelled delightedly, happy to see him living and moving even though he was still manacled to a marble column.

Scooping up an axe Khamsin had dropped, I rushed toward my pal with the intent of chopping through the chains that bound him. Just then, a wild-eyed redhead stepped between me and my bulldog, and she was holding a weapon of her own, a big ol' skinnin' knife with blood channels grooved down each side.

"You peeg," Red shrieked, having apparently misplaced for the moment her cultured way of speaking. "I weel keel you and your filthee mutt. For Khamsin's sake, I weel keel you." And she started swingin' that knife back and forth like she wanted to shave my whiskers all the way down to the gullet.

This put me in a jamb. Hittin' a living statue what looks a bit like a female is one thing, but it just ain't in me to rough up no human woman. Fortunately, Mike didn't feel the same way and Red was standing awfully close to him. The bulldog stretched his neck up a little and took a chomp out of the pert little roundness of Red's bottom, tearing away the backside of her golden robe. She immediately forgot about "keeling" us and started to scream and jump around before running off wildly through the smoke with her hands over her derriere.

I got Mike free of his chains and somehow we found our way through the licking flames, out of the hotel, and onto the street. The building burned behind us until the onion dome came crashing down in a powerful swirl of embers and ashes, but the pair of us didn't wait for the ashes to settle before striding directly to the wharfs.

"Mike," said I. "Vacations is rougher than I imagined. I'm ready to go back to sailin'. And I've learnt my lesson about swearin' off fightin'. That ain't no way to live. But I'm swearin' off redheads and blondes, fer sure. No percentage in 'em."

Mike grrrfed in agreement and we found the first ship headed out for Cape Town where all the *Sea Girl*'s crew was supposed to rendezvous when our bonuses was spent.

Nary a nickel of my own bonus was left, though not because I'd spent it. Somewhere amidst the clouting and the tumult I'd completely lost my poke. Luckily, I had managed to hang onto the golden key Khamsin's red headed priestess had given me for my chains back at the burned down hotel. That would be enough to pay for me and Mike's sea passage.

I took the key outa my pocket where I'd tucked it and held it up to let the sunlight spill all gleaming along it. Right then, someone whanged into me from behind and the key went spinning out of my hand, winked once, and splashed into the warm blue of the Pacific. I watched it through the clear waters as it dropped quickly from sight.

When I turned to remonstrate with the clumsy oaf who had bumped me, I found no oaf but a woman instead. She was prettier than airy angel and neither a blonde nor a redhead. For which I was grateful.

"Oh, excuse me," the woman said. "I fear I'm not used to the motion of a ship at sea. I do hope that key you dropped was not terribly important to you."

"Not in the least, I said, offering her a bow like any gentleman would.

She smiled so sweetly I felt myself smitten.

"By the way," she added. "Did you see the purser come this way? I'm wondering how much the passage to Cape Town is. My elderly father is waiting for me there and I'm not sure I have enough money. I...." She looked down and scuffed a delicately soled shoe on the hard plank deck. "I don't suppose...in an emergency...a big strong sailor like you might have some extra money to loan a lady in need?"

I sighed, hatin' to see a woman sufferin' from worry and thinking of the golden key that was to have paid my passage and would have paid hers as well.

"I'm a mite low on cash," I finally admitted. "But if we could find someone on board who'd be willin' to fight for dough, I could get us flush right quick."

She looked relieved and a brilliant smile curved her ruby lips. "Why I think I DO know someone," she said. And she winked at me with one pretty tiger-yaller eye.

LUCK AND SWORDS

Prologue

Ice maiden with crystal bones, her song like chimes in a silver breeze. Flame lover with torch dreams, her voice like flowers burning. Their music was rain on dry earth, and evening wind playing games with dust and winter killed leaves.

In each of the god's emerald eyes, beauty danced—a distilled and perfect loveliness wrapped in robes of song. The god laughed at his own production, his breath misting the air with power and the faint scent of nectar.

The demon was not impressed. His ivory hands scooped up the dice and spun them across a table as black as a night on which all the stars had died. They stopped flat against the table wall and settled slowly to the polished surface, still showing the loosing image of his last throw. A leering skull, gold like the color of ancient bone, glared up from each face.

"Are we playing," the demon asked, "or making pretty pictures?"

The god made sounds of amusement. He scooped up the dice, whirled and let them fall. Falling, they twinkled like metal tears.

"Watch what happens," the god spoke in thunderings and silken murmurings, "when the skulls show."

The dice splashed on the obsidian table, leaving waves to shatter the stillness. The demon and the god looked down. Emerald eyes and ruby looked through the sea of rippling liquid stone at the world lying below. The ripples ceased. The dice stared back. From the face of one, six skulls leered, mockery in every aspect of their expression. From the other a single skull gleamed. Its grin was acid, and then one empty socket closed in a wink.

"I win," the god said.

* * * * * * *

The twin die skipped and danced their way across the scarred wood of the dicing table. They came up off the back wall and tumbled to a slow stop. Two black eyes gleamed upward.

"Snake eyes," the barbarian cursed, slamming one iron ridged fist into another. He then shoved forward another small pile of square cut coins with the mint mark of Lorlish upon them.

The skimmer pulled back the dice with his long stick and held them out. The barbarian shoved his long blond hair away from his face and snatched the bones with a snarl that left the skimmer's hands shaking.

Grabbing a wine skin, the dicer tilted back his head and gulped three great swallows, the overflow trickling down the corners of his mouth to drip on the stained oaken table. His breath stank of fetid grape when the skin was lowered. He shook the dice and hurled them, and cursed again when their dance turned up twelve spots.

Rail got up and left the tavern. He had been watching the player, who was loosing heavily and drinking even more heavily. Tension had become as taut as a bowstring in the room. It was only a matter of time before the barbarian decided the dice were weighted and began breaking bones with the length of steel sword he wore at his side.

Rail felt no urge to be present at the eruption. Not that he particularly feared the swordcraft of a drunken Turkosh barbarian, but in the crush of people scurrying for safety it would be easy to get one's sword arm pinned in the crowd just as one needed it. Rail could think of no especially good way to die, but that would be among the more humiliating.

A few others with good sense left the tavern also, but quickly moved away down the street. Rail was left standing alone. As he turned away himself, a roar of delight came from the barbarian within. An isolated victory. It would only make the inevitable a bit longer in getting here. Rail walked away, letting the streets flow past and the cool silence enter in.

Rail, dark and lean and tall like all the Chein race, rubbed his eyes. They had become too much accustomed to the clear, clean air of the winter moors, and the smoke of the room he had just vacated had irritated them. The moors had taken weeks to cross, and before that he had been two months coming up the coast from his people's land. His thoughts of those lands were heavy with pain as he considered their beauty, lying like a wounded pearl in the grasp of the conquering Sharr.

From the borders of the Sharr's reign he had crossed the mountains in the last days of autumn, grateful for the dry year that had dumped little snow in the passes. Past the narrow foothill valleys of the Turkosh barbarians he had come, to Lorlish on the Moors, then across the moors' naked expanse to Suidora. Maybe from here he'd go south into Phunial, into the warm lands where he would not be constantly shivering with cold.

Though he tried to endure it stoically and succeeded most of the time, Rail was not fond of winter. He had seldom experienced such bitter cold as ruled here in the northlands, for it rarely snowed along the Chein Coast. Even in the worst winters, when Denius—god of the north winds—swept southward with his trailing hordes, the great current of the Sa Phaeal, which curled up the coast as far north as the most distant Chein settlement, turned all of the winter god's snow and ice to rain and fog before it struck its blows on the land the ocean river protected. Rail had seen little winter until the coming of the Sharr.

Yet, despite the chilling breeze that paved the streets with frost, Rail walked the cobbled ways of Suidora for a bit. He had no wish to enter another tavern. Besides, he had little enough money, and even in this city where prices were high the air was cheap. The coins in his pouch made little jingles of loneliness as he counted them. Only five left. Four were the rich butter-colored gold of Chein. The other was a Sharr coin of an uncertain metal called thenium. Though it gleamed like silver, it was not of that metal. It was much harder and did not tarnish.

Rail's departure from his homeland had been a little too abrupt to seize much more than his father's buried sword and the few hoarded coins his mother had thrust upon him. Where she had obtained the Sharr coin at, he had no idea.

Though it bought him exile, it had almost been worth it to see that damn Sharr, whose skin normally had the appearance of verdigris, turn all shades of brilliant orange and yellow as it died beneath the caress of the garrote. There had been much hate in Rail, born in the rape of his land five years earlier and the death of a father and older brother. Only his youthfulness had saved his own life during the conquest; it had not protected him from the growth of his hate.

Then, a Sharr beast had struck a child in front of Rail, a little girl who had the temerity to cross the street before it. Rail had looked once at the child's crushed face, then had taken off his belt, looped it around the Sharr's neck, and held on until the thing stopped changing colors and lay in pale chalk death.

When the goad of Rail's anger left him, the enormity of his deed struck him like a blow. If they took him he would die in horror, and all his family would die as well. The Sharr paid in tenfold any harm done one of their number. His only choice was to run before they found him out.

He dug up the sword his father had carried, buried for him by his mother when the Sharr had overrun the Chein lands. It still lay within the wooden case that had kept it from rust. He had taken the coins from his mother because he had no hope otherwise, but still the pouch was a regret hanging at his side. He had stolen a horse, and there again he had killed, but it had been far swifter and he'd not lingered to watch the rainbow of the Sharr's passing.

North he had gone, in a direction they would not expect. And if they had searched for him then their search had not come nigh, for he had seen nothing but empty lands and black-winged carrion birds floating like a rapture of death in the bitter sky.

Now in Suidora, Rail walked. His breath smoked as he remembered his home. He strolled in reverie and the stars moved slightly. Once, he halted to watch an old man playing Peth against himself, muttering softly as he shoved pieces about the twin boards. The player seemed as oblivious to Rail's presence as he was to the cold.

Later, Rail stopped again. A woman's figure moved against a curtain, backlit by a hanging lanthorn. For a moment, a few lewd thoughts—born of loneliness—burned in the young man's head, but he shook them away and went on.

Abruptly, he stopped a third time. The architecture about him had changed. Cylindrical towers reached skyward like massive fingers where before the buildings had squatted broad and flat against the earth, as if they feared the heights. There was no fear in the narrow black stone surrounding him now, only sleeping power and untrammeled might. It was as if he had been sleepwalking and had walked out of one world into another and opened his eyes in another city.

For all its brooding presence, though, it was a lightless city. No torches guttered in the brass-wrought sconces that jutted from the huge walls. Darkness hung like a vapor. Even the pavement beneath his feet was of jet, and he should not have been able to see as well as he could. Moonlight, he supposed, then noticed there was no moon in the cold sky.

How far and how long had he walked? He seemed to remember bells sounding the time but had no idea what units they were measuring off. He had been lost so deeply in his memories that he could have easily entered a different section of the city without awareness. But, he wondered, what had brought him to a halt now?

Perhaps it was the music, he thought, but he knew there had been no music. Quite suddenly, there was. It pattered like rain on dry earth, and rustled like the wind playing games with dust and winter-killed leaves. It reminded him of the way ice sounds when it's dropped into water to cool it, and somehow it brought to mind the whisper of flames in a chimney where the night shadows dance.

He followed the sound, not at all sure he wished to. His feet moved and he no longer shivered in the chill breeze. The music warded him. The eldritch chant fled away, but slowly. He went to it, and followed it until the city walls gave away on either side and he found himself on a narrow windswept trail at the foot of a rising hill. To his right lay a cliff—deadly as an ambush—to his left a tree choked gorge. Hoarfrost glittered in a few protected places. The music ran up the scale as it ran up that trail. His feet followed and he did not try to stop them.

The trail opened into a cleared area, like a circle, at the apex of the hill. As Rail entered the clearing his foot struck something that skittered across the stone. A silver die winked at him metallically. Tiny gold skulls marked the rolls instead of the usual black leopard spots. The darkness, which threw a cloak over his shoulder, did not dim the ancient golden light that bled from the inscribed death's heads. He stooped and picked up the die. The music ceased.

A form appeared in the open space before him. Then another. One was crystal ice that did not chill, the other a fire that did not consume. He saw they had no eyes. Yet, they were beautiful. A third form appeared. It resembled an old man but its eyes were a verdant gleam in an otherwise colorless face. Sharp as gemstones, those eyes carved the night. They dominated the world and Rail could not remove his own black orbs from the emerald power of the other's. The being held out a die to match his own.

"Come, mortal," it said, "let us game." And by those words Rail knew he faced a god.

A dicing table appeared between them, black as the night air. The god laid his die upon it.

"Now yours, mortal."

Rail lay his own die beside the other. The two began to spin, moving faster and faster until they formed a blurred silver ring on the obsidian table. The god giggled a bit.

"We were playing," it said. "A demon and I. For the souls of all in Suidora. I won. But the demon offered a bargain. I have always had a weakness for such. The bargain was this. I would choose a representative. He would do the same."

A small figure appeared on the table within the circle made by the spinning cubes. With a start, Rail realized the figure was alive and moving. Its tiny voice tickled in his ear.

"Our champions would battle," the god continued. "If my champion wins, I own not only the souls of those in Suidora but of Lorlish on the Moors as well. And of all who live between. If his champion wins, he owns the same. You, mortal, are my champion."

Rail was about to explain that he was not from Suidora, and that, besides, this all had to be a dream. These things just did not happen. He opened his mouth but his voice was eaten by the rising wind. Dark wings beat in his head and he was whirled aloft, hurled like a leaf across the sky. His cries made no sound to his own ears.

He found himself naked save for a loin cloth and a sword in his hand. A black floor gleamed beneath him, so shining and dark it appeared as if he stood on the night. Silver walls whirled about him, framing an arena for himself and for another. Across the floor from him stood the Turkosh barbarian he had seen dicing earlier in the evening. The blond warrior was clad the same as Rail, and also had a sword in hand. He seemed as sober as the anger in his eyes, and stropped his blade on the air as he spoke at Rail.

"I guess you know why we're here, stranger."

Rail took a few deep breaths and rolled up onto the balls of his feet.

"I've heard," he said, "but I have no wish to fight for other's pleasure. I don't suppose, though, you would be agreeable to laying down our weapons."

"What! And forfeit the gold I've been promised. We Turkosh have always fought other's battles and received little enough pay for it. It's time we were paid what we were worth. Now, defend yourself until I kill you."

"Then let us fight," Rail said quietly.

The blond bared his teeth and rushed. Rail stepped easily aside. The rush was a feint, meant to draw Rail forward, meant to make him think he dealt only with a slasher whom he could easily best. Overconfidence could be deadly. Obviously, the blond was not stupid. Rail did not take the bait and the barbarian's sword cut only air.

They circled then, the barbarian taunting. Rail remained silent, his sword held easily at the guard position. Their steel touched as they moved in and out.

The Turkosh ducked and slashed left. Rail parried, riposted, and drew blood from his enemy's shoulder. The

Turkosh was not unskilled, but the sword he had chosen was heavy, a common fault of barbarian tribesmen. Long, heavy blades were excellent for splitting open the armor or crushing the mail of civilized soldiery, but they were dangerously slow against an unarmored and quick foe.

The two fighters exchanged quick thrusts. Rail scored a slash on his enemy's thigh but misjudged the barbarian's speed, narrowly avoiding the blond's remise. More careful now, Rail began to take advantage of his lighter and quicker rapier. He stabbed and carved until blood streamed like sweat from the barbarian's body.

Even as a child, Rail had been trained by the best of the Chein sword masters in the art of fencing. The Chein fought more individual duels than those in the north, and had acquired through long training under that harsh master skills and tricks that often meant the difference between victory and a maiming, or death and being carried home on your shield.

Rail parried a thrust to the heart, then another, and danced away. The barbarian began to extend himself, cursing as he became angrier. To the blond's credit, however, he did not loose his head. Rail's Chein blade struck repeatedly through his opponent's guard but left cuts no deeper than scratches. The barbarian was too quick to allow a fatal thrust.

Both men were beginning to tire but fatigue told more on the barbarian, who was suffering from blood loss as well. As of yet, his steel had been unable to find Rail's flesh.

Rail used a trick he knew called the kareen-tie-e. It began as an overhand slash that brought his foe up to parry, and ended with a hand switch and thrust. His sword tip lanced the barbarian's cheek, scoring it to the bone. Blood welled like a spring. The blond grunted and stepped back, raising his left hand to his face. The sword in his right dipped groundward. Rail could have struck then but did not. He waited.

"Damn you, man," the Turkosh said. "I can't touch you." He threw his sword down. "Kill me and be done with it. I'd rather not look like a sausage when they bury me."

Rail placed his sword to the other's belly but withheld his thrust. "You fought well," he said. "I won't kill."

The barbarian grinned. "Hey, maybe you're not so bad after all, stranger. I wish there was some wine around. I'd drink a toast to you. And one to me as well."

The blond laughed and looked around as if to see whether a skin or two of wine had materialized. Neither noticed the roaring until it was upon them. Wind buffeted them from their feet and hurled them skyward.

The wind deposited Rail on his feet in the clearing. The table and dice were gone. No sign remained of the barbarian, and of the god there was only a sweet laughter and a few words.

"You won for me, champion," the god's voice spoke. "You shall be rewarded."

Two figures came out of a mist and walked toward Rail. The one with ice-milk skin had cool hands that soothed like water on a hot day. The other wrapped him in arms over which plumed a fire to warm his flesh.

The figures took him by either hand, their laughter stroking his ears, and led him across the clearing to a bed of soft grasses. There was no cold in the air, only the faint scent of nectar, and a music like the touch of rain on dry earth and the wind playing games with dust and winter killed leaves. Rail was drawn down into silken caresses that moved like liquid on his flesh. The music was a breeze that stirred their spirits together.

In the morning, Rail awoke, stiff with cold. He started from sleep to find himself fully clothed. His sword lay beside him, its polished surface showing no sign of the blood that had dried black on it the night before.

In the night of a strange city he must have been bewitched by the eerie music he had heard, and perhaps by the strangeness of his surroundings. Believing he had dreamed, but feeling vaguely as if he'd lost something precious, Rail arose and started on his way. As he left the clearing his boot struck something that gleamed on the gray basaltic stone of the hill. He picked up a die of silver. Gold skulls marked the rolls.

Rail was still smiling, like a cat that had just taken a mouse, as he rode out of Suidora an hour later and turned his horse south for Phunial.

SUNDERED MAN

"They're coming, my Lord!"

From where he sat brooding on the Scorpion Throne, Kellan looked up at his squire. The youth's name was Henris, an earnest lad who fidgeted now with fear or excitement. Or both. He was the last of the King's servants to remain by his side.

"How many?" Kellan asked.

"A dozen, I think, my Lord." He held up a spyglass. "They are still far distant."

"And within the castle?"

"Only the rats guard it now, my Lord. You and I are alone."

Kellan snorted and shook his shaggy head. "So. They send a dozen heroes after a single man." He levered himself to his feet. "Bring my armor. And a crossbow. It is not my time. Nor yet theirs."

Henris nodded and trotted quickly from the room.

Kellan straightened his body. His muscles ached; his neck and shoulders creaked. He was barely forty years old but too many battles and too many days of hard worry had worn him thin. Past wounds tasked him. The crown was a burden he struggled to bear. But still his hand went to the Sword of Kings where it leaned against the throne, and he hefted it with a black anger throbbing in his grip. Immediately, his pain subsided.

His gaze found the blade then, drank from its ivory length. The weapon had the hardness of steel but was not made from any ore Kellan had ever seen. Some said it had been forged magically from the wing-bone of a dragon, and though the King was not sure he believed that he had *no* doubt that the Sword responded to his passion with a power of its own.

Power. Passion. Those twin forces had driven—or riven—his life. They had brought him access to the Sword after the "untimely" deaths of King Geraint and his wife, after their son, Donal, had fled the highlands with suspicion falling upon his golden brow. As cousin to Geraint, Kellan had been next in the succession. The Sword of Kings became his, though until Kellan took the blade to hand it had been merely an ancient symbol of the crown and never a weapon to be used. For a while, life had been…grand.

Henris returned then with tools for a warrior's trade, with plate armor of black steel and a dark helm with a crimson crest, with a gleaming crossbow and copper quarrels. Kellan let his squire dress him for battle, and while the lad knelt to buckle the King's greaves, Kellan asked him:

"Why do *you* stay, Henris? When all else have fled me?"

"I gave my word, my Lord."

Kellan stared for a moment, then sighed. "And you have nowhere else to go. Is that not right? Did you not tell me when you came to serve me that your mother was dead?"

"Yes. She is dead. When I was very young."

"And what of your father? Have I asked of him before?"

"You have not. But he cared naught for my mother. He would not have taken me as his own."

Kellan nodded. He'd paid scant attention to the boy's story when it was first told to him two years ago. He did not know why he remembered it now, except some trifle about the mother's death had pricked him. He shrugged, hefted his sword.

"Show me, Henris. Where you saw my enemies coming."

The youth nodded, then led the King from the still lavish throne room, through corridors stripped bare by fleeing servants, up dusty stairs to a rampart of the castle facing the heath to the west. It was late afternoon, the sun just beginning to fall like a crown of glory before them.

Kellan blinked in the brightness. His eyes watered. Yet, it felt good to be out in the light and the fresh air after the dimness and mustiness of the castle's rooms. It saddened him, too, because from here he could see how decayed the turrets and walkways and walls of his ancestral home had become. He had grown to manhood here but had forsaken it while living at the King's court in Aramish. And now, without servants to keep it up, the place had disintegrated rapidly.

Much like myself, he thought.

"There," Henris said, interrupting the King's reverie as he pointed across the heath to a line of misty hills that huddled like rain clouds on the horizon. "I used a farseeing glass before but they should be close enough now to view with just our eyes."

Kellan looked. And saw. His eyes still worked well.

"No!" he cried out. His heart boomed. "It cannot be!"

"What? My Lord! What?"

Stricken, Kellan glanced at Henris, then back to the distance where it seemed a fist of sunlight had come to earth and was burning its way across the heather toward his castle.

"The sun! Rising from the west! Riding for me!"

"It's only a reflection, my Lord," Henris said. "They must have their shields burnished. The setting sun—"

"It's the prophecy!" Kellan shouted him down. Then more softly, "The prophecy."

He remembered, then: when ambition had first begun to blood him with its spurs, when, as a youth he'd married a wealthy beauty who was years his senior.

* * * * * * *

Kellan's wife was Sarella, she of the vivid eyes and sharp tongue, the latter of which she used for a decade to chastise Kellan for his lack of success at rising in the world. Sarella talked him into going to the witch, who—it was rumored—could tell the future.

He had sought the fey woman in the bogs, and found her in a hut of wattle and daub. It struck him as foolish to believe in the abilities of the witch. If she were so powerful why wasn't she living in a palace herself? And when he entered her hut he found she was young, scarcely out of childhood. But in those days Kellan had feared the disapproval of his wife more than he feared looking foolish. So, he asked for a reading.

The woman/girl told him first of a thing no one but he could know, something evil he'd done at age sixteen and which no one still living had witnessed. He believed in the witch's powers then, and he gave her the promise she asked for. She returned him prophecies.

He would be king and possess the Sword of Kings.

He would remain king until the sun rose in the west and rode in flame to drag him down.

He would wield the Sword of Kings where others could not, and as long as he carried that blade he could only be defeated in battle at the hands of one who had no earthly father.

And he would only die when his head was divided from his heart and his heart torn away from his limbs.

The first of the prophecies came true a fortnight later when he and Sarella contrived to kill King Geraint and throw suspicion upon the king's son, Donal. And since the sun could never rise in the west, Kellan did not believe he would ever be overthrown, or that he could be defeated or die. Such plans he had. And no promise need be kept to any witch. Not after he'd murdered her.

But the kingship had not been quite what Kellan thought it would be. Many protested when he rode at the end of his first year to the sacred grove at Lodinumm and took up the Sword of Kings. That blade had not been carried in human hands since the time of the Druids. Most said it could *not* be carried without driving the bearer mad. The second blood of his reign had been spilled in the days that followed.

And just when the turmoil over the Sword had been beaten down, Sarella became a new thorn in his crown. She never carried the Sword, but it was *she* who went mad. She grew into a tyrant, and to maintain his rule Kellan had to join in her tyranny, in the savagery and debauches that steadily increased over the years. Predictably, revolts sprang up like toadstools after a rain. And though Kellan was never defeated in individual combat, his followers did not have such luck.

In time, Donal led an army to depose him, and at the battle of Ataavis Kellan's troops deserted him. He and a few loyals fled into the hills, fled toward his ancestral castle at Trepismoor. Sarella had died on that road, died insane and raving of past sins, and he had buried her at the castle where he first loved her. After that death, the rest of Kellan's retainers fled, leaving only Henris behind.

* * * * * * *

Kellan returned from the past; it did not seem a long journey.

"Prophecy or no, you should try to escape, my Lord," Henris was urging.

"No," he said. He lifted the Sword. "By this blade I am made King. To take it they must defeat me in battle. But no man born of a human father can best me. So the witch told me. Heroes or no, those who come against me will die."

"Do you wish me to fight at your side, my Lord?" Henris asked.

Kellan shook his head. "You are untrained and will only be in my way. Return to the throne room. Await me there."

Henris bowed, did as he was bade. Kellan made ready.

The heroes rode four abreast through the open portcullis of the castle and dismounted in the narrow courtyard. They were dressed in plate armor of polished steel, with helms that hid their faces but which bore the crests of famous families. Their bronzen shields had been ground to a high shine, but by this time the sun was well down and the shields did not burn so brightly as before. By this time, also, Kellan was on the rampart above the heroes, crouched in shadow behind the crenelated wall where he could not be seen.

"Where?" one of the heroes asked. He wore a hawk's crest of black.

"The throne room, I would imagine," another answered. His crest was a lion, golden and rampant.

"Wrong," Kellan called from the wall above them. He stood, triggering his crossbow as the heroes looked up. The bolt slid past the nasal guard of Hawkcrest, punched into the eye behind it. One hero died there.

But such surprise would not work twice. Kellan tossed aside the crossbow and retreated, not because he had too but because he wanted to kill the rest one by one within the womb of his castle. The heroes followed, as he knew they would. And at each turn of the corridors he faced them for a moment and with his blade took the life of another of their number.

Outside the walls, night had conquered, but the heroes fired the torches in the corridors as they passed, and inside the castle the shadows fled as Kellan led his enemies on a merry chase that could end at only one place—the Scorpion Throne. Kellan turned at bay there. Four of the heroes remained and he had decided to kill them here, in front of the throne they so desperately sought to take from him.

But now the heroes lowered their swords, and the one with the golden lion upon his helm opened his visor to show his face. It was no surprise to Kellan to see the visage of Donal beneath the crest.

Kellan shook his head. "You'll never be king, Donal Geraintson. Not while I hold this Sword." He brandished the dragon-blade and drew greater strength from its white, glittering length.

"Just so," Donal said. "And no man born of an earthly father can defeat you. But...."

From an alcove to one side of the room, Henris stepped forth, carrying a yellow torch in one hand, carrying a large, purple-wrapped object in the other. He crossed to Donal, handed him the object and moved aside.

"Henris?" Kellan called. His eyes found those of his youthful squire and saw only hate there, a ravening hate. "What? Have? You? Done?"

"Betrayed you," Henris answered. "Do you not recognize the act? Is it not familiar to you?"

"Enough!" Donal snapped. "Now it ends."

The son of Geraint unwrapped the thing he held, let the purple cloth flutter to the cold stone floor. Beneath lay a cross of fine grained wood, and upon the cross was the likeness of the Christ, the new God brought to these lands only recently from southern climes.

Kellan laughed. "You think to defeat me with a length of wood?" He shook his head, laughed harder as he brought up the Sword. "I'll kill you now, Donal. As I should have killed you when I slaughtered your father and mother."

The King took a step forward as Donal stalked upon him with the cross held high like a shield. Kellan swung his blade, brought it scything down upon the wood, upon the carved likeness of a dead man.

A gong rang. Kellan heard it, then realized the gong was the sound of the Sword shattering. He cried out, his hands suddenly stinging with fire, his arms gone numb to the shoulders as he gazed stupidly at the broken weapon clutched still in his fists.

"Not. Possible," he muttered, as Donal stepped back from him.

Then Kellan felt another kind of sting, the sharp bite of a misericord sliding between his shoulder blades through a tiny gap left in his armor when Henris had dressed him.

Kellan turned his head, looked down, saw Henris there with his arm lifted. He felt a cold prickling as Henris twisted the knife in his back. Then the broken Sword fell from the King's nerveless fingers and his body collapsed as his spinal cord was severed.

Kellan fell on his side, his gaze seeking and finding Henris.

"Why?" he croaked.

Henris picked up the shattered Sword of Kings. A six inch fragment of blade remained attached to the hilt. Very sharp.

"Now the head must come away from the heart," Henris said, as if intoning ritual. "Now the heart must be divided from the limbs."

"The witch," Kellan muttered. "She was your mother!"

Henris met Kellan's gaze and smiled. The King's squire straightened, and youth fell away from him like layers of tempera to reveal a man grown.

"My twin sister," Henris said. "Though she did not have quite my power."

"Sister?" Kellan whispered. "I didn't...."

"Yes," Henris said. "Sister. And your daughter. From the woman you raped when you were sixteen."

Kellan closed his eyes. But the dragon—that ageless enemy of humankind—no longer protected him, and even with his spine cut he felt his sundering begin.

A FLOCK OF SWORDS

The Lord High King of Vomarius rode south with a tide of carnivores at his back, going down to the newly opened lands beyond the Jibraihn Straights and the isthmus of mud that had recently arisen there. He had held his army back only long enough for the baking hot sun to firm the ground for the horses, and then he'd unfurled the scarlet oriflammes of war. It was a good day for conquest, as sure as his name was Collus the Butcher.

Once, years before, the boiling mist that habitually obscured the Straights had tattered in a black storm and Collus had seen the peaceful coastline lying so near across the acid waters. He'd always assumed the south to be a beastland. Sometimes at night the bellowing of monsters could be heard through the amplifying fog. But, in the hours before the storm-dispersed mist reclaimed its hold, Collus had seen only a placid people who dwelt in ease on the far shore. Ever since, he'd lusted for their soft-bodied females and envied them their comforts. He hated them for the possession of both.

Yet, no ship could cross those angry waves to alight upon that shore. No bridge could ever be laid. The currents that boiled and heaved in the Straights were not just water. They ate anything that touched them.

Then, an earthquake lifted a jut of land between the coasts and the way to the south lay open. The weakling folk who lived there lay open, fitting prey for northern predators who had evolved and hardened through centuries of warfare. Soon, predators and prey would be together.

With the rising of the new isthmus, the usual concealing mist had cooked away, and the Butcher signaled his men into skirmishing lines as they neared the gentle, green slope at the edge of the southern coast. At the head of the slope stood a peaceful village. Quiet. Unprepared.

Though the people there must have seen the dark apparitions that approached through the shimmer of the midsummer sun, they had not fled, nor even erected barriers against invasion. The fools actually seemed dully curious and had come out of their huts to watch the approach of their executioners. Collus could see no weapons among them, and he smiled as he ordered the tocsin bearers to ring the attack. His smile became laughter as his men fell upon the Southerners like stooping hawks.

Even when the Butcher's purpose became absolutely clear, even when northern swords began to redden with blood from hacked away heads, not one of the villagers tried to flee. They just made their deaths easier by dropping to both knees and baring their necks, like domesticated animals used to being killed. The lack of resistance angered Collus, and he cut and slashed with a rage that threatened to tear whole bodies apart.

It was not long, however, before the Butcher began to tire of slaughter and to think of other reasons he had come south. He soon noticed one of those reasons moving dazedly amid the ruins of her world. She was young, lovely—weak. He rode her down, using his horse to shoulder her from her feet. His armor was already half unlaced by the time he dismounted and was astride her. She had blonde hair and smooth, smooth skin that had never seen work, though blood from his gauntlets now marred its paleness.

She made no struggle against him, as if merely waiting for him to do what he wished. Then he made the mistake of looking into her eyes. He expected fear, but what he saw was a bovine dumbness, a placidness of face that might have been at home on a cow chewing its cud. He couldn't perform while looking at such a face. There was nothing in it to push against, nothing to hurt. Not even the remote thought of resistance troubled this female. And he always liked resistance.

He shoved the woman away as he stood up and began retying the lacings of his armor. Then he heard the scream. The sudden explosion of sound made him realize for the first time how quiet the killing had been. There had been no screams until now, nothing other than a gentle moaning among the southerners, which he had taken for resignation. That meant the scream must have come from among his own men.

Collus spun around, almost hoping to find that one of the weaklings had raised a hand in anger. But what he saw did not involve the cowards his men were slaughtering. What he saw was something big, and spotted, something that moved swiftly amid the burning huts of the village. It carried a man in its teeth, a man whose lance glistened red with its blood.

It didn't seem bothered.

More shapes soon loomed through the smoke and dust. More screams joined the first. The war quickly turned real, except it was fought against beasts instead of men, against curved fangs and bone-sharp claws instead of steel.

The Butcher didn't care. He rallied his warriors and they fought back hard. Some of the creatures, like giant tailless cats, bled enough through their wounds to die. But more always replaced the fallen. Steadily, the Northern raiders were driven back toward the isthmus they had so recently crossed.

Collus had just readied a call for retreat when another two dozen beasts moved between his army and their lone escape route. The Northerners were cut off and surrounded, and the fighting lulled as the spotted beasts broke off their attack and sat back on their haunches as if waiting for something.

The Butcher looked around at what remained of his best legion, a few score ragged and wounded men with blood-encrusted armor. He appreciated the aesthetics of the encircling movement the beasts had carried out. They'd even managed to shunt the natives aside. As if protecting them. Or herding them.

Very much like guard dogs, Collus thought.

Whatever the Butcher would have thought next was interrupted by a crackling sound of shattering trees that won his attention. Collus looked up to realize how foolish his plans for conquering the "weak" south had been. For coming at him through the forest rode a horde of armored warriors that were not quite men. Each stood over twelve feet tall and each was hideously scarred. They were mounted on monstrous reptiles whose slaty flanks smashed aside the forest canopy.

It was, Collus guessed, the shepherds coming to see just what scraggly varmints had attacked their sheep.

IN COLD DESERT LIGHT

A failed flier. A Warlord walks,
strides for Helium in the dark,
never caring what rude beasts stalk,
from savage Banth to deadly Thark.

Yet the night is not lorn as it seems.
A hundred eyes are quick to follow.
But in those orbs no light gleams,
for all are empty, the sockets hollow

All those bodies John Carter killed,
risen up from death to seek his life,
stirred again, called up and willed,
by a new mastermind, a lord of strife.

A quick rush of feet stirs the dust,
in cold desert light of Martian moons.
And swords are drawn, black with rust.
The dead are coming across the dunes.

The Warlord hears and spins around,
sees his enemy. Their shadows loom.
And from their throats an awful sound,
calls out John Carter, shrieks his doom.

There is no fear in Carter's face.
He draws his steel and gives a yell.

For the attack, his muscles brace.
His blade swings, rings like a bell.

The air is thin and the lungs quiver,
as John Carter goes to war.
Under wicked skies the swords shiver,
and death, it seems not far.

Though his enemies cannot be bled,
and corpses raised don't die again,
Carter hacks necks, cuts off a head,
kicks away skulls and lunges in.

The moons pass, the dawn it creeps.
The dead lie in pieces on the ground.
Upon the last, John Carter leaps,
then walks on until he's found.

CROSS PLAINS CONJURE MAN

Somewhere from the dust of Texas,
somehow in the denseness of air
  of Dark Valley
  and Cross Plains,
there arose the walls and forests
 of ancient places.

Sometimes in the hot Caddo winds
came the ring of copper bells,
the shout of hooves and the clangor
  of iron on shields,
  and armor.

Even in the fall of waste
from post oaks and mesquite
there grew the seeds of ghosts,
  of painted warriors,
and ships wreathed with smoke,
of braceleted queens panting in the gloom.

But no one listened
  except Robert E. Howard.

Bookish and small,
a little out of step with the flow
of lives filled with cattle and fences,
  with grass and oil,

Bob Howard had an ear
attuned to a slipstream world
   of tigers and jade,
hidden in the sun-blasted landscape
   of West Texas

How did Bob hear the tiger's roar?
How did he see Chinese boxes
   of worlds within worlds?
You can ask it psychologically
   or historically.
You can wonder on the sharp-stained love
   of his mother,
the slow, throbbing heart-drum
   of his father.

You can talk about skies torn with blue
   or the roil of storms that pound
like giants or gods in the earth.
Surely it was all this and more,
   life and love
and an adventurer's soul,
kettled in a gumbo with the scarlet muse
   of Bob Howard.

He built his body,
honed his dreams,
found a typewriter as tool,
and some say he excavated
   the memory of battlefields
   beneath his native soil.

But I say it was magic,
a sorcery of fire and shadows
called forth in a booming voice,
full of incantations and spells

of fury
and beauty.

From a cell-sized room in Cross Plains,
Bob Howard conjured forth alive
   serpents and apes,
barbarians and green-walled ruins.
He sewed up the whole cloth
of cities and sword-jewelled empires,
filled with sandaled kings
and silk slippered dancers.

Howard raised such lands,
gave them meat and screams,
   and far too young,
in sunlight grown cold with loss,
he conjured his death with a bullet,

and passed....

ABOUT THE STORIES

As both a reader *and* a writer, I personally like to hear from authors about where their stories come from. Since I've written such histories for all my stories, I thought I'd include them with this collection but put them at the end so anyone who wanted *just* the stories could skip the descriptions. The order here is different than in the anthology itself because I've generally considered my earlier stories first.

The Evening Rider: When I was barely into my teens, I created an imaginary world called Thanos where I set a lot of barbarian-type adventures. The landscapes were based on the creeks, ponds, woods and fields of the Arkansas farm where I lived. At that time I was reading the Conan books by Robert E. Howard, as well as the Brak tales of John Jakes, and the Kyrik and Kothar stories by Gardner F. Fox.

Thanos was Earth after an alien race known as the Selkrie had colonized it, destroying our civilization in the process and tearing the moon from its regular orbit to send it into a much closer dance with earth. After the Selkrie abandoned Thanos, leaving behind a few nasty remnants, humanity began to climb again toward civilization. However, several other alien races, also losers in wars against the Selkrie, were exiled on Thanos too, making the planet a bit more varied than it had been originally.

I set a bunch of adventures on Thanos at various periods before, during, and after the alien invasion, but most featured Thanos at a pre-industrial level with swords and other edged weapons. I created a huge, sprawling family named Kyrin to use as characters in these stories, and I still have the notebook where I wrote descriptions of them and their relationships. I recall many of them fondly. Essentially, however, none of these adventures were ever written down. I *imagined* them to amuse myself, often while walking on the farm, or at night before going to bed.

The only character from that time to make it into print was Thal Kyrin, who became my first series character. As he exists now, Thal is actually a composite. I'd first envisioned him as a powerful warrior and prince of a country named Sagea. But, somehow, he seemed to lack a little fire. So, long before I *wrote* a story about Thal, I imagined he'd absorbed the ensorcelled spirit of his ancestor, Vaul Kyrin. Vaul was a great warrior and berserker whose spirit had been trapped in a milkstone and driven insane. This composite worked for me and when I *did* actually start writing, Thal was ready to step forward as a living, breathing character.

Although not the first Thal story chronologically, "The Evening Rider" *was* the first piece of fiction I wrote about the character. In fact, it was the first Sword & Sorcery story I ever wrote. This was back in 1981-82. I suspect this shows in the prose itself, which is probably a bit more "purple" than in the other stories in the series. The story won 3rd place in the 1991 Deep South Writer's contest, and was published in 1995 in the magazine *Shadow Sword*.

In the Memory of Ruins: This was the second story I produced about Thal Kyrin, in about 1985. I wrote it after reading Karl Edward Wagner's *Night Winds* collection, and though Wagner's *style* wasn't an influence on the tale, his idea of lone and lonely "Lynortis" certainly was.

My fantasy tales have always been much longer than my horror stories, mainly because of the need to develop the fantasy world background. "Ruins" is no exception. I was lucky to find a magazine in the 1990s called *Shadow Sword* that *wanted* the longer lengths. Most of the Thal stories were first published there.

When this story was printed in 1996, the "the" in the title was inadvertently left out, making it "In Memory of Ruins." The piece had previously gotten honorable mention in 1992 in the Deep South Writer's contest. That contest was pretty good to me.

Coin and Steel: I had an idea in 1986 to do a series about a roving band of mercenaries that would feature *Rhing* Kyrin, Thal Kyrin's son. The "Black Company" books of Glen Cook were an influence on that concept. I roughed out "Coin and Steel" but couldn't find a decent ending and dropped it. I fiddled around with it at various times and extensively rewrote it in 2004, and again in 2008. It appears here for the first time.

Wine and Swords: In my early days as a writer I did a lot of what is called "free writing," where I just started typing and let the images and words roll over me. The opening paragraph of "Wine and Swords" was written that way, and the story took off from there. I'm not sure where the rest of the plot came from, but I remember wanting to write a heroic fantasy with no sorcery in it. It was finished in 1987, and I still remember working on it in my first apartment in New Orleans after I took a job at Xavier University there.

This is my personal favorite among the Thal stories. I like the cast of characters, especially young Minay. I like the twist with Minay hiding in the dead camel, and I didn't get that idea from *Star Wars* but from stories of the Old West.

"Wine and Swords" won 1st place at the Deep South Writers' Conference in 1990, in the SF/Fantasy category, and it was a welcome win that really helped build my confidence. Plus, it paid me $100. The story actually tied for 1st place with "The Horns of the Air," and the conference decided to publish "Horns" in their annual chapbook. "Wine" was first published in *Shadow Sword* in 1997.

Sword of Dreams: "Sword of Dreams" is a Thal Kyrin story but is an exception to the series rules in a couple of ways. First, it's short, and second, it wasn't published in *Shadow Sword*. It first appeared in 1992 in *Fantastic Realms*, which was the same year it was written. Later, part of the premise for this story was extensively reconsidered in the development of "Dark Wind," another Thal tale. This explains why these two stories begin similarly.

At the time I wrote "Dreams," I was intrigued by mandalas and by trying to tell a story in which temporal dislocations would occur in a character's thoughts. I've also used a lot of dream imagery in my tales over the years, but nowhere as strongly as in this piece. Part of the reason is because I have very good recall of my dreams, which are intensely vivid. They often have useable scenes and story lines.

Dark Wind: This was written in 1995 and is the last in the Thal series to be completed. I don't know if I'll write any more about the character. Quite possibly not, although working through this anthology has created a bit of an itch. By the time this story was finished, *Shadow Sword* was no more. I sold the tale to *Genrezone*, but that magazine folded as well and I eventually donated it to an online charity site, for pets, of all things. I remember wanting to produce a really brutal, all out, physical fight scene for Thal. I like to think I accomplished that.

Luck and Swords: This story was written in between "The Evening Rider" and "In the Memory of Ruins." It had a very simplistic plot, and since I didn't think the original version was of publishable quality I never submitted it. About fifteen years later, in 1999, I revised it for the magazine *Classic Pulp Fiction Stories*. I still don't think it's that great, but there were elements created for "Luck" that I later used in the Talera novels. Don't look for many of them in *this* version, though. I changed all but one of them for this publication.

The Horns of the Air: When I first wrote this story about Jys Martel, I conceived of it as part of a series. I never finished more than the one story, however, and probably never will. There's a fragment of a Jys story somewhere in my files.

This was written in 1987, the same year as "Wine and Swords," but the characters of Jys and Thal are very different. Thal is a darker character, and much less innocent. Jys, despite training as an assassin, lacks Thal's brutal edge and is more spiritual in nature. The two tales tied for first place at the 1990 Deep South Writer's conference. "Horns" was published in their chapbook. One influence on the story's "setting" was Peter Matthiessen's *The Snow Leopard*, which is my favorite book. Another influence came from *Teot's War*, by Heather Gladney.

A Gathering of Ravens: This is one of the few stories I've written with a female lead, and the only one about a female warrior. It was the first female protagonist story I ever wrote, back in 1991. The tale is quite dark and I generally like the writing. I particularly like the opening scene and consider it the best opening I've ever done for a fantasy tale. Of *all* my fantasy pieces, this is probably my favorite, although "Wine and Swords" is a close second.

I don't know where the idea and plot came from. I wanted to stretch my abilities by writing a female lead, and also wanted to submit something to Marion Zimmer Bradley's "Sword & Sorceress" anthology series, which always featured women as main characters. (I did submit, and she said it was perfectly good but far too long.) The story won 1st place in the 1991 Deep South Writer's contest, and was published in their chapbook.

Of Sake and Swords: I had no plans originally to submit this piece, which was written as an experiment in 1993 or 1994. But I had some fantasy poetry published in *Warrior Poets* and found some prose poems in the magazine. I thought "Sake" might work as a prose poem and sent it in. It was published in 1997. (By the way, I mentioned in the Author's Note for this piece how it resulted from a challenge by a member of my writing group. I might add that none of the other group members completed *their* challenge! I sometimes allow myself to feel a bit smug about that.)

A Flock of Swords: Though *Twilight Zone* type stories seem to me to work best in horror fiction, "A Flock of Swords" was my attempt to put the same kind of twist into a Sword & Sorcery tale. The story is quite short and I think it works. It was written in 1991 and was accepted first time out. However, that magazine never published it or paid me for it. I sent it to *Warrior Poets* in 2000, where it was published after the editor suggested a few revisions that helped make the story clearer and stronger.

Worms in the Earth: Barbarian's Bane: I had to grow up pretty substantially before I was willing to try any humorous fantasy. In 2001, I saw the guidelines for a magazine called *Dragonlaugh* and wrote this piece for them. It sold right away, and was published online. It was actually a blast to write, but I never would have tried humor like this when I was in my serious twenties and thirties.

Mirthgar: I resubmitted "Worms in the Earth" as a reprint to a publishing group called *Flashing Swords*, and they liked it well enough to ask for more of the same. "Mirthgar" was the result, and I again had fun doing the humorous riff, although this one was harder to write than "Worms." It was written in 2008 and published that year in an anthology called *Strange Worlds of Lunacy*.

Slugger's Holiday: I wrote this in 2003 as a pastiche of Robert E. Howard's Sailor Steve Costigan fight stories. I intended it as a kind of experiment, to see if I could get into Howard's style at all, and his humorous fight story style is really much harder to master than it might seem. I had a lot of fun with it, though I really had to read the Costigan stories carefully to pick up the lingo. I spent two weeks just reading the stories before I even tried any writing.

I printed the story for REHupa, the Howard fan group I'm a member of, and thought that'd be the end of it. Then, author/editor Bret Funk decided to publish an anthology from his Tyrannosaurus Press imprint and asked me for a story. I didn't have anything except for this and "Dark Wind," so I sent him both. He decided he wanted to use "Slugger's," and it was published in *Beacons of Tomorrow* in 2006. There are some folks who really don't like the exaggerated sailor lingo in the story, and I can understand. It took quite a while for Howard's Costigan stories to grow on me.

Sundered Man: I helped my son, Josh, with a Shakespeare project for high school and ended up writing this story as a retelling of a Shakespearian play. You can probably guess which one. It was another experiment, since I'd never done this kind of retelling before. I finished the piece in 2006, although I let it languish on my computer for a while before ever submitting it. It appears here for the first time in print. (It's *Macbeth*, by the way.)

ABOUT THE POEMS

Recompense Reprise: My favorite poem by Robert E. Howard is "Recompense." I've read it over a hundred times, and this is my response. It was written in 2006 for REHupa, and then published in 2008 in *Niteblade*.

You Were There: This was written in 1998 and is actually my favorite among my own fantasy poems. It has a reincarnation theme, which *could* have come from Robert E. Howard via Jack London. I sold it once but it was never published. It's been submitted to a lot of other places but no one seems to like it as much as I do. It appears in print here for the first time.

Smoke in the Blood: This was originally a "Thal Kyrin" poem, written in 1992. I changed several elements in it before it was published in *Warrior Poets* in 1997.

In Cold Desert Light: This poem is a bit incongruous among the rest of the offerings here. It's a Sword & Planet pastiche featuring Edgar Rice Burrough's character, John Carter of Mars. It was written in 1997 and appeared that year on a Barsoom fan site.

Cross Plains Conjure Man: I wrote this poem in 2001 in honor of Robert E. Howard, and it was published in *Star*Line* that same year. It was nominated for the Rhysling Award in speculative poetry, but didn't win.

ABOUT THE AUTHOR

CHARLES ALLEN GRAMLICH grew up on a farm in Arkansas, near the foothills of the Ozark Mountains, then moved to New Orleans area in 1986 to teach psychology at a local university. He's since sold four novels, two nonfiction books, and numerous short stories. His tales, while mostly in the genres of horror, science fiction, and fantasy, have also included westerns, children's stories, mainstream fiction, slipstream works, and experimental pieces. Charles has also published poetry and nonfiction, the latter ranging from reference works on science and psychology to articles on writing.

Charles is a member of REHupa (the Robert E. Howard United Press Association), HWA (the Horror Writers Association), and SFPA (the Science Fiction Poetry Association). He is an editor for *The Dark Man: The Journal of Robert E. Howard Studies*, and currently lives in Abita Springs, Louisiana with his wife, Lana. He has one adult son, Joshua. His blog can be found at:

http://charlesgramlich.blogspot.com